I0684930

Also by J.A. Sanborn

The Orion Factor

Available in Kindle edition or softcover at Amazon.com

THE LOST CIPHER

Swift River Publishing, LLC
P.O. Box 30965
Savannah, GA 31410
swiftriverpublishing.com
swiftriverpublishing@gmail.com

ISBN: 978-0-9968082-0-0

THE LOST CIPHER

To JoAnn

248474170331058285
T_HE_LOST_CI_P_HER

A Karen Hunter Mystery

A novel
By
J.A. Sanborn

Acknowledgements

My heartfelt thanks to Ann LaFarge who graciously slogged through the original manuscript. Her advice and comments were invaluable.

I am grateful to Kathryn and Marc Sanborn for taking much time out of their busy lives to review this manuscript. Their patient, thoughtful critique, and many suggestions are greatly valued.

I am also indebted to my friend, Leonard Capobianco, for all his advice and help with this project.

I am very beholden to my friend, Colonel Norman Laird, for his advice and patience listening to my ideas over Saturday breakfasts.

This book could not have been written without the understanding support and love given by my wife, JoAnn, who spent many hours in the final editing of this book.

Prologue

Write the things, which thou hast seen, and the things, which are and the things, which shall be hereafter. Revelation 1:19

The city of Middlefield is located near the center of Georgia, giving rise to its name of incorporation in the county of Twiggs. It is a city of thirty-five thousand, determined by the 2010 Federal census covering fifty-eight square miles. The population demographics are a healthy mix of race with a range of cultures. Women outnumber men by 3.6%. The overall population has a mean population age of forty-one. The average annual income is $42,000.

The city has a government design with a mayor backed by a city council of eight civic-minded, elected servants who wield the power over the souls of the city. The city has a well-paid manager to oversee daily operations.

Middlefield abuts the smaller city of Jeffersonville with its population of eleven hundred souls. Middlefield's nearest neighbor of size is Macon, located in Bibb county lies to the northwest, a short drive up the interstate highway, I–16. Middlefield's proximity to Atlanta has made it a bedroom community. Those workers employed in Atlanta often live Middlefield to rear their children in a slower paced environment. The population of Middlefield grows at a slow, but steady rate.

However, the lure of city life does draw many of the

younger citizens out of Middlefield, who return only for holidays and deaths.

Middlefield is zoned light industrial having no heavy industries by city ordinance. The city enjoys an arms manufacturing facility bordered by other soot-less industries employing approximately a thousand locals joined by commuters from surrounding towns.

Middlefield College is a significant component of the city's vibrancy. It provides solid employment to over five hundred residents. In lieu of taxes, it contributes monies to finance many projects critical to the city. Its facilities are available to Middlefield citizens at no cost when not in use by the College.

The College is also responsible for enhancing the economy of city businesses as several hundred academics migrate to Middlefield for the yearly Archeology Conference in mid-March.

Middlefield is home to the *Patriot Bugle*. Published as a morning daily, the *Patriot* generally covers news of the city with bylines of its local reporters.

One arm of the Middlefield government spotlighted by the *Patriot* for particular review is the Middlefield Police Department. Reporters are particularly critical of the MPD's efforts to lower the city's crime rate.

The city has its share of damage to property, sexual offences, violent theft crimes, and several murders each year driven by the usual motives–money and drugs. The Major Crimes Unit of the MPD usually solves these ‘common-place murders’ by good forensic work, or in some cases, witnesses come forward or anonymous leads are received.

However, severe criticism by the citizens and the press reached an intense level with the two mysterious murder cases that had remained unsolved for more than two years after the police had found two young women dead under similar, but unusual circumstances, a year apart in the month of March. The citizens demanded security from their police.

The Medical Examiner believed the death for each woman was due to cardiac arrest, or asphyxia caused by some means he could not determine, since both women appeared to be in good health without signs of any brutality, which could have been responsible for their deaths.

Since no physical violence was evident, the Medical Examiner, with considerable uneasiness, believed he had no choice but to list the death cause in his final autopsy reports as Undetermined.

Road workers had found each young woman, one nineteen, the other twenty-one, within several hours of their deaths along the Georgia, I–16, which runs northwest from Savannah to Macon. Toxicology tests of blood and tissue samples taken at their autopsies showed evidence of drugs in their systems, but otherwise yielded no useable clues to identify the cause of their deaths. Blood tests did indicate that drug overdose was not a factor. There were no physical signs that the women had fought for their lives. There was no indication that the women had been strangled.

Subsequent criminal background investigations of the victims discovered that neither of the two murdered women were Middlefield residents. In fact, each had recent prostitution convictions in Atlanta.

The ME determined that both women had had sex sometime before their deaths. Semen samples were taken and tested. After DNA profiling, submission of the profiles to the National DNA Database provided no ties to a name.

Since the women were prostitutes, having sex before their deaths was not evidence that that person may have caused their deaths. When found, both women were fully clothed except for their underwear, and someone had cut a small lock of hair from each. Though interesting, the police did not consider these facts vital clues. A decision was made to withhold that information from the public for future use by the police should a suspect be identified.

The profiles revealed that it was one man sexually involved with both women. Police questioned whether it was just bad luck for the man that the women had died shortly after. If not, was he responsible for their deaths? That question remained unanswered until an unexpected event happened early in the year of 2011. By then, three more women's mysterious deaths that had occurred.

In the end, the police would find the killer, but at a terrible cost to their personal and professional lives.

Chapter One

Behold, he cometh with clouds; and every eye shall see him, and they *also* which pierces him: and all kindred of the earth, shall wail because of him. Even so, Amen. **Revelation 1:7**

The crime site investigations yielded no witnesses to the women's last nights, nor any useable clues. Despite pleas from the MPD, no one ever stepped forward with useable information. Activity of the Major Crime Unit was at a standstill with little hope for solving the murders. Since there was no progress evident in the foreseeable future, the Mayor and City Council decided to replace Lennox, the current police chief.

Therefore, in January of 2008, the Council hired an exceptional deputy police chief, David Tate, to restore the Middlefield Police Department's effectiveness after the disastrous leadership of Chief Lennox. Tate was a transplant out of the suburbs of Chicago. His experience in high crime areas was essential to manage the crisis facing Middlefield.

David Tate was a slender, handsome man in his fifties, facing a life alone after the death of his wife two years ago. Her death provided the impetus to search for another world beyond Chicago.

Standing six foot three, Tate was a head taller than most of the officers who would be working for him. His size dictated an easy relationship when working with both males and females.

Before Lennox's firing, the Department was in a state of rebellion. General ineffectiveness had been the standard under Chief Lennox. The most experienced officers had threatened to quit. The loss rate of competent officers was such that the department had become nearly dysfunctional. Chief Tate was needed to restore citizen trust. His other marching orders by the Mayor were that he needed to focus resources to clear up the unresolved murder cases as well.

By January of 2008, Detective Green, head of the MCU had led the murder investigations of the two prostitutes without significant results. Chief Tate knew that he had to replace Detective Green to revitalize the critical Major Crimes Unit. He dreaded this task; progressing cautiously until he could find a way to make the replacement less of a wrenching experience for Green.

Sadly, but conveniently for the Chief's decision, Detective Green became seriously ill in March of 2008, and retired early the following month forcing an immediate need to backfill Green's position.

Further, to ensure positive changes to the entire MPD, Tate planned and ordered a total reorganization of the seventy-person police department resulting in the wholesale transformation of management positions within every operating Unit. In particular, because of the two unsolved murders, Tate restructured the Major Crimes Unit to place the brightest and most dedicated officer that he could find into that leadership position.

As Tate looked over the personnel files of all his

detectives, he decided that one officer, currently within the MCU, met his requirements to head the Unit. His choice was a thirty-five-year-old detective who had been with the unit for the past eleven years. He noted that the annual evaluation reports expressed opinions of this officer who was highly regarded by supervisors and teammates. More importantly, this officer was well aware of the murder cases at hand.

Lieutenant Karen Hunter had received her master's degree in criminal justice from State University in 1997 with a specialty in forensic science. That year, Chief Lennox had hired her in the spirit of equal opportunity by adding females to the ranks of detectives, or so he told her, but Hunter was never certain if Lennox had hired her because of the excellent academic record, her striking beauty, or pressure from the City Council.

Immediately, and rather suddenly after graduate school, Karen Hunter, nee LoPorti, had married a handsome man, Bill Hunter, who promised her a rich and fulfilling life. It had been a sudden, whirlwind romance with her future husband, which was scarred to some extent by her abrupt breakup with another graduate student, Joe Romano, a serious suitor who had planned to marry her after graduation. Their breakup had not ended amicably, but later Karen believed that her old beau had gotten on with his life without her.

Karen LoPorti had had a hard, early life. Because of her strong personality, she had overcome the pain of those years, and her formidable will had led to success in her professional life. Karen, however, never shared with anyone a deep, family secret that she carried, not even with her husband.

Initially, as the new kid in the Unit, Lennox had assigned her the lowest priority cases hoping the boring experience would discourage her. However, her handling of the assigned work was outstanding, forcing Lennox to admit begrudgingly that he had hired an exceptional officer. At five foot nine, the brown-haired woman had poise, personality, charm, and high intelligence that encouraged friendships and camaraderie.

Hunter's ability to work effectively with the senior detectives within the Unit soon earned her the respect of her workmates. Karen impressed her peers, so that she had become the go-to person in many instances. Her steady bearing with indispensable instincts especially when handling difficult cases made her a valuable asset to the department. From personnel records, Tate knew Karen's expertise in managing crime situations had resulted in an outstanding record for the department except for the current mysterious murder cases, but then she had not been the lead officer. However, Karen's direct involvement in other murder cases the Unit had investigated during her tenure showed that she was a first class detective.

When Chief Tate made Karen's promotion to Major official, she began to re-assemble the Major Crimes Unit. Her first appointment to the MCU was a solid performing, well-respected detective named Grace Carpenter. Lieutenant Carpenter had been one of the hard-working, much underappreciated officers in the Vice Unit under the old regime. Her career spanned twenty years in law enforcement; she had moved after five years with the Atlanta PD when her divorce forced a decision to seek another position outside of Atlanta. A well-seasoned detective, she was celebrating fifteen years with the Middlefield Police Department.

Grace stood five foot eight inches, and at forty-five years of age, she was a dependable, valued asset at the MPD. Similar to Karen, her annual fitness reports were well above average. Grace was a seasoned cop who Karen believed could be depended upon to serve as co-director for the Unit whenever needed. Grace was promoted to the rank of Detective Captain becoming second-in-command. Karen had a good sense of people and Grace, she knew, would be a valuable colleague and friend. Grace had many qualities, which fit perfectly with the Unit including her expertise in DNA forensics. This skill was one area the Unit needed badly for the murder investigations now underway.

Married at twenty, Grace had divorced after a marriage of five years. Recently, she married a man after having lived with him for two years.

The second person on Karen's hiring roster was Sergeant Martinelli. He had been with the MPD for eight years, transferring from the Vice Unit when Karen appointed him. Karen considered him an 'up and comer'. At Vice, Don had proven himself to be a solid, clear-thinking detective. His ability to cut through turmoil to see the critical issues was his greatest asset. Don's fitness reports were exemplary. He worked well with males and females in the department and always seemed to have a kind word for everyone.

Don, a native Georgian, was raised in Attapulgus, where his father, Clayton, was a supervisor at the local attapulgite quarry. The town's name, Attapulgus, which was due to the attapulgite in the area, came from the local Indian word meaning "Dogwood."

Don's early life was sheltered in a family of loving parents. He was born in 1985 long after the upheaval of the civil rights demonstrations in the sixties. His mother, Henrietta, was famous for sharing her cooking; she always lent a hand to any who needed it.

Don attended schools in nearby Bainbridge where he excelled in his classes. At six feet two, Don played basketball and football; earning letters in each sport during his junior and senior years.

After high school graduation, Don went to Fort Valley State University where he received his bachelor's and master's degrees in criminal justice. There he met the love of his life, Kim.

Clayton wanted Don to return to Attapulgus, but that was not what Don planned for his life. He applied for a position in the Middlefield Police Department, which hired him as a detective in training. Don married Kim soon after, and two children followed in due course.

Karen filled out her four-person team with the hiring of Corporal Susan Ramos. Susan was new to the MPD compared to Don and Grace having been hired only three years earlier after she had completed her Master's degree in Criminal Justice. Shortly after graduation, she had met and wed Carlos Ramos, who was completing his medical internship at Middlefield General Hospital.

Susan had worked in the GBI forensics lab for three years before coming to Middlefield. Because of her experience at GBI, she brought much needed lab skills to the Unit. Karen promoted both Don and Susan to the rank of Detective Lieutenant.

Chief Tate's instructions to the new manager of the MCU were to solve the two cold case murders resting on the Department's books. Nevertheless, even with the newly structured MCU, solving these murders would take the Karen and her investigators on an arduous journey.

* * *

Early Tuesday morning on March 18, 2008, the body of Alejandra Mendosa was found along Interstate-16 within the Middlefield jurisdiction. Mendosa's clutch bag with identification lay near her body. It was apparent from the condition of her body, that she had not been dead very long before her discovery.

Tragically, she was the third young woman found under similar circumstances in the past three years, but as

Middlefield was to learn, she would not be the last.

When Karen and Grace arrived at the site, they observed that Mendosa looked as though she had simply lain down for an unlikely rest by the breakdown lane of the highway.

The dead woman's long, dark brown hair partially covered her face. She was dressed in a black skirt that reached slightly above her knees. She wore a white blouse that was clean except where contact with roadside dirt had smudged the clothing. Without a coat or jacket, she was underdressed for the weather this time of year.

Her body showed no evidence of a struggle. Lacking defensive wounds on Mendosa's arms, Karen's initial thought was that light, possible ligature marks around her wrists could be attributed a sexual bondage escapade with a lover. However, that was only speculation.

The ligatures, if that's what they are, wouldn't be able to incapacitate the woman. In any event, it is something for Gordon to evaluate.

Grace called the Twiggs County ME, Dr. James Gordon, to the scene as was required before the body could be moved. Gordon examined her neck for any evidence of violence. After bagging her hands, he unbuttoned the midsection of her blouse. He then plunged a thermometer into her abdomen. Although a procedure not meant for the timid, the internal body temperature reading could help to determine the time of death.

Since the night temperature on the morning of the 18th was twenty-eight degrees, that temperature would increase cooling rate making the woman's internal body temperature lower than the expected body-cooling rate, thereby distorting the time of death calculation. Gordon estimated that the twenty-eight-degree night temperature probably increased the cooling rate from 1.5 to 1.7 degrees per hour.

"I measured Mendosa's internal body temperature to be 92.3 degrees Fahrenheit. At the estimated rate of 1.7 degrees per hour, she had probably breathed her last sometime after two this morning," Gordon told Karen, promising he would try to refine the time later. As in any case, of this type, Gordon would not commit his thoughts to Karen without a full autopsy performed. He scheduled one for the following day.

Gordon's autopsies of the two previous women had determined their deaths were due to internal suffocation; he had not found the cause for the women to die by asphyxia, but it was clear strangulation was not the cause.

There were no marks on their necks as generally found in cases of strangulation. Had they been smothered in some fashion, there would have been indications of violence.

Gordon noted as contributing evidence for this belief that neither woman had shown petechial hemorrhaging of the blood vessels in their eyes. Additionally, the hyoid bones in their necks were not fractured, which he knew was frequently found in strangulation cases, but, not always.

Doctor Gordon had been the Twiggs County ME for the past twenty years. A slight, balding man of fifty-five, his demeanor was no-nonsense. For him, it was depressing to have to examine people who had died so early in their lives. Gordon had seen many changes during his lifetime, and to him, violent deaths of so many young across the country in recent years were an indictment of the lack of societal respect for law and life.

The autopsy, scheduled for Wednesday morning, would follow the same process as was done for all autopsies of mysterious deaths. Gordon had scheduled the examination of Mendosa for 9:30 a.m., and the police had not yet shown up.

Impatiently, he and his assistant, John Bard, began to record the physical details of the woman as a preliminary activity while waiting for the police. Photographs were taken by Bard at each step of the autopsy for the permanent record.

At 9:50, Grace and Karen came into the room.

"This examination was scheduled to start at 9:30."

"We apologize, James. Traffic held us up."

"Well, we need to start moving. I have another one at 2:15 scheduled."

"Thank you, James. I apologize again."

"Before we are done today, I will give several evidence bags to you, so that you can maintain a direct chain of evidence control."

"I will remove the bags from her hands to scrape beneath her nails. Any detritus will be sent for testing to the GBI Forensics' Lab to aid you in your investigation."

Gordon then began the formal process tape recording his words for future reference:

"A full report will be made available to the Middlefield Police. I will maintain a permanent copy of this voice recording along with certified copies of any associated documentation at the Medical Examiner's office."

Gordon continued with his procedure.

"From the roadside body temperature and ambient temperature of the site, I estimate the time of death somewhere between the hours of two and four a.m., Wednesday morning (3/18/2008)."

Gordon then began the physical examination of the woman.

"I will document a list of clothing and Alejandra Mendosa's physical features as follows:

- **Skirt: Black leather, slightly dirty at the points of contact with the ground**
- **Blouse: White cotton, slightly dirty at the points of contact with the ground**
- **Bra: White cotton**
- **Underwear: not present**
- **Physical features:**
    - **Hispanic**
    - **Complexion: Fair**
    - **Eye color: Dark brown;**
    - **Facial shape is oval**
    - **Small nasal features**
    - **Hair color: Dark brown**

- **Length: eight inches below shoulder**
- **Weight: 120 pounds;**
- **Height: 5 foot 6 inches**

- **Notable features:**
  Syringe puncture wound on her left arm.

Gordon then proceeded with coarser aspects of the process by removing organs and noting their important physical features. Her heart and all other of her organs examined appeared normal.

He chose samples of blood and urine for testing along with sections of organs, including her brain for toxicology testing. Gordon then selected additional organ and brain samples to label and freeze for re-testing should the need arise.

Based on her stomach contents, Gordon noted Mendosa had not eaten for the past twenty-four hours. He also observed evidence of recent sexual activity; he designated semen samples to be sent to GBI for DNA profiling.

Additionally, Gordon found that her uterus contained a fetus, which he estimated to be nearly nine weeks in development.

"It is heartbreaking to realize that two lives were lost here," Gordon lamented.

"I know, James; it is tragic. We are trying to locate her family, but we aren't having much success," Karen replied.

"Let me know what to do with her body."

"Send her over to the Parker Funeral Home. The station

has taken up a collection for her. She'll be buried in St. Mary's Cemetery on Canton Street."

"Karen, I believe that we are finished with this. I will have the test results sent to you as they are received."

"Thank you, James. We will be waiting."

When Gordon had completed the autopsy, he completed the necessary government forms noting a few critical items he knew were required for the report.

- **Alejandra Mendosa was approximately nine weeks pregnant.**
- **Semen samples found in Mendosa will be sent to the GBI lab for profiling.**
- **Blood and tissue samples will be sent for toxicology testing.**
- **Victim's clothing will be sent to the GBI Crime Lab for fiber analysis.**

* * *

Three weeks later, the toxicology results came back; Gordon completed his final report by stating that Mendosa's death was <u>Undetermined</u> as to cause.

For the 2006/2007 autopsy reports, Gordon had likewise checked off <u>Undetermined</u> as the cause of their deaths. Back then and now, Gordon could not offer anything more concrete for an official opinion.

Without undeniable proof, he could only hint to Karen that someone, the killer, must have administered a drug to each of the three victims. His private opinion was that this drug was the source of the asphyxia leading to their deaths.

When the DNA testing of the semen sample in Mendosa was complete, it was clear and disconcerting that this profile matched the profiles from the other two unsolved cases. There was no longer any doubt that the man involved with the three women was most likely their killer. For Karen, however, another problem arose. A second male had left his DNA profile in Mendosa along with the presumed killer's semen.

With the lab reports and after conferring with Karen, Gordon now indicated that he believed he could state that all three women were murdered in the medical sense. As a result, he listed Homicide as the mode of death in his amended report of Mendosa. He then revised his autopsy findings for the deaths of the other two women from Undetermined to Homicide.

As Gordon knew well, in Georgia, the medical definition of homicide was different from the legal one. Medically, homicide did not indicate murder, manslaughter, or negligence as to the cause of death. It meant that a death might have occurred by unintentional, direct, or indirect actions of another person or persons. The legal definition of murder did mean the intentional killing of a person by other person or persons.

Consistent with Gordon's amended autopsy report, the Middlefield Police continued their pursuit of these women's deaths as murder using the legal definition. This change by Gordon did not aid the police, or offer new evidence to solve the Mendosa murder, but it did clear an obstacle, which had bothered the District Attorney should the cases ever come to court.

Karen knew one man having had sex with two women murdered may have been a terrible coincidence, but three women murdered with the same man's semen inside them nailed him as the killer, without doubt. However, what about the second profile? Who belonged to that? How did he fit in this murder?

No profile match existed in the National Database for either man. Since neither man's profile could be matched, Karen knew that identification of the killer was going to be backbreaking labor without much chance of success.

The MCU continued to conduct a thorough murder investigation of the Mendosa case without success. The MPD found a few witnesses who were certain they had seen Mendosa going into a Savannah bar alone on Sunday night before Saint Patrick's Day celebration, but no solid evidence connecting viable suspects was ever determined.

Appeals to the public had led to a general waste of precious police time. Some telephone tips speculated names of people who might have committed the crimes. Sometimes, callers were settling old scores or just plain troublemaking. The problem was that any possible suspects so named either had solid alibis or had no opportunity or no motive to kill the women. Worse, police had wasted much time following those leads that led nowhere.

Karen believed, also without any proof, that the

murderer must have known Mendosa. Could her murder have been committed due to her pregnancy? Did the killer love her? If so, why kill her? Was this display a need to satisfy his ego? Was this an act of revenge?

Did this murderer feel compelled to take Mendosa's life over an unplanned pregnancy? If so, what would have been the cause for the other two women? Was there any connection?

As for the dumping location, in Karen's opinion, the killer had chosen the busy I–16 corridor rather than the much less traveled state highways branching off of I–16 to ensure the police found her body quickly. Why was that important to the killer?

It was unexplainable that they found Mendosa in the eastbound direction of the highway. She was known to be in Savannah, which is southeast of her discovery location. Had she been in Atlanta, the dump location would make more sense. For the other two unsolved cases, police also found their bodies lying along the eastbound lanes. An interesting fact, Karen thought, but did it have any known value to this case, but then again where had Mendosa been from the evening of the 16th to the 18th?

Obviously, no one in the MCU wanted to allow the cases to go unsolved, however, without real leads; there was no hope of resolution. After exhaustive interviews, nothing had stood out enough to deliver a case that the district attorney would accept. Even with assistance from GBI, the three cases remained open, having gone cold.

The re-investigations of these cases had barely begun when there was an additional murder in March 2009. Road workers discovered Arlene Lonergan, age twenty-one, under the same circumstances as the previous three women. Four murders presenting similar circumstances were unheard of. This killer did not fit any profiles with which the police were familiar.

The police were no closer to finding the killer of these four women than they had been in 2006 when the nightmare began. Citizens could not believe that with all the available tools in forensic crime fighting, these cases should have dragged on for this long without the killer apprehended. The citizens knew their police had failed.

The public was calling for resignations at the Police Department. The *Patriot* stated in one of their scathing articles that the city had spoiled the police with fancy benefits.

The impression held by some was that the police did not want to leave the station houses to protect people. The *Patriot* reminded its readers constantly of the lack of progress in solving serious cases.

Every thinking citizen realized that a serial killer was on the loose. Publically, and for political reasons, the police had deliberately avoided the use of that word.

Politics had blunted a formal announcement voicing a serial killer. Since there were no answers or explanations for the crimes, police feared alarming the citizens.

Karen assigned the MCU staff to re-examine the two

mysterious deaths of Louise Fletcher in March of 2006, and Patty Sunberg in March of 2007.

It was clear to the investigators that the killer was incredibly skilled, very lucky. With no witnesses or no new clues, there was a high probability this case would also go cold.

The MCU understood that March was a deadly month for young women in their jurisdiction, but they were not close to an explanation. Why did the killer only murder in March? Was there any connection to the annual Archeology Conference held at Middlefield in March?

The College invited scholars from around the world to the conference. College planners had selected the middle of March because of the large Saint Patrick's Day festivities in Savannah primarily for the benefit of attendees' families.

In 2008, Grace had looked carefully at the attendees' list provided by the college. She submitted names to the National Criminal Records, but nothing had turned up.

The College was incensed that the police had done this threatening to withhold any future lists. Karen threatened search warrants if they did.

Worse, in March of 2010, Rose Smith was found on I–16 making her the fifth murder victim. A background check showed her conviction of prostitution in Atlanta in 2009. The unfortunate tally of dead prostitutes counting Mendosa's, now numbered five.

Chapter Two

And when they have finished their testimony, the beast that ascendeth out of the bottomless pit shall make war against them, and shall overcome them and kill them. Revelation 11:7

For police, pressure was building each day to find the killer until the MPD received an unusual letter in early 2011.

On January 20, a renovation crew was clearing a book storage room at the Middlefield College Library. While they were removing the books, an envelope containing a letter slipped to the floor. Unable to control their curiosity, workers opened the envelope. The content of the letter was so sinister; they turned it over to the College administration, who in turn gave it to the Middlefield Police for evaluation.

Chief Tate read the letter; then he called Karen Hunter to his office.

"Karen, I've just received a most disturbing letter. The College found it yesterday. I'm not sure what to think. Take a look at it."

Karen carefully took the letter and read:

March 18, 2008

Detective Karen Hunter,

I want to tell you about Alejandra Mendosa. She was found along I–16 this morning. She was murdered. I am the one who did it. It is important to me that you found her quickly. I want you to see that she died in an odd way. I know the coroner will

not be able to tell how she died.

Do you realize that the other women you found in the last two years are my doing? They have gone terrified, but peacefully to their reward. Well, not exactly peacefully….

I get much satisfaction in helping these young Ladies to reach the other side. They all have terror in their eyes as they expire. I like to watch them die.

I make this prediction: you will never catch me. I will be victorious. You are a loser and I despise you. You are going to die.

I am just waiting for the right opportunity. It will come when you do not expect it.

I have included some codes for you to work on, because I know you love codes. I have included clues in this letter to help you solve them. You need to do some more research on codes, Karen. See if you can overcome your lack of education.

<u>My name may be in the last two code lines.</u> A further clue: <u>the alpha codes may help solve the numerical codes</u>. Good luck!

Your able, devoted helper…

MIRHCAHTVZ XZNVJABY KKNPOWHZ
MKNYKWBY KKGUQQBTBZWNKZELOXE

519091241387394638384902781928 17
0327414018506232968283622766 1443
635004167291335952859828431753 78
682179468439731000128610661130 80
096143212700468283630280022623 60
110863010130329174882737651755 27
163313244368561580541792844583 58
434837926884641383599105451031 94

"Karen, as you can see, the writer refers to Mendosa's murder, and he seems to have accurate information concerning her death. Notice the date of the letter. The writer seems to know you well, although he does not say how or why, but he makes a clear threat against you."

"Chief, there have been so many strange things around all these cases that I am not surprised about anything that happens these days."

"Well, what do you think?" Tate asked.

"I am astounded that he addressed the letter to me. What is his real motive? As you noted, this letter is nearly three years old; he wrote it March of 2008. This is almost the end of January 2011. Where has it been all this time?"

"President Burns from the college sent it over. It was in their library stacks."

"He may have tripped himself by doing this. We have had nothing at all to work with for these cases. The code stuff at the bottom is something I think we should be able to handle, I hope."

"Is there anyone in your group that knows something about codes?"

"I know Don has some military experience. He may be able to coordinate resources to work them. I spent some time in the past researching code writing for some projects I had in college. Codes have always been more than a passing interest for me. I'll start considering it again."

"That's interesting. I didn't know that. Don is a smart detective. Have him look at it. I don't believe you can fully devote your time to solving them."

"Chief, I believe that this is the break we've needed, but I honestly cannot say how it might help right now. The person has thrown in stuff that does not make sense to me. I am not sure what we will need for support yet, but we may require a lot of it. One thing this letter does is give me a feeling that we now have something that may help solve the Mendosa case; perhaps it may also lead us to solving the other murders. It looks like I am the bait, though."

"This guy is pure evil; you need to be careful, Karen."

"I will. I must admit he makes very nervous, but I think I can handle it."

"You need to recall anyone who may have a grudge that is strong enough to want you dead."

"I'll spend time on it. Right now, I have no idea who it could be."

"Are you sure you going to be able to work this in light of the personal issue involved?" Tate asked.

"Chief, I can't let this stop me. The Unit has been working these cases for a long, miserable time. This letter is a new avenue for us."

"As I asked earlier, can you remember anyone in your life who bears this sort of grudge against you?"

"Right now I'm stunned. I need time to absorb what I have read. I'll need to spend time to answer your question about someone's possible hatred."

"Keep me informed of the Unit's progress. When you need more help, ask immediately."

"Chief, we know we have a serial killer operating here. We have not had the courage to announce that fact. What do we do to let the citizens know? We have to warn the women in Middlefield. In fact, the news should be spread throughout Georgia."

"There's a problem with that, Karen. The Mayor wants to play down this idea of a serial killer."

"But we believe it's the same guy committing these murders. The method of operation and the semen profiles are the same for the five women; and now, thankfully, we have his confession."

"I understand. We have to be careful how we announce it. It may backfire on us."

"Our five murdered women were found a year apart. To top it off, we think he kills only in mid-March. It is the same MO. He is the serial killer. We have to admit that to the people."

"We don't know if he will continue, or even why he has this strange pattern. In addition, what is to say he does not kill any time of the year, only changing the method of operation to mislead us? The question will be how we tell the citizens," Tate said.

"Chief, you have to listen to me. People must be told that we have a serial killer operating in the area."

"I have to plan how I get the Mayor's attention."

"Chief, I understand what you are saying, but I can't sleep at night thinking that an announcement may save another woman's life. We should at least warn women to be vigilant."

"Give me a chance to try. I will call the Mayor to tell him we must have a press conference. I'll let you know."

Karen returned to her office, to reflect on the situation she and the MCU had faced for the past five years.

This is 2011. Since the murder of Louise Fletcher in 2006, we have not made a single arrest. We have five murdered women, and not a clue who murdered them. We have no viable leads other than DNA profiles that have no name match. We have failed. There's no doubt. I hope this letter is the break we have been waiting for.

Karen made herself comfortable in her chair. She knew there was value in mentally reviewing the sequence of events, so she continued her journey of thought:

The Mendosa murder had transformed the urgency of the investigation in 2008. The woman was an archeology graduate student at Middlefield College preparing to write up her dissertation and graduate within a few months. Pressure from the press to solve these murders was intense because of the murder of a woman of 'value.'

It was not that Middlefield citizens were particularly callous, or did not care about the murder of two prostitutes back then. It was, perhaps, that they simply could not relate to those women's deaths. They may have been sad for them, but it did not elevate the community's blood pressure the way Mendosa's death had.

The citizens of Middlefield were alarmed at Alejandra Mendosa's murder, but they suppressed outrage for the

prostitutes' murders. Outrage should have been there for all of them.

Perhaps, parents consider their young daughters to be pure, wholesome creatures on their way to successful careers. Their daughters are different from the other four unfortunate young women, even though many of their daughters above the age of sixteen are not exactly virginal in behavior. However, those other women had made life-degrading decisions, which may have contributed to their deaths, so it is a world they cannot fathom.

Even though we worked diligently to solve all the murders, the fact that four of deaths were 'women of the street' resulted in minimum press coverage.

Back then, Green felt this lack of press coverage was a major reason the usual volume of good phone tips never materialized. It was one more way for the 'good' to avoid worrying with regard for the 'bad' folks.

For the Mendosa case, we had identified a few possible suspects from Middlefield College who worked with Alejandra in her research.

We had found no reason for Mendosa's friends or work-mates to harm her. However, Mendosa's pregnancy was a possible motive for someone.

Using that reasoning, we asked for swabs from those associated with her. Most had refused on First Amendment principles to give samples.

For those who did, we had paternity tests done. Much

to my chagrin, we discovered that the father was none of those who had volunteered their samples. We had cleared Devin Schneider and Nathan Schott who were close associates with Mendosa.

Devin Schneider denied any intimacy with Mendosa. He said they did not like each other from the day they met.

Nathan Schott readily admitted Mendosa was his lover. They had split amicably when they realized they had different goals for the future.

Then, we concentrated our efforts on Mendosa's associates who had refused to give DNA samples. Top on our list were Assistant Professor David Marino and Chad Jenkins.

We were well aware of rumors that Marino had been intimate with Mendosa over the past year. Marino denied any relationship other than professional.

Jenkins was her current boyfriend, so it would not have been a surprise if they were intimate. What was a surprise, though, was his denial.

Since Jenkins denied intimacy with Mendosa, finding his DNA in her presented a serious problem for him to explain. Did he know she was pregnant? I wondered if that was the reason why Jenkins had not volunteered a cheek swab.

We never fully vetted Jenkins. His alibi was that he never left the college that weekend. He said he had spent his time in his room, so no one could vouch for him. Without any proof to connect him to the murder, we reluctantly eased the pressure on him.

Under questioning, Dr. Marino swore he had never been intimate with Mendosa. I felt it was a lie, but it was the kind of lie to save embarrassment. Still, I hate it if people lie to me.

We did press Marino's alibi for the weekend Mendosa died. Again, I was not able to verify it because Marino could offer no witnesses. He said he had been in his apartment the entire time; no one had come to visit him.

Frustrated, we obtained their samples using an old trick. During separate interviews of Jenkins and Marino, we offered drinks. After their interviews, we sent the containers to the GBI crime lab to profile the samples, if possible. Two weeks later, we had results.

We then knew that Jenkin's semen was the other profile found in Mendosa. I had paternity tests done. The result was an earth shaker. Marino was the father of her baby!

Then I had had a serious problem on my hands. Either man might have had a reason to kill Mendosa, but we could not arrest them both for Mendosa's murder.

My strategy was to tell them we had their profiles. I told them we had paternity tests done. I thought that maybe the pressure would make one of them crack, but it never did. Because they had lied, I decided to withhold the fact that Marino, not Jenkins, was the father.

We have asserted that Mendosa knew her killer. Were we correct? Was it possible that the other two women

knew the killer also? Wait a moment; did none of them know the killer before he murdered them? At the time, it had been an assumption that finding a connection to the three women could move the investigations forward. It had not. The reason for the murders remained a nagging question.

I believe it had been a special love or hatred to dump Alejandra's body the way the killer did. In 2008, I had had the same feeling regarding the other two women. Worse, someone had killed two more women using the same MO in 2009 and 2010.

However, Alejandra was different. Alejandra's pregnancy was particularly sad. A mother and child lost to an evil person. What a waste.

Karen's thoughts turned to her present, personal situation.

Bill and I have been trying for ten years to have a child with no success. Here was a woman who had what I always wanted. Someone simply snuffed out the lives of Alejandra and her baby. Life is so unfair.

We know that a serial killer has committed all five murders. From 2006 to the latest in 2010, we know it is the work of one man, but attaching his name to his profile has been impossible so far.

These murders must stop. I need to energize the Unit, so we can put this murderer on death row. This letter may do it. I need to have the Unit spend time with this letter.

* * *

The next morning, Karen assembled her detectives to discuss the "Mendosa" letter.

"I called you here to review the letter given to me by Chief Tate. First, I need to make you aware that on Friday, he will have a press conference to talk officially concerning our serial killer. I warn you now that he may not use that phrase. Politics, I am afraid; I want you to be prepared. Tate is the mouthpiece, so no one from MCU is to talk to the press. Do you understand?

"For this meeting, I've made copies of the letter," said Karen.

While the group read the letter to themselves, Karen watched their faces for signs to see how they would consider its value. She saw smiles. She saw frowns. She thought it was going to work for them. More than ever, Karen wanted the investigation to succeed with the new information they now possessed.

"Well, what do you think?" she asked.

"This is the break we've needed for years. I am excited. Why is he targeting you, of all people?" Grace asked.

"Frankly, I have no idea."

"Karen, the part of the letter he wants us to read is only to taunt you. The rest he has put in code, which he believes cannot be broken. If you agree, I'd like to work the code part of the letter," Don suggested.

"Don, I think you are the right person for that. Start as soon as you can. I have had experience with codes and will work with you. Let me know immediately if you need any assistance."

"This letter has shades of the Zodiac killer. If you recall, he was a serial killer who operated in northern California in the late 1960s and early 1970s. He sent many coded messages during his reign of terror. Many were decoded, but the one with his name was not. However, the MO of our killer is different. Their egos are similar. They both believe they are more intelligent than we are," said Don.

"I agree. The e-mail I will send to you identifies some preliminary ideas I have for how we can approach the investigation. I want each of us personally involved. Most of us have been in the department long enough, so that we understand what that means. This job ain't going to be easy, if I can use street language."

"Karen, should we call in the FBI to lend a hand?" asked Susan.

"Not right away. Turf always gets in the way of cooperative police work. They have not been much help to date. We can always revisit that idea later."

"I ask that now because I worked with the FBI on a case some years ago. It was a mess. They always want to control investigations; it is not satisfying. I wanted to know your feelings," Susan explained.

"Good, we agree. Earlier, I asked our document clerk, Betty, to gather up the existing files on all our cases. She will put them in the conference room for your use.

"I think we should lay out the five cases again; scour them for any commonalities we may have overlooked in the past. We should develop a profile of the killer based on the letter. In the meantime, Don and I will try to focus on the letter content."

"I feel there is tremendous drudgery re-looking over the files again," Susan complained.

"I know. We seem to be in an endless loop, but we have to overcome it," Karen said, less than sympathetically.

"I would love to do what was done in Britain to solve these murders. Of course, our Fifth Amendment does not allow it. Wouldn't it be incredible to order a sample of every male's DNA in the area?" Grace ventured.

"It's just wishful thinking. We have no information to say the person is local, but let me make myself extremely clear on this topic. We are not going to have a repeat of 2008. We never solved the murder of Mendosa. We never solved the four prostitutes' murders. We are meeting today to figure out how to work these cases. We have to be creative in our approach," Karen emphasized.

"The readable part of the letter gives us an idea what happened. He confesses he did it. He writes that breaking the numerical code will provide us his name. The four-part alpha characters are puzzling. He is extremely sure of himself," Don said.

"I would ask forensics to look at the letter for any latent fingerprints, but since it has been handled by so many, it's probably not worth the effort," Susan offered.

"Have them check it, anyway. He may have left a print, which we will need when we catch him. We know his profile isn't in the system yet, so he's safe for now."

"Karen, this guy is strange. He's careful concerning how he murders; then he leaves his semen without worry."

"It seems that there may be clues to his identity buried in the letter. Can we try to sort them out, and put them on the white board?" Grace asked.

"I like that suggestion," Karen said.

"Why don't we put down the most obvious things first? We can try to build to something from the letter's content," Grace suggested.

"The letter was typed on plain paper with no watermark. No clue there at all," Karen said.

"The letter is dated March 18, 2008, the day she was discovered along the highway. I have no doubt the murder was premeditated," Susan noted.

"As Don noted, the coded part of the letter has two different types of ciphers," Karen added.

"Can we break them?" Grace asked.

"I hope so. Don and I will spend much of our time working them," Karen said.

"We haven't a clue why he is doing this. Obviously, he has a vendetta against you. Does he hate other women? Does it satisfy his rage to take revenge on them, or is it something else?" Grace asked.

"Well, what should be our non-cipher approach?" Don asked.

"Yesterday, I asked Susan to contact other Georgia police departments to see if they have any unsolved cases with similar MOs. I have a list of my former boyfriends. In addition, I have asked Susan to do a thorough research of their pasts. That research should include anything judicial. However, I can't believe I dated someone who would turn to killing over a relationship with me, but who knows," Karen said.

"Is it just your old lovers that we should be concerned about?" asked Grace.

"No, we have to look at other situations I was involved in as a police officer," Karen said.

"What other situations?" Grace asked.

"Well, in 2005, Lennox assigned me to work a rape case of an undergrad at the College. It turned out the perp was a professor attending the annual College Conference. However, an appeals court overturned his conviction on a technicality. But he lost his position at NYU, and his life was a mess after that."

"I understand. We need to find him and interrogate him," Grace said.

"I agree. He does bear a grudge against me, but there may be others involved. I had made quite a number of arrests for various crimes early in my career. We have to check them all out. I would like you, Grace, to lead that effort. Let's move on to other clues in the letter."

"The letter is written using a word processor, not a typewriter. Assuming it was done at the College, it is not traceable," said Don.

"Well, since it was found at the College, was the person

who wrote it associated with the College?" Susan asked.

"It could have been someone who simply used the library. Perhaps the person is not associated with the College beyond that," Grace added.

"The coded part of the letter will require a lot of work to solve," said Don.

"We will deal with that in a bit. Let us try our hand at profiling the writer from the letter. It may not help much, but it's a start," Karen suggested.

- **The writer is clearly educated.**
- **The writer has a huge ego–the smugness.**
- **The writer shows no remorse.**
- **I believe the killer wrote the letter just before we found Mendosa.**
- **This person is comfortable with codes**.

"Obviously, the MOs of these murders show they are well planned out. The way he selects victims may be random, though," Grace said.

"This killer shows a single-minded purpose to kill you, Karen. That's not random," Susan said.

"I guess he is practicing for the day he catches up with me," Karen said.

Since 2008, Karen had never viewed the Mendosa murder as a random act. She was less certain regarding the prostitutes' deaths, considering the women's profession. It had been hard to concentrate the MCU energy on those murders. They could have been blind meetings that just suited the killer's plan. Perhaps it was simply a case of "wrong place; wrong time."

"They may have been unfortunate meetings with a psychopath honing his skills," Don said.

"Who knows? For some reason, I believe that our killer does know his victims before he selects them," Grace added.

"Perhaps, but because four out of five of the women were prostitutes, we can't be certain how they met," Karen said.

"Sorry. Change of subject. Speaking of code writing, I heard that some researchers encrypt their sensitive data to protect it from colleagues who might plagiarize credit for their work," Don informed them

"God only knows why they think their data may be so secret," Grace said.

"Don's point is that practice of that sort may not be as unusual as we think. Perhaps it is someone associated with academia. We ruled that out three years ago, but maybe we were wrong," Karen replied.

"Ah, our College connection?" asked Grace.

"Remember, the letter was found in the College library. Mendosa was a graduate student," Susan added.

"So perhaps it challenges our assumption that we should not be looking for a professor or another graduate student," Don said.

"The Mendosa case reeks of a love triangle or some sort of relationship that did not end well," cautioned Grace.

"We certainly did not rule that out in our investigation

in 2008. We just couldn't find any evidence to arrest anyone," Karen reminded.

"Why do we think the letter has to point to a professor or some academic type? Couldn't it be just any educated person?" Susan asked.

"Sure, but we can't limit our view to the academic world. We are only focusing on it because that is where they found the letter. However, it is a mistake to jump to conclusions. We can start there again, but we spent a lot of time back then with no results. We should quickly move beyond the College, if nothing pans out," said Karen.

"With the age of the letter, we can't even say the person is still at the college," added Don.

"Again, I'm not optimistic that reviving the College connection will be fruitful. We have had nothing to work with over the years. Maybe the letter will improve our luck," Karen added.

"Karen, we should call the GBI folks to develop a professional profile for us," Grace asked.

"Well, our little attempt today isn't especially telling. Perhaps an experienced profiler can work with the letter. We'll need to make the files of our crime scene analysis available," Karen said.

"I've read criticism about the whole idea of profiling. Profiles run from fifty to ninety-eight percent correct. Infamously, the FBI booted it with the Green River killer along with some other high profile cases. In fact, it might lead us in the wrong direction," cautioned Don.

"I think we've been going in the wrong direction for a long time. It cannot hurt. Let's try it," Karen said.

"All right, Karen. I will call GBI for a name."

"Also, it may be useful for us to ask a psychiatrist to guide us. We never tried this before. Perhaps they can give us an idea of where we could focus our investigation. It is another way to look at the things we know. It's way to try to understand his thinking," Karen said.

"Could we have someone come here to talk to the group?" Grace asked.

"I have someone in mind. I will call him."

"The whole tone of the letter is strange. I think he wanted us to have this letter three years ago. We've had four murders with similar MOs as Mendosa's," said Grace.

"We don't understand the guy's motives. However, for whatever reason, he is acting as judge, jury, and executioner. In any event, we have to capture whatever tidbits of clues he has sent to us to identify him. Unless you have anything further, I think we are finished for today."

"I'll call GBI now," Grace said.

"Don, why don't you start looking at the code while I talk to Grace?"

Grace followed Karen to her office.

"I want you to review the murder case files again. Start with Mendosa. We had a good investigation in 2008, but another review may turn up something we missed."

"I've actually started on them. The DNA profiles were the only thing we had. Do you remember the problems we had? Only some of the males associated with Mendosa voluntarily gave samples."

"We had two possible suspects: Jenkins and Marino. We knew that Marino was the father of Mendosa's baby, but neither of their samples matched the profile of the killer's. However, with Jenkins, we also found his DNA in Mendosa at the autopsy. He clearly lied. He denied being with her that weekend." Karen added.

"I remember we pressed the idea that Mendosa tried to get Jenkins or Marino to marry her providing a motive for her killing. They were the only ones to refuse lie detector tests. We wanted to arrest Jenkins because he had lied to us, and we could not verify his alibi. Of course, we never could verify Marino's alibi either," added Grace.

"Yeah, the DA took the circumstantial evidence to the grand jury, but they returned a 'no bill.' That ended the probe of Jenkins. That effectively shut down the Mendosa case," Karen agreed.

"Marino's alibi wasn't that solid, but it wasn't enough to arrest him, either. The DA felt another 'no bill' would result for Marino. We didn't have enough for a case."

"I have to spend more time with the files. Maybe there is something we missed," Grace said.

"Good. Let's continue our discussion in a few days, if need be."

"Before you go, change of subject. I think it may be important to know if Mendosa was having any prenatal care. Was there anything in the case file that indicated who

Mendosa's doctor was?"

"I don't remember anything relating to that in the file."

"If not, check the College infirmary. Find out if she went there for her pregnancy. We should be able to obtain her records without a court order," said Karen.

"I read somewhere that they refer student pregnancies to a doctor in Atlanta. I'll have Susan verify that."

Chapter Three

And when the dragon saw that he was cast unto the earth, he persecuted the woman which brought forth the man child. Revelation 12:13

On Friday, January 25, Chief Tate stood before interested citizens along with assembled reporters. City officials stood behind him as moral support giving the citizens a sense of solidarity from their leaders.

"The city is dealing with multiple unexplained killings. We do not have a solid suspect. We are looking at several people of interest. Recently, credible evidence has come into our possession, which may help us to put closure to these murders soon."

"Can you tell us what that evidence is?" a reporter interrupted.

"Not at this point. It has to be examined before we can release any further details," Tate responded.

He did not mention that these murders appeared to be planned annual killings. The Mayor insisted that Tate not use the word serial in the announcement. Therefore, Chief Tate's speech was less than forthcoming.

The Mayor's political precaution was silly. Anyone following the news for the past few years knew there was a serial killer operating in the Middlefield area. Rumors always fly around before officials have fortitude to say it.

"One person may be responsible for all of the killings. We need to explore that further. I want to alert all women to be on their guard. Do not to accept open drinks from people unknown to you at bars, or any other places where you buy drinks. I recommend women develop a buddy system. We encourage men in the community to support our women. The police have set up a hot line that will respond to any woman calling for an escort. Primarily, this service will be made available for any women needing accompaniment to their cars. We plan to have officers stationed at the mall. If citizens request other venues, we will try to accommodate them," Tate continued.

Chief Tate closed his communication with a spirit of hope by saying we would catch the evil person soon. After Tate had finished his statement, Mayor Hampton promised to form an ad-hoc Citizens' Committee whose singular purpose would be to provide progress reports to the city. He appointed the City Attorney, Jeffrey Benton, to chair the Committee. Five additional citizens chosen by the Mayor would complete the panel.

Chief Tate was tasked with providing weekly updates to the panel. If there were no results in a reasonable span of time, the Committee could recommend the removal of Chief Tate. Given the progress to date, the residents' reactions to the speech were "wait and see."

During the Q & A period following Tate's speech, the word that the Patriot journalists keyed on was <u>soon</u>.

That word would come back to haunt all City officials as the weeks dragged on without a single arrest.

After Tate's news conference, the Mayor approached Tate with a threat. The City Council would be patient, but there had better be results.

Later, Karen approached Chief Tate.

"I think your message was well delivered. It had the right touch. I am a little worried that people will believe we will catch the killer in a few days. It is still going to be a while."

"I know. The Mayor insisted that I add that word. He thought it might tamp down some of the general criticism, but I doubt it."

"Did you know what Hampton planned to do with his committee?" Karen asked.

"He never said a word. He's trying to slide the monkey off his back before the election in November."

"It's going to be that much tougher with him breathing down our necks."

"I have no doubt. Our announcement may have eased the City's fears, but it puts intense pressure on us."

"I have a feeling that the committee may be a vehicle we can use to our advantage. It may be the way to supply information to the city without giving away the details of our investigation," Karen said.

"Yes, this process may help. The way it is now, the reporters just record what we say; then blow it up to suit their agenda. In the end, the story they print is nothing remotely similar to what we've said," growled Tate.

"The information we release has to be so clear the reporters can't mess it up. Also, it has to be benign or it may tip off the killer," Karen added.

“Karen, you will write the weekly message we provide to the committee. Please set your calendar so we can meet at noon each Wednesday,” Tate ordered.

“I will put together some ideas concerning how we plan the reports.”

“I am going to talk with Hampton. We must have the right people selected,” Tate added.

“Good. I have invited a psychiatrist friend of mine to give the MCU some things to think about the killer’s psyche. Care to join us?”

“I think I will concentrate my efforts on the Mayor’s committee, for now.”

The following day, the MCU assembled in the conference room. Karen had arranged for coffee and Danish for the special meeting.

“Good morning, folks. I invited a visitor to our meeting today. I want to introduce you to Dr. Henry Adams. He is going to assist us to understand the type of person we are dealing with,” Karen said.

“Good morning. What I am going to share with you this morning is not profiling. The best that we can do is to try to understand what clues the killer is giving us from the letter. Like you, I have assumed that the letter writer is the killer. Detective Hunter supplied me with a copy of the letter last week. She also supplied me with some other information regarding the murders committed by this man. As you already know, this individual has a personal grudge against Karen. He does not clearly state the reasons in the letter. By showing his detailed knowledge of you, he hopes to control and terrorize you."

"I'm not giving any credence to his statements regarding our inability to work these cases, nor his comments about me," Karen said.

"Good. This person has some working knowledge of police procedures. He is disdainful of police abilities. He exhibits a trait other criminals have, that is, he believes he is much more intelligent than the police."

"He's certainly been very lucky so far. Is there anything you see in the letter that would help us identify him?" Grace asked.

"Not directly. His hatred of Karen and his statement around killing other women is a sign of the rage he can't control. Clearly, he is striking out at females to satisfy the need to avenge. This leads me to believe that he may have feelings of abandonment by someone crucial in his life. He has some idea of betrayal by someone who is or has been close to him. This person could be his mother or some other woman who was a protector, and then betrayed him."

"Many people have lost their mothers, or been abused by someone close for one reason or another, but they don't go around killing people," Karen voiced.

"That is true. Many people have experienced dreadful childhoods. They overcome the pain; they become useful contributors to society, not killers. There are those, however, who fixate on a feeling of abandonment, which feeds hatred. He did not say whether he knew Mendosa before he murdered her. It could be that all the women he killed were just pickup opportunities.

"In general, these types of killers lash out at women, but may focus on one woman in particular. The person who becomes the target is someone he perceives has betrayed him. His killings of other women are substitutes for the betrayer. I have no doubt in my mind that he means to try to kill you, Karen."

"Is there a name for this type of behavior?" asked Karen.

"It is called the Madonna-whore or Madonna-prostitute complex. Freud suggested this is something that develops in some men who divide women into two categories. These men see women either as Madonnas or as prostitutes.

"The Madonna in his life may be his mother. It may be someone else. He may have the feeling she abandoned him by dying or, for instance, marrying someone he dislikes. He pictures his mother or this person as pure, undefiled by sex. He loves his mother. He may hate his mother, but he does not want to admit it.

"His other category of women is driven by his sexual needs. Those women who are easy conquests for him are sluts in his mind. He despises them, but he needs to use them. He may become especially fixated on one woman with whom he was intimate. She betrayed him somehow. This may be the point at which he decides to wreak vengeance. That may be what we are facing here."

"Whew. This is enlightening," Grace exclaimed.

"I am not stating this as a known fact. It just appears that way to me. Obviously, there are probably other things involved."

"Doctor Adams, thank you for your time. Sharing this scenario with us today helps a lot," Karen said.

"It is not my pleasure that I had to tell you this. I hope it makes a difference.

"Karen, if you please, I have a suggestion."

"What would that be, Doctor?"

"If you can, try to think of men you have been involved with. Try to remember how they felt about their mothers. Think of their views of women in general. That may assist you to spotlight someone."

"Thank you, Doctor. I will try to give it as much thought as possible. Susan is checking my arrest records for my rookie years here." Karen replied.

"What are you looking for?" Adams asked.

"Anything that that points to arrests involving moral crimes, etc. Since most of my arrests occurred when I first joined the force, we're looking at the first three years."

"Also, in the letter the killer offers clues for solving the ciphers. Obviously, I'm not an expert in those matters, but don't overlook common words, names etc."

"You may be right, Doctor. As I dig further into the ciphers, that will be one area of focus," Don said.

"Thank you again, Doctor. We appreciate your time with us," Karen said.

Chapter Four

Reward her even as she has rewarded you, and double unto her double according to her works: in the cup which she hath filled fill to her double.

Revelation 18:6

"Don, prioritize your work on the ciphers. Do not let anything else get in the way. Without the ciphers, we have nothing. Right now, the DNA isn't giving us a name."

"I've already started looking at the alpha characters he gave us. He knows you are familiar with ciphers, so that means he is somehow close to you."

"I know. I will personally work these with you. Meet me each morning at ten in my office."

"Should we ask the GBI if they can support us with the code?" asked Don.

"If they have someone on board that can assist, sure."

"I am going to do a review of the College's functions as well as the professional staff. In addition, I want to meet at eight a.m. on Wednesday to review what we have learned. I will set our tasks," Karen added.

Karen went to her office, which was the typical fifteen by fifteen-foot space with floor to ceiling walls and a locking door, as befitted a Major.

She had replaced the drab, gray steel desk used by Detective Green with a smart wooden credenza that gave the room a sense of respectability. Her desk chair was a large leather roll around.

There were several side chairs for use by visitors. The

walls had been re-painted before she moved in. They were still looking fresh, probably due to the 'No Smoking' ban imposed several years earlier. Of course, that made no difference to Karen who had never smoked in her life.

Karen placed her college degrees prominently on the walls along with two paintings of forest scenes. Pictures of her husband with Thor, her dog, were on her desk.

Although Karen felt that reviving the College connection was a waste of time, she decided a short report of the College to the MCU would help. It would focus on the activities of the College beyond the local academic work including the annual Archeological Conference. Using as much on-line information as available, she found enough general information to include in her report to the staff.

The next morning, Karen went to Grace's office.

"Grace, back in 2007, Green had interviewed a guy named Joseph Romano. It was Green's feeling that Romano was a bit too interested in the two prostitute murders, so he checked him out."

"Why is that important now?" Grace probed.

"Romano and I were very close. Well, to be truthful, boyfriend and girlfriend. We split when I met Bill. I hadn't run into him again until the Sunberg murder when Green interrogated him."

"Did anything come of it?"

"No, Green just felt he was a bit too nosy, so he went after him for information. Green never felt comfortable with Romano, but there was nothing solid he could put his finger on.

"Green did try to find out things concerning his life: hobbies, friends, associates, family, etc. Nothing was notable there. Green thought Romano was lonely. He did get him to admit that he had had a relationship that had gone sour."

"Karen, did you ever tell Green you had a romance with Romano?"

"Of course, I did. Green eventually dropped Romano as a possible suspect. He had no evidence or anything approaching a case against him."

"Karen, maybe we should look up Mr. Romano to see what we can get for any updated info."

"I agree. It may be worth a trip to Atlanta."

"I think I should go to see him, Karen."

"No, I should see him. If he does have anything to do with these murders, it wouldn't be good to spook him now."

"I think you're wrong, but you're the boss."

"I'll give him a call this afternoon. I will check him out. If I get negative feelings, I'll suggest we both go."

"Suit yourself, but be careful."

After Grace left, Karen stood at her desk while dialing Romano's phone number.

"Good morning, Dr. Romano."

"Hi, Joe, this is Karen Hunter here."

"Hello, Karen. It has been a very long time. How are

things with you these days?"

"They are going well," Karen lied.

"How are things with you and your husband? Any kids yet?"

"To be truthful, Joe, I am trying to work some marriage issues out with Bill. His work requires him to be out of town often. He is currently at a pharmaceutical show in Chicago this whole week, so I called to ask if we could have dinner sometime soon."

What did you have in mind, Karen?

"Is there any special reason?"

"Yes, I have an old murder case that you discussed with Detective Green sometime ago. I would like to talk to you again in relation to it. New information has come to us. Some of it is disturbing."

"Really, how can I help?"

"We are puzzled by this new information and have some questions, with which you may be able to help us. I know you were tangentially involved sometime ago, which was the reason Green interviewed you."

"Am I a suspect again?"

"No. Green did not feel that way. I also didn't feel that way back then, and presently I don't put you in the suspect category either. I am just looking for some help. Perhaps there's something you may not have thought of back then."

"Okay. Well, you know bachelors, Karen; they never turn down dinner dates. By the way, you timed your call perfectly. My birthday date, as you may remember, happens to be on Friday this week. Could we have dinner that day to celebrate it? I had planned to spend it alone, but… Does that work for you?"

"Yes, Bill will still be in Chicago then. I want you to understand, Joe, that I coming for a business meeting."

"Okay, that's great. It will be very nice to see you again."

"On Friday, I could be in Atlanta by seven. Do you have any preferences for restaurants?"

"One of my favorites is Roma Posta. Have you ever been there?"

"No, I haven't even heard of it."

"That's right. It was not open when we were together. It does have delicious food. See you at seven that day. I'll call for reservations."

"That sounds great. See you then."

Karen sat at her desk letting memories whisk through her mind.

It sure was fun back then. If I had not made that decision to leave him, how different things might have been. It is strange that he never found somebody to love over the years.

They had been serious lovers while they were at State. They had planned to be married. Karen had broken off the engagement abruptly when she met the true love of her life, or so she thought.

Romano was now a full professor at Tech. Joseph Romano stood over six feet with a swarthy Sicilian complexion of his familial roots. His wavy dark brown hair complemented his dark brown eyes. He was slender for a man in his early forties. He was someone who caught a woman's eye.

Still, it is unusual for a man of his stature, professional position, and general affability to be unmarried. Not that everyone has to get married, fool.

However, his experience with Karen had apparently put a stop to any idea of seriously romancing women.

Karen pulled herself out of those thoughts.

"Grace, do you have a minute?" Karen called out. "Something has been nagging me concerning one of the professors Mendosa worked with."

"Be right there," Grace called back.

"Was Susan able to procure all the case files for you?"

"Yes. And she also found that Middlefield College refers their students to the Adelphi Family Medical clinic in Atlanta."

"Oh, I'm familiar with the Adelphi clinic. Doctor Culver has been my gynecologist, although I haven't been to see him for several years."

"Why go to Atlanta? I stay closer to home. My gyno guy is here in Middlefield."

"I went to Doctor Culver ever since my days at State. The University referred its female students to him. I just have been going back to him."

"I know. Once you establish a connection, it is not easy to break away from a doctor you trust."

"It's only been a couple of days. I know I have been pestering you. Anything new to discuss that were contained in the original case files?"

"I haven't completed my review of them. I've seen nothing yet that sends up red flags. How do we handle this professor, Karen?"

"I've changed my mind from the time I called you. At first, I thought a professor in another department might have been involved with Mendosa. In fact, now I do not think there is a College connection with any of these women. I am just reaching for straws. Forget I mentioned it."

"I agree. We should stay focused on your old boyfriends or others who may have had associations with you."

"Yes, we need to explore those more. After our discussion earlier, I decided to have dinner with Romano on Friday. I'll be looking for some insight to his earlier interest in the cases."

"That was fast! As an old friend, Karen, can I give you some advice? Be sure it is just insight."

"Grace, you are no one to talk, but I do try listening to advice. Joe and I go back years. I know he has gotten over our breakup years ago. Don't worry."

"I do worry. I know you. I know Bill. I also know things have been rough between you two. I know you are lonely, it shows."

"Thank you, Grace. I know you are concerned. You need to relax over this."

"Okay, Karen I will, but..."

"On Friday, I will have to leave work early. The Atlanta traffic at that time of day will be a killer even by the back way, but I'll see you the following Monday with some details."

"Some details?"

"Okay, Snoop, all the details."

* * *

As Karen walked out the door on that Friday afternoon, Grace knew this meeting would not be a good thing for Karen or Bill. Pretend business meetings did not generally work out well. She knew that from her own sad experiences.

As Grace walked to her office, Don approached her.

"Have you seen Karen?"

"She just left. Anything I can do for you?"

"No, I just wanted to tell her that I have gotten a code contact at GBI lined up. I have started to do my research of codes. I'm finishing my presentation of codes for the group."

"Good. She will be back on Monday. Keep at it."

Chapter Five

Behold, I will cast her into a bed, and them that commit adultery with her into great tribulation, except they repent of their deeds. Revelation 2:22

The drive to Atlanta was not as grueling as Karen thought it might be. Arriving at the restaurant, she gave her keys to a valet who parked her car.

Joe had arrived early; he already had their table. He rose upon seeing her; took her hand in his; pecked her on the cheek; and pulled her chair for her.

"It is so nice to see you again, Karen. I've missed you."

"You know, lately I feel the same way, Joe. It would be nice if we could meet more often. I'm not implying anything beyond that."

"I understand, Karen. It's just dinner."

"This restaurant has a subtle aura I love."

"Yes, and as I said, the food is terrific."

"How are things at the MPD?"

"You know, 'così e così.' Bill is Bill. MPD is MPD," Karen replied.

After relaxing for a few minutes, Joe asked, "Is the old Mendosa murder the case you are working on? The Atlanta Journal had a brief blurb as regards to the case being re-opened."

"That's why I wanted to talk to you," said Karen.

The waiter arrived at the table.

"Buona sera, Giuseppe. Come state?"

"Bene, grazie. Antonio."

"E lei?"

"Bene."

"Vorresti bere qualcosa?"

"Vorremo una bottiglia vino della casa"

"Questo vino e' molto buono, Giuseppe."

"Grazie."

"Antonio, this is my dear friend, Karen Hunter."

"I apologize. I am Antonio. I am pleased to meet you, Ms. Hunter."

Antonio returned shortly with the bottle of wine. After tasting, Joe declared it suitable. Antonio filled their glasses.

"Antonio, we will order our dinners now. Please allow us some time to enjoy your fine wine. And when that one is empty, please bring us another."

"Take it easy, Joe. You remember what wine does to me."

"I do. You'll leave with your honor intact."

Karen ordered the Filetto Di Manzo all' Aceto Balsamico. Joe had the Scaloppine Con Salsa Ai Capperi E Limone.

"After you called the other day, I began to think of our college days. You were completing your master's degree in criminal justice. I was finishing my doctorate in forensic science."

"It was a carefree time for us back then," replied Karen.

"Yes, but when you're going through the exams, it never seems carefree. It was in retrospect, though. It was also a time of heartbreak when we went separate ways."

"I know, but you moved on from me. I am not sure I completely got over you. I am not alluding to anything now, Joe, but the pain of my decision bothers me more often these days. At times, a person regrets the decisions they've made," said Karen.

"I never asked you before. How did you meet Bill?"

"Believe it or not, we met in the *Ranger* bar on River Street during the Saint Paddy's celebration in 1998."

"That was it?"

"Yeah, you know the rest of the story."

"Karen, I know you didn't invite me this evening to discuss us. What is it you wanted to see me for tonight?"

"Something has been bothering me since we re-opened these cases. As I recall, you were vocal at the time with your theories concerning the two prostitutes. You called us in 2007. You said to check the College rumors out. Do you remember what else you told Green at the time? You told him that the women probably knew the killer. Why was that?"

"It's a hobby of mine. I read many crime books. Because of rumors, it was not suspicious to me that the two prostitutes' murders had something to do with Middlefield College. I believed they were probably sex crimes, but I had no idea who was involved."

"You also told Green that they were probably missing something unusual. So, what made you think that?"

"Trophies, I guess. In crimes, I've heard that sometimes it's a trait of killers."

"Does that idea come from your true crime books?"

"It doesn't exactly."

"The trouble is there was nothing written in the *Patriot* or the *Atlanta Journal* about the deaths being associated with sex, or anything concerning their having a sexual nature. We thought that it was important not to let that fact out to public."

"Everyone knew it, Karen. The College was alive with rumors."

"You remember how Alejandra Mendosa went missing from Savannah? Her body was discovered along I–16; she was a graduate student attending Middlefield College; she supposedly went to Savannah for Saint Paddy's Day."

"I don't remember all the details concerning it."

"You called one of our people to say we should check out Professor Marino. Why was that?"

"As I've already said, I had heard rumors from some folks I knew at the College. Apparently, the prostitutes were servicing some professors and others there. Later, when I read Mendosa was murdered, my sources thought she was having an affair with some married person. The rumor had no names, though. I knew she was in the Archeology Department."

"What about Marino?"

"Karen, I don't really know why I thought that. If you remember, there weren't many options."

"Still, your statement that the killer was definitely known to Mendosa is odd. We weren't certain that idea was valid, but we didn't let that information out," Karen said.

"Then I have no explanation," Joe replied.

Perhaps Grace is closer to the truth than she realizes. It could be the killer did know each of his victims.

"In Mendosa's case, it could have been someone in the academic world, or someone she was connected to socially. Who knows, she probably was pregnant. Maybe she pushed the father to marry her. That can be a career ender for a grad student, Karen."

How does he know that? Perhaps it is not that strange for Joe to have known Mendosa was pregnant. She did tell Jenkins and Marino. I am sure that hit the rumor mill.

"I am going to level with you, Joe. Green really suspected you. I was able to talk him out of it because I was convinced you simply were not the type. He was not fully convinced, but without solid evidence against you, he let it go. Your alibi for the dates the prostitutes died was like so many others; it couldn't be positively verified."

"Yes, but many times that is a true situation," Joe pushed.

"He wanted me to stay close to you, but, of course, I didn't. He did keep you on the radar, though."

"I know he became pretty rough with me; I told him I wouldn't cooperate anymore."

"At the time, we had semen samples from the autopsies of the two women. The profiles showed it was one man. We now have five dead women having his profile in them."

"So why don't you nail him?"

"Joe, the killer is careful. Then, he is wantonly careless with the one thing, which you know is much better than fingerprinting to identify him. He doesn't make any sense with that behavior."

"So, he isn't in the National Data Base. What do you think I can contribute to the case?"

"Joe, we made assumptions regarding several people at the College. All had alibis, but we could not verify many of them. With this new information, we have to check a few of them again. That is not our focus, though. We are checking old contacts I had in my past."

"Are you saying I need an alibi?"

"Not unless things change, Joe. Are you aware that we recently received a letter?"

"No, there has been nothing in the papers that I've seen. Just that the Mendosa case had been re-opened. What's so special about an old letter?"

Karen hoped Joe did not see her reaction. She had said nothing about it being an old letter.

How does he know that?

"What made you think it might be old?"

"I don't know. How would I know?"

"I suppose that you wouldn't. Well, the stacks at the College library were being cleaned out for renovation; workers came across a letter. The letter is dated the day Mendosa was discovered. It has a part we can read, but the rest is in some sort of code."

"What will you do to decrypt the code?"

Decrypt? That isn't a word I hear often.

"Don mentioned today that he heard some researchers code their sensitive data to protect it until publication. I knew that from some work I did a few years ago. Have you ever coded your work, Joe?"

"Believe it or not, that is true. I have coded some of my work. My codes simply provide minimal security of my work for a short time."

"What research information of yours would require it to be coded?"

"Karen, the issue is that many academic institutions are extremely focused on image. That means untenured faculties are at high risk for unemployment during their early years. The system functions on the 'publish or perish' philosophy. This situation has led to plagiarism, or recently, falsifying of research data to get something into print. It also suggests some researchers bend to politics to please funding groups."

"I am aware of the pressure schools put tenure track people under. Don and I are developing our own ideas around the codes we've received, but I want to get your ideas concerning codes."

"Why focus on me?"

"I remembered that you had some interest in codes back when we were together. If you are willing, I want you to take a look at the letter codes we received."

Joe read the letter and told Karen he would be unable to

decrypt the code.

"Do you have any idea why he hates you, Karen?"

"No, it creeps me out. He hates me for some reason."

"Maybe you unknowingly hurt him. Perhaps you affected his whole life. Now he can't forgive you."

Would you think that, Joe?

"It's a mystery to me right now."

"What are you going to do? Whoever wrote this letter is obviously dangerous."

"We'll nail him if we can, but we need to break the code."

"I'm telling you I am not able to help with this code breaking. My codes were very simple, really. I could check with a couple of my frat brothers who love this type of game, but I doubt they can really help. You are going to need professional support here."

"That's what I was afraid you were going to say."

"Let me check with Dave or Charlie to see if they are still into this type of gaming, okay?"

"Joe, I can only send them the code, not the prefacing letter part. Don't tell them what this code pertains to."

"If you feel more comfortable, I will e-mail their phone numbers. You can talk to them directly."

"That might be a more appropriate way," said Karen.

They finished their meal with inconsequential chitchat.

"Karen, do you have to rush back?"

"I do, Joe."

"Can you stop by my condo for a minute before you

head back? I have something from our old days to give you."

The second bottle of wine was starting to do its work. Karen felt herself weakening. Joe's suggestion to stop by his house before she left should have been a warning. She knew she could handle it.

"I'll stop for just a minute."

On the drive to Joe's home, Karen sobered up a bit. She nearly decided to head for home, but the lure was too much, and she had said she would stop by.

He said he wanted to show me something. I am curious. Our love had been strong before Bill entered the picture. Was it love or something else? I had always thought Joe would marry me. I was impulsive back then, not thinking through the consequences. Be careful, Karen.

Arriving at Joe's condominium, Karen had a feeling that she should not be doing this. Perhaps Grace was right.

"You should have a cup of coffee before you drive back to Middlefield."

"After all the wine, that's a good idea."

Joe leaned close to Karen as he set the cup down near her. The smell of his aftershave sent shivers down her spine. Karen knew that this was forbidden territory, but her hand moved to caress his face unable to stop herself. Slowly she wove her fingers through his hair and she could sense his maleness becoming ready.

He slowly ran his fingers over her lips as she opened her

mouth inviting him. He brought his face closer to hers and their lips met in a heated kiss. Joe kissed her as he had many times before. As he cupped her breast through her blouse, she could feel his hand faintly trembling; beckoning them to an intensity they both knew. It excited him and her to the point of no return.

Karen looked into his eyes. ***Oh, I don't think I can stop him or myself. I don't want to stop!***

"Joe, we can't do this."

"I know, I know, Karen."

"Oh, I want you so badly."

Joe moved his hand and slowly reached inside her blouse feeling the warmth of her breast. He gently pushed her bra aside. The memories of days past engulfed him as he felt the powerful urge overcoming him. The smell of her hair; the warmth of her breasts urged him on.

Karen did not push his hand away. She slightly moaned. Her defenses were low. She knew she was doing something very wrong, but she could not stop. She now eagerly kissed Joe pulling his hand to the hem of her skirt.

Joe's hand moved up her thigh. She moaned again. Karen urged him on as she moved her hips inviting him to touch the place that he had touched so many times before.

His hand reached her panties slowly pulling them away. They both knew that it would not stop here as they went to the bedroom. They undressed each other with the urgency that neither could nor wanted to stop.

Joe gently pushed her back on the bed and slowly began

to enter her. The feelings, the memories of a love so long ago returned. It drove them both on.

There was no time for protection. Karen felt the hot surge within her. After, they lay on the bed gently caressing each other.

"I'm sorry, Karen."

What have I done? What have I done?

When it was over, reality of what they had done shamed Karen.

"Oh, Joe, it was so wrong of us. I am so ashamed. I am married. I have broken my vows."

"I'm sorry. You have to admit it was a good time."

"Is that what you thought it was? It was just a good time?"

"No, bad joke."

"Why did you say that?"

"I don't know, Karen, it just slipped out."

"You're pathetic. It's time for me to leave."

I am sorry, dear Karen, but it was a great birthday present. One more time in the future...

* * *

On the drive back to Middlefield, Karen felt the stinging guilt of her unfaithfulness. She had never cheated on Bill, not once during their marriage thirteen years ago. Now she had.

What will I do if Bill finds out? Should I tell Bill? No, the experts say no, never! I am so ashamed of myself. Tonight was as delicious as it was when we were going

together. I feel shame and desire at the same time. How do I handle that? Was I so lonely that I set this up? Did I see Joe just for a one-night stand? He was callous about it, though. Did I give him a birthday present like in the old days? Is that what he thought? Huh? I guess I was just another conquest for him.

On Monday morning, Grace greeted Karen on her arrival at the station.

"Good morning. I hope you are going to tell me it was just insight last Friday," teased Grace.

"Just insight, although it gave me ideas to think about," Karen lied.

I'll bet it did, Karen.

"Well, that is a relief. I spent a restless night worrying that you two may have not been careful."

"Grace, be ready for today's meeting. Check with Don; see if he is ready. If not, tell him he can present any findings today even if they aren't complete."

"By the way, Don came to see you after you had left on Friday. He said he had some thoughts that he wanted to share with you. I think they concerned his progress on the code."

"Well, he can fill us all in at the meeting, so I want everybody to be prompt. Is there anything else?"

Grace noted the difference in Karen's mood from Friday.

Yeah, sure, Karen, just insight. I know damn well, what happened. You did exactly what I thought you would

do. Do you think this is going to help your marriage? Do not ever tell me I have loose morals. Do not ever preach to me.

"I'm going to my office, Grace. Joe gave me two contacts for the code stuff. I want to call them before our meeting at ten o'clock."

Karen checked her morning e-mail. Joe's response came along with some words he should not have written. She noted the numbers. She deleted the e-mail.

"Good morning, David. This is Detective Karen Hunter from the Middlefield Police Department. I had a conversation with Joe Romano recently. He gave me your phone number. He indicated that you might be able to assist us in a case I have re-opened. Is this a convenient time for you to talk?"

"It is, Karen. What can I do for you?"

"I have an encrypted code that I would like to have you look at, if you have time. Joe said you liked this type of gaming. It would be a tremendous benefit if you could read it. I will provide some information that our code guru says may help you. Can I fax it over to you?"

"Sure. I love these challenges. How is Joe doing these days?"

"He appears to be doing well."

"If you can make heads or tails of it, will you call me back as soon as possible?"

"Yes. I will do my best. Nice talking with you, Karen,"

The call to Charles Davenport gave the same result.

Chapter Six

Remember therefore from whence thou art fallen, and repent, and do the first works; or else I will come unto thee quickly, and will remove my candlestick out of his place, except thou repent. Revelation 2:5

At ten o'clock, the MCU assembled in the conference room for Don's discussion of the letter codes.

"As you know, Don is going to present some ideas to us that we have discussed regarding the coded part of the letter. I think we all need to have an understanding the grave problem we face. Get your coffee now, so you can give him your full attention. Please start, Don."

"Thank you, Karen. Along with the legwork we are doing, solution of the code may be our best hope for solving this case. What I am going to say today involves many terms not familiar to us. As you know, our writer wants to confuse us, so that we cannot easily see what he is thinking. That is obvious. What is not obvious is how he has done this. His ciphers include both an alpha character code and eight lines of numerical code."

"Don, go slowly with us poor souls," said Grace.

"I will do my best. The first thing I want to mention is the difference between ciphers and codes. In the Mendosa letter, we are dealing with ciphers, but first I want to introduce you to the notion of codes. Codes are substitutions of messages that work at the level of words to confuse a message. Ciphers, on the other hand, are substitutions of messages that work at the level of the individual letters making up the message."

"If we have ciphers to solve, Don, why bother showing us codes?" Susan asked.

"It's simply for our education. We don't want a defense lawyer explaining to a jury that we have no idea of the difference between codes and ciphers."

"Susan, I agree with Don that this process is the best way for all of us. I want us to keep focused to the task we have. Sometimes education has to take twists and turns that seem unrelated. Don, please continue," Karen added.

"The use of codes is a way of hiding messages by using some method, a codebook for example, which both the sender and receiver of the system possess. Codebooks usually assign a huge number of phrases or words to a random string of numbers or letter characters. For example, **ADVANCE** could be the code for 'Send help now.' For a time, this type of encryption was used by commercial companies to reduce the number of words when sending a telegram."

"Was it their purpose to hide the content of a message, or just save telegraph costs?" Susan asked.

"Both. The drawback to such a system is the portability of the codebook. For the system to work, revisions to the codebook must be available to many people nearly simultaneously. It is not a trivial task, especially if one uses the codebook system in the espionage world. You can imagine the problems this system can develop. We believe it is unlikely that our code writer used this method."

"Yes, the 'code method' isn't the type of system we would have any chance of solving without his codebook. However, the letter is challenging us to decipher his codes, so he must be using a system that gives us a shot at solving them. Of course, he may be lying. We will only know that after we spend much time working on them," Karen added.

"Karen, are you familiar with codes?" Grace asked.

"I have a very good understanding of ciphers and codes. Don and I are meeting daily to work out ideas that may help us solve them. We hope that will speed up the solution process."

"Since the writer thinks he is more intelligent than we are; he has to allow us a fighting chance to solve his ciphers. If he does not do that, there would be no way for him to say he outsmarted us. It would be extremely difficult for us, if not impossible, without some knowledge of his codebook," Don continued.

"Don, is the codebook method easy to use?" Grace asked.

"In some ways, yes, but it has the problems I've related to you."

"Can anybody do ciphering work?" Susan asked.

"It depends on the system being used. In some cases, it takes a skilled person to do it well. For our ciphers, we believe this person may have amateur crypto interest or experience. We believe he used a classical cipher of some type."

"Ciphers used in the modern world by governments, rely

on sophisticated algorithms driven by computers of tremendous computing power to encrypt and decrypt messages. We believe that would be too much for our killer," Karen answered.

"Also, we don't know this guy's background; it looks as though he used a less sophisticated system. Most likely, he would not have the heavy computer equipment required. Plus, he couldn't say he'd beaten us if we don't have the same level of equipment," Don added.

"Well, then, we can eliminate the codebook idea and the computer driven systems. What else?" Grace asked.

Don continued, "A cipher doesn't have the drawback of the codebook process. Nevertheless, it has its own sets of issues for encrypting. As I said before, a cipher is a method of concealing the content of a message by substituting or transposing letters of a message with other letters, symbols, or letter pairs. In addition, there are combinations of substitution or transposition schemes to create ciphers. I will try to explain as we go through this. Ciphers versus code systems are beneficial to us."

"How does that benefit us?" Grace asked.

"It's a tremendous benefit to us because the system gives us something we can work with. We can try to identify cipher types, which maybe breakable," Don answered.

"Still, Grace, this is a formidable task because there are fifty to sixty ciphers, which use various algorithms exist. Worse, some ciphers exist that we obviously do not know.

Don, please explain 'breakable'," Karen added.

"Okay. An encryption algorithm is breakable if a systematic process allows extraction of a message or useable parts of a message. Encryption breaking may include using methods called 'brute-force,' which consist of systematically checking all possible keywords until it finds the correct one. In the worst case, this process involves testing the entire search space. The keyword length of an encryption is extremely time consuming to solve even for the brute-force process. The crypto world considers an encryption to be strong if no process other than brute-force can break it."

"Do you have a feeling about the strength of our problem codes?" Susan asked.

"Let's start using the word ciphers instead of codes," Karen directed.

"To continue, the letter writer included both alpha and numerical type ciphers," Don said.

"Beyond the statement that he is trying to make it easier for us, I am not sure I can appreciate the significance of the two types," Susan said.

"The alpha type may be easier for us to solve. If so, it may aid us solving the other lines."

"Are you able to tell if that is true?" Grace asked.

"Not yet. Many, if not most of the 'pencil and paper' ciphers of these types can be broken somewhat easily. At this point, Karen and I aren't certain what we have."

"I feel we're going around in circles with this. How will

we ever fight our way through this?" Grace asked.

"In a general sense, the feeling of going around in circles about these ciphers is real, but many encryption algorithms are breakable. The process requires us to try all keywords systematically. If the decryption process is able to glean out some plaintext from ciphertext pairs, the task may be a bit easier," Don explained.

"What is plaintext? Ciphertext?" asked Grace.

"Sorry. Plaintext is a message someone wants to deliver to another. Ciphertext is the encoded plaintext disguising the plaintext to make it unreadable. That's where our decryption or ciphertext breaking effort begins."

"That being said, sometimes being breakable doesn't mean that it is worth the resources to break it. It may take years to decipher the plaintext message. Spy messages are generally time critical, so if it takes a very long time to decipher the plaintext, the message has probably lost its value. In our case, we have the time urgency, but from a different perspective," Karen said.

"I'm not trying to pin you down at this point, Don. How will you manage to break this?" Grace asked.

"There are various known techniques. Many algorithms exist to do this. I contacted Dr. Marcus Strong at GBI. He agrees with our opinion that our ciphers are the classical types. He is going to try to brute-force it. If it is successful, we still need to do our best police work to catch this person, but decryption could speed up the solution of the case. We have to assume this isn't a prank being played on us."

"That's a fair assumption. From the information in the readable part of the letter, it is obvious the writer has considerable knowledge of the Mendosa murder. He also admits that he murdered the first two prostitutes. We know he murdered two more after he wrote the letter," Karen said.

"One item I need to mention. We have to understand that GBI has its hands full with current cases. It cannot immediately react to murder cases that are cold. GBI has too much work to do these days. Marcus is requesting his supervisor, Julius Bennett, to re-assign his time to our code work, now that we are actively working these cases. In the meantime, he will do this work in his spare time, so we cannot push him. I know he will do his best," Don added.

"I understand. Please let him know how much we appreciate what he is able to do. Let me know if I can help with his supervisor," said Karen.

"What if our efforts are unsuccessful?" Grace asked.

"There may be some goodness in initial failures. If trying to find possible ciphers solutions results in gibberish or messages that do not match our case, we can assume we don't have the right cipher type. I say assume because we may have the right cipher type, but the wrong keyword, or something else is wrong with our method," Don explained.

"Don, better tell them that there are some ciphers to date that defy decryption. We don't want to discourage you, but they exist," Karen said.

"There are a number of ciphers known, which have

never been solved to date. The Kryptos ciphers at the CIA headquarters courtyard in Langley, Virginia, for one example."

"What are the Kryptos ciphers?" Grace asked.

"Kryptos is an encrypted sculpture by the American artist, Jim Sanborn. It has four ciphers inscribed on the sculpture. Richard Gay, an ex-CIA operative, has solved three of the four ciphers. The fourth remains an enigma."

"Are there more?" Susan asked.

"There are the three Feynman ciphers, of which only one was solved. A few of the twenty Zodiac messages sent by the killer have been solved. Unfortunately, a critical one with his name hasn't been."

"Our killer's ciphers are nothing like the Zodiac's, so he isn't trying to copycat the Zodiac killer," said Karen.

"I agree, Karen. Our perp is different. The Zodiac killer operated in California in the late 1960s and early 1970s. He randomly picked out men and women for killing. If I remember correctly, he had different methods of operation depending on the situation. However, our killer focuses on murdering young women in a specific way. He hasn't used firearms or knives, etc. as Zodiac did," Don added.

"I'm sure the Zodiac team faced similar problems in their investigations," Grace said.

"Most likely, but we can't let that discourage us. This person says he left clues in his letter to help us. Since he regards us as having low intelligence, he must believe that it is not much of a risk for him. We will do our best to prove him wrong," said Karen.

"Don, can you spend some time to explain, in general, how this ciphering actually works? Right now, this subject is overwhelming to me. It is critical, though. I need to have a crash course," Susan asked.

"I can, Susan. A crash course probably will not benefit us. Many people have what I would call a natural gift of insight when it comes to working this type of problem. A person has it or does not. I am not casting any aspersions on our abilities in this room. Mathematicians, computer scientists, even linguists often have an edge in this area. Even those amateurs who are able to solve ciphers have abilities in the areas I just mentioned. Those of us who majored in Criminal Justice may or may not have it, sorry to say."

"Let me describe the two major types of historical pen and paper ciphers known as classical ciphers. Generally, they are not secure these days. They can be broken with computers assisted by deciphering skills, which many people have. My guess is our killer did not rely solely on these types. It would be too risky if he did put his name in a cipher easily broken.

- The first type is the substitution cipher. With this kind, a person replaces the plaintext letters with other letters or groups of letters from a ciphertext alphabet. One can scramble both the plaintext letter and ciphertext alphabets, or they can be used in their natural sequence.

- The second type is transposition. In this cipher, the plaintext letters are in alphabetical order. The order of the cipher alphabet is scrambled in a defined way."

"Don, please show them an example of each," Karen said.

"I'll put a simple mono-alphabet substitution cipher on the white board. I will explain some terms cipher people use. According to legend, Julius Caesar used a similar cipher. His method used a plaintext alphabet unmixed. He also kept the ciphertext alphabet in its normal sequence. His process was to shift the cipher alphabet relative to the plaintext alphabet by three characters to the left. To make a cipher stronger, a person could design different shifts and alphabets."

"For Caesar's time period, his system worked fairly well. But his method is a limited system, and today is easily broken," Karen added.

"I'll show an example where the plaintext alphabet is the normal sequence, but the ciphertext alphabet is scrambled. Here we deviate from Caesar's because there is not a discernable shift of the cipher alphabet. We will hide our plaintext message by substituting cipher letters for the plaintext letters to get a ciphertext. Our system could be set up as follows:

Plaintext	a	b	c	d	e	f	g	h	i	j	k	l	m	n	o	p	q	r	s	t	u	v	w	x	y	z
Ciphertext	p	z	x	b	c	f	l	o	u	e	m	g	w	y	a	k	h	s	q	d	j	i	t	r	v	n

Don continued, "Notice that the plaintext alphabet I put up on the board is in its normal order. You could also scramble the alphabets for both plaintext and ciphertext. In my example of Karen's name, I can put the ciphertext in uppercase just to make it a bit more complicated to hand decipher, but a computer can do it relatively quickly."

"In this case, Karen Marie Hunter would encipher to **MPSCYWPSUCOJYDCS**. By omitting the spaces between the names, it would appear to be more difficult to decipher by hand."

"Would that make it unbreakable?" Grace asked.

"No, our example of a mono-alphabetic system can be solved rather easily, primarily due to idiosyncrasies of language. By that, I mean letters in a written language have an unequal use rate, or different frequencies of use. The first known recorded explanation of frequency analysis was determined in the 9th century by an Iraqi, Al-Kindi," Don replied.

"The frequency of letter usage in English was determined years ago. Therefore, statistical analysis of a cipher's characters often allows discovery of the plaintext, however, a writer's style can affect the analysis. A novel published in 1939 with title of *Gatsby* startled the crypto world. Written by Ernest Vincent Wright, the novel has over fifty thousand words, none of which contain the letter 'e'," Karen added.

"That is right, Karen. Wright's novel made the world

aware that spies could write messages in such a way to confuse anyone trying to test the ciphertext using frequency analysis. Based on the usage of letters in the written English language, as you can see from the letter frequency chart, the letter 'e' is the most often used; followed by the letter 't.' That is the weakness of this type of cipher. It falls victim to statistical analysis."

"It's simple enough as an idea," Grace said.

"Folks, you can see why these systems have proven to be insecure," Karen added.

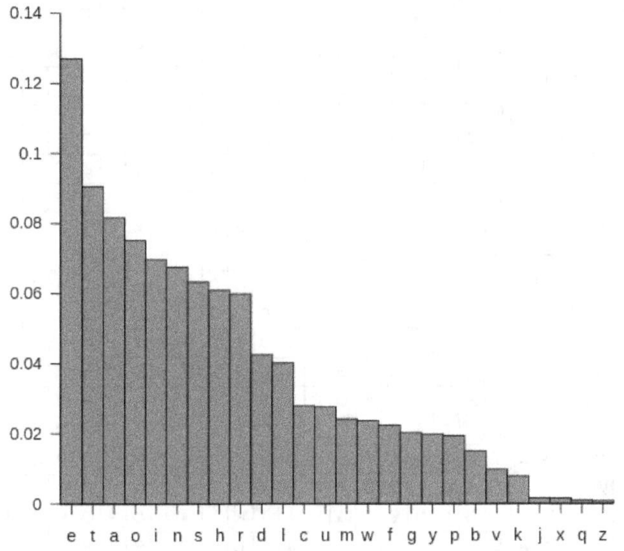

"Yes. Polyalphabetic substitutions of various types do exist. The Vigenère square is the type of cipher where twenty-six substitution alphabets are used. They are Caesar ciphers with different transformations," Don explained.

"They are confusing, but with effort, generally not

secure," Karen said.

"The following picture is what a Vigenère square, a 26 x 26 array, looks like. I'll show you how it is used when we discuss the letter ciphers," Don said.

		PLAINTEXT LETTER																								
		A	**B**	**C**	**D**	**E**	**F**	**G**	**H**	**I**	**J**	**K**	**L**	**M**	**N**	**O**	**P**	**Q**	**R**	**S**	**T**	**U**	**V**	**W**	**X**	**Y**	**Z**
	A	A	B	C	D	E	F	G	H	I	J	K	L	M	N	O	P	Q	R	S	T	U	V	W	X	Y	Z
	B	B	C	D	E	F	G	H	I	J	K	L	M	N	O	P	Q	R	S	T	U	V	W	X	Y	Z	A
	C	C	D	E	F	G	H	I	J	K	L	M	N	O	P	Q	R	S	T	U	V	W	X	Y	Z	A	B
	D	D	E	F	G	H	I	J	K	L	M	N	O	P	Q	R	S	T	U	V	W	X	Y	Z	A	B	C
K	**E**	E	F	G	H	I	J	K	L	M	N	O	P	Q	R	S	T	U	V	W	X	Y	Z	A	B	C	D
E	**F**	F	G	H	I	J	K	L	M	N	O	P	Q	R	S	T	U	V	W	X	Y	Z	A	B	C	D	E
Y	**G**	G	H	I	J	K	L	M	N	O	P	Q	R	S	T	U	V	W	X	Y	Z	A	B	C	D	E	F
W	**H**	H	I	J	K	L	M	N	O	P	Q	R	S	T	U	V	W	X	Y	Z	A	B	C	D	E	F	G
O	**I**	I	J	K	L	M	N	O	P	Q	R	S	T	U	V	W	X	Y	Z	A	B	C	D	E	F	G	H
R	**J**	J	K	L	M	N	O	P	Q	R	S	T	U	V	W	X	Y	Z	A	B	C	D	E	F	G	H	I
D	**K**	K	L	M	N	O	P	Q	R	S	T	U	V	W	X	Y	Z	A	B	C	D	E	F	G	H	I	J
	L	L	M	N	O	P	Q	R	S	T	U	V	W	X	Y	Z	A	B	C	D	E	F	G	H	I	J	K
L	**M**	M	N	O	P	Q	R	S	T	U	V	W	X	Y	Z	A	B	C	D	E	F	G	H	I	J	K	L
E	**N**	N	O	P	Q	R	S	T	U	V	W	X	Y	Z	A	B	C	D	E	F	G	H	I	J	K	L	M
T	**O**	O	P	Q	R	S	T	U	V	W	X	Y	Z	A	B	C	D	E	F	G	H	I	J	K	L	M	N
T	**P**	P	Q	R	S	T	U	V	W	X	Y	Z	A	B	C	D	E	F	G	H	I	J	K	L	M	N	O
E	**Q**	Q	R	S	T	U	V	W	X	Y	Z	A	B	C	D	E	F	G	H	I	J	K	L	M	N	O	P
R	**R**	R	S	T	U	V	W	X	Y	Z	A	B	C	D	E	F	G	H	I	J	K	L	M	N	O	P	Q
	S	S	T	U	V	W	X	Y	Z	A	B	C	D	E	F	G	H	I	J	K	L	M	N	O	P	Q	R
	T	T	U	V	W	X	Y	Z	A	B	C	D	E	F	G	H	I	J	K	L	M	N	O	P	Q	R	S
	U	U	V	W	X	Y	Z	A	B	C	D	E	F	G	H	I	J	K	L	M	N	O	P	Q	R	S	T
	V	V	W	X	Y	Z	A	B	C	D	E	F	G	H	I	J	K	L	M	N	O	P	Q	R	S	T	U
	W	W	X	Y	Z	A	B	C	D	E	F	G	H	I	J	K	L	M	N	O	P	Q	R	S	T	U	V
	X	X	Y	Z	A	B	C	D	E	F	G	H	I	J	K	L	M	N	O	P	Q	R	S	T	U	V	W
	Y	Y	Z	A	B	C	D	E	F	G	H	I	J	K	L	M	N	O	P	Q	R	S	T	U	V	W	X
	Z	Z	A	B	C	D	E	F	G	H	I	J	K	L	M	N	O	P	Q	R	S	T	U	V	W	X	Y

"Why would anyone use a code that is not secure," Grace asked.

"For many kinds of situations, it isn't important. Who

cares if lovers are exchanging hidden messages, for example," Don answered.

"It could make a difference if a couple was trying to hide an illicit love affair. Maybe their wives or husbands would like to know," Grace said.

I guess that would be your style, Grace. I am not that clever.

"Karen and I do have a thought that the alpha ciphers put in the letter are Vigenère type. At this point, we do not know. We do have the feeling that they will play an important part in our deciphering the numeric cipher lines."

"This is getting complex," Grace said.

"Perhaps it's just the killer's way of further taunting us. I don't think he tried to make them crack-proof for all the reasons we've stated before," Karen replied.

"Well, that's something in our favor," Susan said.

Don continued, "If you were attempting to truly hide a message, there are better methods than the Vigenère."

Karen added, "Interestingly, you could probably make a Vigenère cipher very close to crack-proof by doing the following when planning out your cipher:

- **Use no spaces or punctuation marks.**
- **Use only uppercase letters. Mixing upper and lower cases may give away information.**
- **Add random characters to the plaintext to conceal the message length.**
- **Use keywords having random characters.**
- **Make the keyword as long as the message.**"

"It's becoming pretty clear to me why this may be so tough for us," Grace said.

"Yes. We police types don't tend to think in terms needed for cipher solving," Don agreed.

"I felt you needed to have a basic understanding of what we are facing. These meetings will help us. They will also probably prevent us from beating unmercifully on people we rope in to help us break these ciphers," Karen said.

"Please continue with your presentation," Grace urged.

"I have a simple transposition example. For this type, a keyword is needed."

"Is that the nursery rhyme you're showing on the board?" Susan asked.

S	E	X	Y	H	U	N	K
19	5	24	25	8	21	14	11
M	A	R	Y	H	A	D	A
L	I	T	T	L	E	L	A
M	B	I	T	S	F	L	E
E	C	E	W	A	S	W	H
I	T	E	A	S	S	N	O
W	A	N	D	E	V	E	R
Y	W	H	E	R	E	T	H
A	T	M	A	R	Y	W	E
N	T	T	H	E	L	A	M
B	W	A	S	S	U	R	E
T	O	G	O	H	A	L	E

"Yes, let's look at the rhyme: 'Mary had a little lamb,

with fleece as white as snow. And everywhere that Mary went, the lamb was sure to go, Hale.' "

"Who is Hale?' Grace asked.

"She's the author."

"Sorry for the interruption."

"You would set up a table as I have shown here.

"Then arrange the message in rows from left to right, top to bottom on an array. Then assign some keyword such as 'SEXYHUNK', for example."

"Don, there are three women in this room. 'Sexy hunk' may get us excited. I'm not sure you could handle us all," joked Grace.

"He's so cute when he uses those words, don't you think, girls?" Susan teased.

"We're just playing with you, Don. Please go on. This is a bit intense for us so a little levity is welcome."

"Not a problem, Grace. Now that you brought it up, my ego says I would have to try to handle you all."

Now there's the male ego at work.

"Can we continue, please?" Karen said.

"As I was saying, for this type, the keyword should not have two of the same letters in it. Doing so may render the message ambiguous. From the array, the letters in the keyword correspond to their place in the alphabet: **A is 1**, **B is 2**, **C is 3**, etc. I have shown the letter positions in the first row under the keyword.

"Next, choose the letters in column order to transpose the message. Since E of the keyword has the smallest alphabet position number (5), it becomes the first column used to begin the ciphertext.

"Select the letters under column E. Place the letters horizontally: **AIBCTAWTTWO**. Continue the steps in the following order with columns: H, K, N, S, U, X and Y to get this crazy looking ciphertext:

AIBCTAWTTWO–HLSASERRESH–AAEHORHEMEE–DLLWNETWARL–MLMEIWYANBT–AEFSSVEYLUA–RTIEENHMTAG –YTTWADEAHSO

"Folks, note that Don has put dashes between the ciphertext groups to make it easier for us," Karen added.

"Yes, I've put them between the ciphertext columns only for our benefit. A person would send the ciphertext without the dashes making the message more difficult to a third party. The receiver would have to know the key word to decipher the ciphertext."

"That's wild," said Grace.

"To decipher this message, work in reverse.

- Write down the keyword and count the number of letters it has.
- Count the number of letters in the ciphertext.
- Divide the number of keyword letters into the total number of ciphertext letters.
- The result of that division tells you the number of characters in each column.
- **SEXYHUNK** has 8 letters, and the ciphertext has 88, so each column must have 11 characters under each keyword letter.

- Write down the keyword. From the keyword, you know that **AIBCTAWTTWO** must be from column E of the keyword.
- Knowing this, you would place it as the second column in your table.
- To complete the decipher process; continue to place the ciphertext groups in columns under each letter position of the keyword.
- The plaintext is then read from left to right, top to bottom."

"These types of ciphers are inherently breakable. Even if you were to write your plaintext message in reverse, there are ways to break the cipher," Karen added.

"That looks as if it would be very tough to break."

"It can be tough, but not impossible with the right tools, Grace. There are many different methods to arrange the transposition ciphers. To understand what this entails, I would like to give you a simple transposition cipher to solve on your own time later. Suppose you like encryption games. You want to share a message with a friend. You pre-arrange with your friend that the keyword in your message is **HARDTIMES**. As an exercise, try to decipher the following message:

ONAFOHNE RSSTGNIN RNOSOSTO FAERRTON CVGETHET OEORFINI UDRAUOTW EYUBRCAN SEAHHTNA

"Set your table up as we did in the previous example and see what you get. Let me know how it is going."

"Are you serious?" asked Grace.

“First one to do it earns ten of my hard earned dollars.”

“This could be time consuming,” said Grace.

“Well, I encourage you to try it. It will help,” Don urged.

“Karen, I’ve had enough for today. Can we continue this topic for our next meeting?” Grace asked.

“We’re all tired at this point,” Karen agreed.

“I’ll have another presentation for you. I feel I need to explain enough background, so that we all understand how difficult this whole process is,” Don said.

“Well, you’re doing just fine explaining this subject. Okay, folks, that is it for now. I will schedule another meeting,” directed Karen.

Chapter Seven

And he shewed me a pure river of water of life, clear as crystal, proceeding out of the throne of God and of the lamb. Revelation 22:1

Karen went back to her office to take a sorry pill.

Who was going to pull her spirits up? I am trying to keep the group pumped up, but it is exhausting. Chief Tate is a dependable person, but there is not much direction here. He will have resources, and that is a help.

My personal life is nose-diving with Bill being the ass that he is. Where did the love go? I do not know if Bill loves me anymore. Maybe he never did. Moreover, maybe I never did love him either. Everything went so quickly. We had such plans, hopes. I always thought babies would come along in that comfortable, old house with the white picket fence. It's corny, but I always thought it would happen. After thirteen years of marriage, there was not a pregnancy once. There was not a miscarriage to blame, nothing. Now I am running out of time. I wanted to go to doctors to see what the problem was. Bill did not. He wanted none of that fiddling with privates by doctors. If God wanted us to have kids, it would happen. Well, it did not, even though Bill had afternoon delight as often as he wanted it. Even that has dwindled down to twice weekly. The passion evaporated years ago; just the act, get it over with, nothing more; he could manage that from a whore.

I blame Bill for everything that is wrong in our marriage. However, what did I do? I went to Atlanta on

the pretext of getting information for a case from Joe. What did I do? I wound up sleeping with him. I am married, but I'm not sure I want to be. On the other hand, do I want to give up all I have? Hey Lady, your libido is talking. I want to leave all of this, or do I? Honey, you cannot just walk out of your marriage. You have too much to lose. Your job, reputation, most of all, your self-esteem is on the line. Do you think, for one moment, that if your mother or father were still alive they would praise you for screwing around on your husband? However, what is he thinking and doing? Men always have the right to screw around; they can beg for forgiveness; they can't help themselves. Isn't that what you were taught? Well, I have had enough of that thinking. Do I want something new in my life? Wasn't this the same feeling you had when you dumped Joe for Bill?

Were you thinking then, or was it an irresistible draw of sex with someone different? I know that Grace knows I was lying about what happened with Joe. Well, that is just too bad. Grace is no angel herself. She has been screwing around on her husband for years. Last, I heard she's due to ride into divorce court.

Some Lady I am. I guess I can't gripe too much, where Bill is concerned. Nevertheless, he is a snake, too, with his affairs on the road. I wish I could come to grips with this. This is tearing me up. I need to feel wanted. I need to feel I am accomplishing something. I am lonely, with no place to turn.

Karen glanced at her desk calendar. It was March 2011.

Almost three years ago, we discovered the Mendosa woman. Now that damn letter has opened up the whole mess again. It is wearing me down; I don't know how well I can deal with this now. What kind of leader am I, anyway? My staff is grumbling at the pressure of the work. They don't gripe to my face, but behind my back; that's where it really hurts. Friends don't do that. Workmates do. Things are spiraling out of control. It is 2008 all over again.

Karen knew she was starting to forget important things. Her personal life was taking up brain space needed for her duties. She should have already talked to the chief about getting additional funds to work this case. The Unit was depending on her. What had she done? Nothing of value. It would not be long before the public would wail regarding the progress of her cases.

Karen's phone rang pulling her out of her thoughts.

"This is Karen Hunter, Middlefield PD."

"This is Denise Lee from the *Patriot*. I have heard of the strange letter found at the library. I wanted to see if we could meet to talk?"

I guess the Mayor has been flapping his gums again.

"Weren't you at Chief Tate's press conference? A meeting with you at this time is premature. We are still working on the content of the letter. When we have something to distribute to the press, Chief Tate will have a public briefing, otherwise check with the Citizen's

Committee. Thank you for the call. Goodbye."

Karen fumed over the call.

That snotty nosed twit is just digging for the 'police aren't doing their jobs' line. Good luck, sweetie you are not getting anything from me. Who in the group is talking to the press off the record, or so they think?

Karen's phone rang for the second time in ten minutes that morning.

"Karen Hunter, Middlefield PD."

"Good morning. This is Mayor Hampton. I just received a call from Denise Lee at the *Patriot*. She is feeling that you are not cooperative. She tells me you are too busy to see her to discuss this murder case we have in our city."

"Mayor, you need to speak with Chief Tate. You know we are giving you weekly updates. Why do I personally have to discuss things with her? We are balls to the wall in this investigation, so I don't have time to talk to a reporter who, I think, is just looking for a way to discredit us."

"Why do you say that?"

"You weren't mayor three years ago when we were working the Mendosa murder. The screaming from the press, in particular from that reporter, was so debilitating it influenced our entire investigation. That reporter went around to people we needed to interview. It took the edge off our ability to question possible suspects."

"You know as well as I do that it is a First Amendment issue with them."

"I am aware of that, but interfering into a police murder

investigation is not a First Amendment right. This call wouldn't have anything to do with her being your niece, would it?"

"Don't be snippy with me. I will bring this up at the City Council meeting if I don't start hearing the right answers."

"Mayor, I asked you at the start of this call to talk to Chief Tate. He is the person who determines where I spend my official time. If he says to do it, I will. I won't commit to you or any other person without his direction."

"Connect me to him."

"Chief, Mayor Hampton is on the line. He wants to speak with you."

Karen hung up.

What an ass. To think the voters of this city selected him is beyond me. Talk about low information voters. I have lost my faith in the system since the last election. We are continually voting jerks into office from the lowest positions to the highest in the land.

Karen's phone rang again.

If I don't stop getting these calls, I won't finish anything today.

"Yes, Chief."

"I just had my butt reamed by you know who. Could you not rough up his ego? I want you to talk to the witch. I do not want to give anything away about our code difficulties. I might accidentally give out names or details of the letter, which you don't want disclosed. You know how I work. Is there any way you can move yourself through this situation to meet with her?"

"Are you ordering me to meet with her? I have to hear that. She is nothing but trouble. It will not serve us well whether I meet with her or not."

"I am sorry. I do appreciate how you feel. We have to do it."

"Okay. I will call her. I'll let her know that political pressure on the police force works."

"Come on, Karen. It's part of the work. It's the responsibility of your role."

"Wouldn't she be satisfied if the information came from you?"

"Maybe, but I have enough information concerning your team's activities to be dangerous. I may spill something you definitely want out of the papers."

"Okay, you win. I may omit answers to the typical stupid questions that some ding dong reporters ask."

"Thank you, Karen. I always know I can depend on you to paint a flattering image of the department. Again, I am sorry this has become a political problem."

"Chief, I am calming down a bit. I will call her right away."

Karen did call her back to arrange a luncheon meeting–on the department, of course.

"So Ms. Lee, what did you want to say to me?"

"Detective Hunter, the Mendosa case has been unsolved for nearly three years. What have you been doing?"

"First of all, to you it's Major Hunter. I want your secret

recorder disabled. Put it on the table. If that does not happen, there will be no more conversation. Also, put your cell phone on the table with the battery removed. Put your pad away."

"How do you expect me to take notes of this meeting?"

"I don't; you can listen for a change and not use some scribbles to back up a sorry story you may want to write."

"You don't take any chances do you?"

"Not with people I can't trust. As you may know, we worked this case exhaustively back in 2008. Let me tell you what we had back then. We had the body of a woman that we easily identified. We had a semen profile from her. We had no crime scene. The crime was committed somewhere else, not where she was found.

"We had no witnesses to any activity that would have led us to a suspect. We developed a few names of potential suspects. We thoroughly investigated them as to their possible motives. We tried to prove their whereabouts during those critical times.

"There were no DNA matches of any of the people we felt who could have been responsible. We did have some support from the FBI. They did not do much. It was not their fault, just a paucity of evidence, if I might use that big word with you. The case went as cold as cases can go. Also, you aren't too concerned that four other women have met the same fate as Mendosa."

"Weren't they whores? A graduate student sells more papers than run of the mill people who put themselves in harm's way daily."

"That's just the point. You choose those who you think are the valuable people of the world. You might be shocked to know many people put journalists in the 'insensitive,' or 'dumb as rocks' categories. One-step above rag pickers.

"Reporters call themselves journalists. Being a reporter allows you, Ms. Lee, to choose minuscule facts; then blow them up into a story, which is only a biased editorial trying to pass as news. A reporter describes the news based on feelings; a journalist tells stories based in facts, without structuring the story with their personal bias."

"I understand."

"I don't think you do. You worked at the paper back then. You dissected us. You had the same information that we had. You did not solve the case either. I know it was not your role. You showed no understanding of the enormity of the problem. We were just a group of incompetents in your eyes. No, you do not now, nor did you back then understand anything."

"Can we move beyond that? I would like to find out why you re-opened the case. Who is a person of interest?"

"I can't tell you that. You know that a letter was found at the College. We think the killer wrote this letter. We do not know. The person taunts us with clues. Nutcases have fooled us before. However, we have to examine all the clues. Once we are able to glean information from the letter, we will be in much better shape."

"Can I see the letter?"

“Not a chance at this point. Right now, it is too sensitive. As far as we are concerned, the killer might be the same man. Why do I say it could be the same man? Just because the same man had sex with each of the women killed, does not prove he killed them. It is called circumstantial evidence; it is strong, but still circumstantial.

“I will tell you that we believe, without a doubt; one man did kill all five women, but we have to prove that. The letter is the only positive link we have to the Mendosa killing. Other than semen profiles, we have no suspect to link to the prostitutes. It is the predicament we have in the past and currently find ourselves. We have many suspicions but very little facts to pursue. This piece of information that only one man’s DNA profile is connected to all the murdered women is off the record for now. I ask you to not print anything more around it until I contact you.”

Karen did not tell Denise that the killer had confessed to murdering other women in the letter, or that she was a target of the killer. To convince Denise how difficult police work is, she posed a question to her.

“What were you doing on the night of March 17th three years ago?”

“How the hell do you expect me to remember that?”

“Bingo. Now you can understand how difficult it is to prod people to talk. Even at that time, people had a difficult time remembering what they did, where they were, what they saw. With all the booze consumed during the Saint Paddy’s festivities, we never obtained any useable information from 'witnesses'. Your intrusion by contacting people we wanted to interview did not help, by the way."

"Is there anything else you can tell me?"

"I will contact you if any significant information we can share becomes available. I will call you, I promise. Because of circumstances and a dearth of information, this interview is over. You understand dearth, don't you? Did you enjoy your Reuben sandwich?"

"Can we quit the sniping? I will commit to providing your homicide group as much information as I can. Any relevant information I come across, I will send to you. The payback for me is, if you have developments in the case that you can share, you share them with me first. Let me have the scoop, as they say. Is that a deal?"

"The *Patriot* is our local newspaper, so I can agree to some extent. You have to be sensitive to what we are going through when you paste an article in the paper. There will be no hitting below the belt to sell papers. In addition, how can I trust that you will not share information with your uncle, the Mayor? He is a nice person, but he is a political animal. You know what happens then. If you agree to this, we have a deal."

"Okay Major, a deal. Mayor Hampton will obtain his information from the paper, not from me. Thank you, Major. I know this will work for us both. We do, after all, want the guy brought to justice."

"Remember our deal."

"You too, Major."

Back at the office, Grace asked, "How did your meeting go with the enemy?"

"I think we've reached an agreement–only time will tell. She has promised to withhold off-putting comments about us in her stories in exchange for a scoop when we have one. I don't fully trust her."

"I'm not sure I do either. It is safer to have her as a potential friend than an enemy, though."

Chapter Eight

And the serpent cast out of his mouth water as a flood after the woman, that he might cause her to be carried away of the flood. Revelation 12:15

"Morning folks, let's continue with our cipher study. Don, are you set to go?"

"I am, yes. I should tell you a couple of other things I did not discuss at the last meeting. There are computer methods that we are sure our perp did not use, but I feel my presentation is incomplete if I don't tell you. Modern encryption methods are incredibly difficult, if not impossible, to break. We divide modern methods into two criteria as:

1. **Type of key used**
2. **Type of input data**

The **'Type of key used'** divides into two categories:

- **symmetric key algorithms that use the same key word for encryption and decryption,**
- **asymmetric key algorithms that use different key words for encryption and decryption**

The **'Type of Input Data'** also divides into two categories:

- **block ciphers encrypt data packs of fixed size,**
- **stream ciphers encrypt continuous data streams**

"It is highly unlikely that our killer had the necessary computer platforms to use the **'asymmetric method'** of the

‘**Type of key used**’ or ‘**Type of input data**’ criteria. These methods require heavy computer support, so we can safely eliminate them. In addition, it would go against his idea of giving us a sporting chance to solve his cipher.”

“I agree with Don. I believe he wants us to solve most of his ciphers, but it is not clear to me why he would want to take that chance. Of course, if he didn’t put his name in the last lines, he is in no danger there,” Karen added.

“Would he design part of the cipher to be complex, the one with his name, and the rest not so difficult?” Grace asked.

“He may very well have. Symmetric key algorithms work well with pen and paper encryption. We are convinced that this is the method used by the killer,” Don asserted.

“Don, please continue,” said Karen.

“Let me discuss two types of paper ciphers. A perfect paper cipher would be one for which no decryption advantage is gained from knowing what the encryption algorithm is, or the ciphertext itself. For the perfect cipher, the likelihood of guessing the plaintext of the message is extremely small, whether or not the decrypter has access to the ciphertext.”

“This is becoming depressing,” said Grace.

“Patience, Grace.” Karen admonished.

“I know, Grace. I am sorry. There is no easy way around it. What I am going to explain briefly is the ‘one-time pad’.”

"Don, make it as brief as possible. We know he didn't use this method because it goes back to our assumption that it wouldn't give us a sporting chance," Karen directed.

"I'll do my best to make it quick, Karen. The one-time pad contains a long sequence of random letters. It is common to assign numbers to the letters, but it is not required. Here is an example of a one-time pad:

```
ZDXWWW EJKAWO FECIFE WSNZIP PXPKIY URMZHI JZTLBC YLGDYJ
HTSVTV RRYYEG EXNCGA GGQVRF FHZCIB EWLGGR BZXQDQ DGGIAK
YHJYEQ TDLCQT HZBSIZ IRZDYS RBYJFZ AIRCWI UCVXTW YKPQMK
CKHVEX VXYVCS WOGAAZ OUVVON GCNEVR LMBLYB SBDCDC PCGVJX
QXAUIP PXZQIJ JIUWYH COVWMJ UZOJHL DWHPER UBSRUJ HGAAPR
CRWVHI FRNTQW AJVWRT ACAKRD OZKIIB VIQGBK IJCWHF GTTSSE
EXFIPJ KICASQ IOUQTP ZSGXGH YTYCTI BAZSTN JKMFXI RERYWE
```

"One-time pad characters must be truly random; must be used only once (hence the name), then destroyed. I should note that true randomness is not a trivial requirement, but if destruction of the pad after its use is always done by both users; this is the first encryption algorithm that has been proven to be unbreakable."

"Don and I know our letter writer did not use this method. If our assumptions are valid, the person wants us to try to decrypt it. The one-time pad would not let him have the satisfaction of defeating us. He would know that we could not do it. This method would be similar to the code-book method in that respect," Karen explained.

"To continue, let me explain briefly how the one-time pad process is done. The users each have an identical pad. Each letter of the alphabet is assigned its normal number sequence minus 1, so **A = 0, B = 1, C = 2, D = 3, etc.**

"Suppose you want to encipher the word, **DONALD** as your message. If you look at the pad, the sequence starting with the letter D is DGGIAK, which is located in the second row of the pad. Starting with the **D** from our message, **DONALD**, we now add **D** of our message to **D** of our key, **D**GGIAK. Since **D** is assigned the number 3, (3+3=6), which is equal to the letter **G**."

"Again, how does the number 6 equal the letter G?" asked Grace.

"Remember that G is normally the seventh letter in the alphabet, but here it is equal to 7 minus 1 or 6."

'The remaining letters of our message, **DONALD**, are done exactly the same way. Thus, **O**=G=(14+6=20), **N**=G=(13+6=19), **A**=I=(0+8=8), **L**=A=(11+0=11), and **D**=K=(3+10=13).

	D		G		G		I		A		K	
	D		O		N		A		L		D	Message
3	(D)	14	(O)	13	(N)	0	(A)	11	(L)	3	(D)	Message
3	(D)	6	(G)	6	(G)	8	(I)	0	(A)	10	(K)	Key
6		20		19		8		11		13		Message + Key
6	(G)	20	(U)	19	T	8	(I)	11	(L)	13	(N)	Message + Key (mod 26)
	G		U		T		I		L		N	Ciphertext

"As you can see from the table, the ciphertext becomes 6 = G, 20 = U, 19 = T, 8 = I, 11 = L and 13 = N, or **GUTILN** for **DONALD**.

"If the 'Message + Key' sum is greater than 26, subtract 26 from it. That is modulo 26. If the number is less than 26, use the number as it is.

"To decipher the message, a person cracking a message must have an identical copy of the one-time pad to reverse the process. The required keyword must be used only once. It must be the same length as the plaintext."

"Wouldn't there have to be a pretty sophisticated spy to use this?" asked Susan.

"You can appreciate that it is a bit complex, but most people can do it once they are trained. The unbreakable part of this method is that if you do not know the key, it is impossible to decipher out of the ciphertext any message having the same number of characters. No information in the ciphertext would allow a person to identify the various possible readings of the ciphertext to achieve the real plaintext. For the counterspy, it would have to be sheer luck to hit upon plaintext making sense. Properly used one-time pads are secure in this sense even against code breakers having infinite computational power."

"It has the added ego problem for our killer. If he doesn't allow us a sporting chance to decipher his code, he can't say he beat us," Karen said.

"How does that concern our ciphers?" Grace asked.

"I believe the alpha ciphers he gave us were to provide us the sporting chance. Again, the numerical cipher may be tough for us to solve. It's his idea to play with us," Karen explained.

"I am starting to feel that we will never solve this case unless he slips up, somehow. This situation is getting much too complicated," Susan said.

"It is becoming hopeless. With our regular police work, memories have faded or been influenced by time. Worst of all, we can't seem to pin any things down," Grace moaned.

"Grace, have some faith, please. We have to do our part to find an approach. We will make every attempt to solve them, but it takes time," Don replied.

"Folks, we can't give up. We have to take every opportunity to solve these cases. The ciphers we have are our best chance," Karen said.

"I have one last item of note for you. A person can design ciphers as combinations of substitutions and transpositions. It is tough, but not impossible to understand. Bear with me on this," Don added.

"Change of subject for a moment, Don. Grace, have you tried getting a profile of the person who may have written the letter?" Karen asked.

"I've been talking to an FBI profiler in DC."

"What have you found?"

"Well, there may not be enough information, or useable information from the dumpsite. It was three years ago. I doubt it, but we may have overlooked something vital. Even with our best information, it may be difficult to generate a true method of operation for the killer. As Don has said, profiling often yields an inaccurate picture," Grace said.

"On the other hand, the FBI has made some remarkably accurate profiles," Karen added.

"Karen, we have developed nothing in this case that helps to paint a portrait of the killer. The only things we can say are listed here."

- **We know that the killer had written the letter just after we found her.**
- **He intended for us to have the letter shortly after he wrote it, but it did not surface until three years later.**
- **We believe that all of the murders were pre-meditated, but we do not know whether he randomly selected them or not.**
- **The killer wrote that the women's deaths were terrifying to them.**
- **For whatever reason, he bears a personal grudge against Karen.**

"Except for his tirade against me, his intent may be to simply kill. Who the victim is does not matter to him. That may explain why prostitutes, as well as, someone like Mendosa were included in his murders," Karen said.

"We do not have much, forensically speaking, except the profiles to provide us any direction, but the National data base is of no use." Grace voiced.

"But as you said, we have his profile and that will be his Achilles heel. Unfortunately, today we have no name to match. So we'll put resources in this cipher direction," Karen insisted.

"At this point, the FBI profiler feels uncomfortable trying to project an image that would be of any use to us. We know he is able to code or cipher with some skill. Big deal," Grace said.

"All right, Grace. Please continue to work with them.

Don't let the whole situation depress you. Don, are you finished with your presentation for today?" Karen asked.

"Karen, I'm done today if you don't want to hear the idea of combination ciphers."

"I think we all are a bit overwhelmed by what we've covered this morning. Schedule another meeting to finish this discussion."

"I'll check schedules and plan one ASAP."

"Grace, on second thought, let's forget about the FBI. Ask the GBI folks to continue trying to develop a profile. I know it may not be accurate, but it may come in handy later. Don, thank you."

"Karen, at our one-on-one morning meeting tomorrow, I may suggest another way of how this may be cracked. I need to research it more before I could share the idea with the MCU."

"Okay, Don. Let's talk in the morning. Thanks everybody. Keep your spirits up. Remember, Don will set up another meeting. Please make room in your calendars for it."

"Grace and Susan, please come to my office. I would like to find out what you learned; are there any other missing women in Georgia that are similar to our cases?"

"I need a few minutes for us to put our material together," Grace replied.

When the three were in the office, Karen asked.

"Susan, what did you find out?"

"Since we are dealing with young adult women, I only

found one case similar to ours. She was a young, black woman found in the north section of Atlanta. Highway workers found the woman on the morning of March 19, 2003. The ME stated that her death had been sometime in the late hours of the previous day. Her body was placed at a dumpsite soon after. She was a student from State scheduled to graduate that year. She was a chemistry major planning to attend Middlefield College for a Ph.D.

"Similar to our cases, there was no definitive reason for her death. They found no evidence of drugs in her system. She was fully clothed, and missing a small amount of hair that had been cut from her head. It was similar to our other victims.

"The coroner's report indicated that the woman recently had had intercourse. The ME had the semen sample profiled. For whatever crazy reason, the profile had never been put into the national database."

"The killer's method of operation certainly sounds similar to our cases. Was the drop site the scene of the murder? Was there anything else similar to our cases?"

"The murder did not occur along the highway. It is a busy road during most hours of the day and night, so someone would probably see anything taking place. Plus, there was no evidence of disturbance at the site."

"What about the DNA sample? Can we get the profile from them? Is there any sample left to do our own profile on it?" Karen asked.

"After I notified the Atlanta Police, the profile was

uploaded. I went back to check our profile to that one. As you will probably guess, it matches the profile of our perp. They don't have a name attached to the profile either, so we are back at the square one in trying to identify the guy."

"Have you anything else?"

"Yes, a letter was attached to the inside of her blouse. The letter was taunting the police to solve the murder. However, unlike our case, the letter had no code in it; it was typewritten, so it was premeditated. There was no name on the note."

"What do you mean?"

"Our letter was addressed to you. It did have the same tone as ours. It simply said that the murderer was not sorry for what he had done; he defied the police to catch him."

"I wonder if that was the first time for the killer," Karen said.

"He was arrogant. He wants the police to understand how smart he was. I don't know why, but I am struck by the fact that the murder was three years earlier than our first similar case in March."

"I'm so involved with the details of the circumstances of the case, I didn't make note of that," Susan said.

"Well, it was just a thought. I am not sure if it has any relevance. It does look like our killer is responsible for her death. Let me know if anything else pops up from the case."

"It is very unnerving to think he is operating in a wide area. We have been thinking that Savannah or Middlefield were the murder venues. Now we know that we were wrong. He's working in many places," Grace said.

"Okay for now. Thank you."

Three days later, Don set the next cipher meeting.

* * *

"Don, let's roll with this. I need to hold today's meeting to one hour and a half if that is possible. The Chief wants to go over a few things before he sends his weekly report to the Citizens' Committee. I need to be ready for that."

"I can't finish this in less than an hour and a half, so I will just present the overview. I will omit some details. I'll have more for the next meeting."

"That's all right. Continue."

"Another category of ciphers is called Nihilist. These ciphers are done manually. That is why they are useable for agents working in the field. They are undemanding to encipher, but not terribly secure. I suspect that these types of ciphers are ready-made for our killer. Effectively, they are numerical versions of Vigenère cipher. Multiple digits are the enciphered symbols instead of letters.

"I will show you a simple example of a Nihilist cipher. An encipherer could create a Polybius square with a jumbled alphabet. The one I have here is not mixed.

	1	2	3	4	5
1	M	U	R	D	E
2	R	A	B	C	F
3	G	H	I	K	L
4	N	O	P	Q	S
5	T	V	W	X	Z

"The agent would use this square to convert his plaintext message with a keyword to a series of two digit numbers."

"That sounds familiar. You mentioned them before. I hope we don't have a test after this," piped up Grace.

"Grace, let's stay on track, please," Karen said, an edge in her voice.

"I am sorry, Karen. I'm just letting off some tension."

"It's okay. Please continue, Don."

"What's a Polybius square?" Susan asked.

"For our present example, the Polybius square is a '5 by 5' array as I have shown here. The array can be larger if needed.

"To use it, a keyword; for example, **MURDER**, would be put in the first row of the square. If the keyword were longer than the first row, our coder would complete the keyword on the second row. He would finish the rest of the Polybius Square with letters of the alphabet in mixed or alphabetical order, but omitting the letters used in his keyword.

"For a plaintext message, **I HATE WOMEN**, he would convert both the keyword and plaintext letters to two digit numbers from the Polybius square. He would repeat the keyword to the length of the plaintext message. Then he would add the plaintext to the keyword numbers together to yield the cipher shown in the last row of the chart shown next:

	I	H	A	T	E	W	O	M	E	N
Plain Text	33	32	22	51	15	53	42	11	15	41
Keyword	11	12	13	14	15	11	12	13	14	15
Cipher	44	44	35	65	30	66	53	23	28	55

"To decipher, he would subtract the keyword from the ciphertext, and use the Polybius square to retrieve the plaintext.

"If the plaintext message is **I LOVE WOMEN** with a key of **MARRIED**, set up a Polybius square as we did before.

	1	2	3	4	5
1	M	A	R	R	I
2	E	D	B	C	F
3	G	H	K	L	N
4	O	P	Q	S	T
5	U	V	W	X	Y

"Again, he would encipher the plaintext by adding the key to the plaintext to get:

	I	L	O	V	E	W	O	M	E	N
Plain Text	15	34	41	52	21	53	41	11	21	35
Keyword	11	12	13	14	15	21	22	11	12	13
Cipher	26	46	54	66	36	74	63	22	33	48

"That's all there is to it."

"These are the most straightforward examples you have presented yet," Grace said.

"There have been improvements to this method of encryption, but my discussion on those will take considerably more than the time we have left, so I will stop here."

"Okay, folks. Continue working on our assignments. Saint Patrick's Day is on Thursday. We know the killer strikes then. We have no idea where these killings actually occur. I will need two of us to remain in Middlefield this week. I want one person to be in Atlanta on Thursday and one to be in Savannah."

"I volunteer for the Atlanta duty. Jake and I will go up on Wednesday night," said Grace.

"Do I have a volunteer for the Savannah watch?"

"I will be staying here in Middlefield. Rob's parents are coming in for a week's visit," Susan said.

"I intend to be here. I want to spend more time on the letter this weekend. I'm going to keep working to see if I can spot some keyword clues," Don said.

"Don, since you are going to be here, perhaps you could monitor the College conference for anything suspicious. I know it is a stretch, but the College has never been fully off my suspect list."

"I can't imagine anyone there is responsible, but I'll spend a fair amount of time there," Don said.

"I guess it's me for Savannah, then. I plan to leave here Wednesday afternoon. I will be back here by noon Friday. I will let the Chief know so he can plan," Karen said.

After the meeting, Grace went to Karen.

"If you don't mind my saying, Boss, I think you are musing too much about the pleasures with someone not Bill. I know who it is. Can I give you some advice? We have all seen how these triangle situations work out. Please be careful."

"Let's keep this professional, Grace. You may be right. I do not put my nose into your personal life. I want you to stay out of mine. Let me know how the interview goes before I leave."

"I will, Karen. I apologize. I am just concerned around you as a friend."

"I understand. What you are doing is intrusive. I won't stand for it."

"Perhaps I am wrong concerning you and Romano."

"You are. I have no idea if Romano is planning to go to Savannah. I am not going to meet him. Savannah is my surveillance area, remember?"

"Yes, it is. I know that. I was only trying to help."

"Why don't you try to manage your own area? Let me do my job, my way."

Your way, unfortunately is going to land you in big trouble. Eventually, you will come crying to me.

Chapter Nine

And the woman was arrayed in purple and scarlet, and decked with gold and precious stones and pearls, having a golden cup in her hand full of abominations and filthiness of her fornication. Revelation 17:4

On Wednesday afternoon, as Karen drove down the highway to Savannah, she pulled into the breakdown lane on I–16 where Alejandra had been discovered so long ago. She had not been here since 2008. Now an old thought sprang to mind.

Why was Alejandra found on the <u>eastbound</u> lane of I–16? She was supposedly in Savannah. Wouldn't the killer dump her as soon as possible on the <u>westbound</u> lane?

Karen made a mental note to have Susan double check the other case files for the exact locations where we found the other four women. An unexplainable force pushing her to stop at the site gave Karen an eerie feeling. It was as though Alejandra were reaching out to her.

What is it that have we missed, Alejandra? What is it about your death that we do not see? Did you innocently walk into something you could not control? Did your behavior lead you to your death? Did Chad do this to you? Was it Marino? Who else was involved? Why did you let them do it? (There are no answers, of course.)

Is it just my own guilt preying on me? Is that Alejandra's message? Be careful how you treat your lovers. Do not trifle with men's feelings, or they may hurt

you? Did you hurt someone so much they had to kill you? Was it because of your baby? Send me a sign, Alejandra. Let me find your killer. What am I doing? I am talking to the wind.

Karen pulled back into the traffic continuing toward Savannah. The thoughts continued.

Should Grace have a right to worry about what I did to Bill? Is this just as Alejandra did? Did she play men against each other? Who knows what can happen if egos are mixed up with emotions of a man over the favors of a woman? I hurt him years ago. Am I now committed to him? Is Bill such a miserable guy that he deserves a wife who cheated on him?

To calm her thoughts, Karen started the CD player as the soothing piano of Jim Brickman flooded the air.

Some people have such talent! Some people are in this world to soothe the souls that others have wounded deeply. Dear Lord, why do we fill this world with such tension and hate? We know we are imperfect. Why do we kill each other in the name of loving you, Lord? Did Alejandra reach out to you? Did she think of you as she lay dying? Please give me a sign, Lord. Let me avenge Alejandra's death. Let me stop the killer.

A much-subdued Karen reached Savannah, and parked her car at the garage next to Planter's Hotel. After checking into her room, she showered to refresh herself from the long drive. Dressed in her jeans and a form-fitting blouse, she needed to blend with the crowds. After all, she was here on business.

As the time neared 5 p.m., Karen walked next door to the Pink House for a drink. Entering the lounge area, she noticed there were no available table seats or chairs at the bar.

I will get a beer and just stand around to see what happens.

Pushing her way to the bar, she felt a pair of eyes looking at her. Turning to her left, she was very surprised to see someone she knew.

"Joe, what are you doing here?"

"I guess I should ask you the same thing, Karen."

"I'm here to have a little fun and relax a bit from the things back home."

"How much fun were you planning? Is Bill one of those to get away from?"

"Don't get any ideas, Joe. I am here by myself for a reason. Where are you staying? I had a tough time finding a room this late. If it weren't for an old friend from State who manages a hotel, I wouldn't have one now."

"Believe it or not, I booked a room the last minute at Planters. I know the manager."

Now there is a coincidence. Oh right, we both know Jim Butler from State days.

"Where are you staying, Karen?"

"I am at Planters. I guess we both hit Jim for a favor."

"Well, that puts us nice and close."

"Listen, Joe. I made a mistake with you one night. It will

not happen again. My conscience has been bothering me ever since."

"Well you must admit it was good and you didn't resist."

"You know how to work someone's guilt, don't you?"

"I think we should celebrate together. Bill's not here and we are free as birds."

"Joe, we need to talk. You have the wrong idea about me."

"Are you okay, Karen?"

"Fine, Joe. Well, that is not true. These murder cases are driving me crazy. I have not been able to sleep a full night. I am so tired. However, it is much more than that. I thought that at first I could handle the thought that someone is out to kill me. It is now preying on my mind. At times, I think I should turn the responsibility for the Unit over to someone else. Find myself an island to leave my troubles behind."

"I guess we all need that thought occasionally," Joe agreed.

"Yes, it's that fanciful flight we construct to soothe our tortured souls. It's not practical at all, though."

"We all need the ability to tamp down reality; let the other side of ourselves out when it's overwhelming."

"I admit that's where I am now. I am not sure what to do." Karen reflected.

"We all have live with it. It is the light and dark sides of us. It's the Jekyll and Hyde within us."

"I suppose you may be right."

Does he think all people live their lives with dual personalities?

"You look delicious, Karen."

"Joe, you just are not getting it. I am not here for you. I did not know you were going to be here, nor did I care if you were."

"Okay. I will stop, but I think there is something on your mind that is really bothering you. I think it's not the murder cases."

"I am feeling somewhat lost in my thoughts. I'm not able to stay on track."

After their drinks, Joe suggested, "Let's get out of here. We can go to a quiet barbecue place on Bay It will be packed but we'll talk there."

As they ate their meals, Joe decided to let Karen have space to unload her feelings.

"Karen, I will just listen. Tell me what is bothering you."

"We need to discuss what we are doing. I am so lonely. That was what made me weak with you. I do not want to hurt Bill no matter what kind of a jerk he is. I do not want to hurt you again. I don't want to be hurt again."

"We don't need to rush into any decisions."

"Thank you for understanding, Joe, but what makes you think we have any decisions to make? You are pushing, and I am sure of your motive."

"You aren't ready for anything else. I know that."

"Joe, there is nothing further for us. There is Bill. I love and respect you both in different ways. Our mistake that night is a scourge on my marriage. I feel so guilty. My parents did not raise a daughter to screw around, but without benefit of marriage, that is exactly what I did–just like when we were dating. You did not know it, but I did it also with Bill, before you and I finally broke up. I deceived you. Now I am deceiving Bill. How do I reconcile that? How do I rationalize all that with my conscience?"

If you knew my secret, Joe, you would not have anything to do with me.

"Karen, I said I would listen."

"Joe, this situation does not just concern you. I was as willing as you were. Our mistake that night does not seem to influence your conscience. I suspect that for you it was just a piece of ass. At least that is what I have believed where men are concerned."

"Wow. You believe that of me?"

"You certainly acted that way. I don't intend to hurt you, Joe. I am in pain over this. I'm saying things out of frustration."

"I will not bother you again. I think it is best. This is such a mess."

"Yes Joe. It is probably best to stay away. I just need time to sort out things."

"I guess you're right."

Joe, I have to spend some time in River Street, and I have to do that alone. What are you going to do?"

"I'm going to scout around for some action. I'll probably hit several places before I turn in tonight."

"I may bump into you later. Stay sober."

"Right, Karen."

* * *

Joe's cell phone rang later that evening.

"Joe, this is Karen. I had a strange incident after you left. I went down to River Street. You know how crowded it is there, so walking means constantly bumping into revelers. I had a strange feeling that someone was watching me, that a man was following me. Everywhere I went, he seemed to be there. I'm not imagining this, it is spooky."

"Did you get a look at him?"

"He evaporated each time I turned to look."

"Did he do anything?"

"No."

"Are you armed? After all, you are a cop."

"Of course, I still carry it when I'm not on duty."

"I am glad you called, but I don't see that I've been helpful."

"Just being able to talk is comforting."

"Where are you now? Is there anything you want me to do?" Joe asked.

"Not really, I'm back at the hotel."

"Perhaps I will see you tomorrow. Sleep tight."

* * *

Joe's thoughts turned to Karen.

What has happened for Karen to become so irrational lately? What's this story about a mysterious stalker on River Street? Is she losing her grip? Why call me? Am I

becoming a crutch for her problems in life? Can she handle what a divorce would bring? I think not. I should just forget this whole mess with her. Chalk it up as a serious mistake on my part. The one-time sex we had recently was very good. That is probably all I wanted from her that night. Nevertheless, there is more to come and I will win at the end.

* * *

Karen fell asleep thinking of Joe.

Why is it that you injure the person you have feelings for, or think you do? What are my feelings? Why does he keep pushing? I know it has to be the sex, but I've told him enough times that there is nothing else for us. Why do I call him? Is it because I feel vulnerable and guilty? Be careful with him, Karen. Be very careful.

Later that evening, Joe quietly slipped out of his bed, dressed, and went down to the hotel lobby and looked at his watch. ***It's only twelve-thirty! I still have time for a drink. Perhaps I can find a little fun as usual.***

The River Street revelers were continuing the party they started early in the day. Joe walked down the access stairs from Bay blending into the wall-to-wall, noisy, drunken crowd.

Friday morning the sun rose to a cloudless sky. Karen checked out of the hotel; drove down Bay Street turning left onto MLK Boulevard. Reaching the highway ramp, she headed northwest to Middlefield. It was time to return to work. It was time to know if the killer had struck again.

Chapter Ten

For without *are* dogs, and sorcerers, and whore mongers, and murderers, and idolaters, and whosoever loveth and maketh a lie. Revelation 22:15

Early on Friday morning, March 18, 2011, a call came into the Middlefield Police Department. Road workers had found another woman's body lying alongside the breakdown lane of I–16 within Middlefield's jurisdiction. As with all of these horrible murders, the killer had staged the site to make it easy for the police to identify the woman. Her wallet with its paraphernalia lay beside her body. Her physical condition looked similar to the five other women found lying beside the highway.

Her name was Lauren Reuben, 22, daughter of the prominent Middlefield physician, Dr. Samuel Reuben.

The most attractive of all the Reuben daughters, Lauren had a beautiful figure accented by her dark brown hair and brown eyes. At five foot six, she was the shortest of Dr. Ruben's family.

The Reuben daughters were Rachel, Lauren, and Shira in order of their births. Dr. Reuben's wife Rimona had died in 2006 when Lauren was sixteen.

Of the three children, Lauren was the most emotionally impacted by her mother's death. Normally an obedient youngster, she had become noticeably rebellious in the past few years. She had sexually liberated herself in her late teens. She often fought with her father over her behavior, but men continued to flow through her life. She degraded herself to become popular socially.

Nevertheless, her achievement in college was well above average where she earned an overall 3.7 average during her four years at Middlefield College. She was due to graduate in May with a bachelor's degree in Physical Anthropology.

As required by law, Gordon came to the site to review the scene before moving Reuben's body. By his rough estimate, she had died earlier that same morning, probably within a few hours of her discovery.

After the last young woman had been found murdered in March 2010, it was no surprise to Karen and the MCU that the killer had struck again. This murder made the sixth one that would continue to test her strength and skills of the MCU.

As part of Karen's duties, she and Grace made plans to visit the Reuben family. She dreaded this task of telling a family in cases like this. After delivering the tragic news, she began gentle questioning of Lauren's family.

"How did she die?" Dr. Reuben asked.

"That is something we still do not know," Grace said.

"Why does the killer put them on the highway?"

"Again, these are questions that we do not have answers for. We have a sense of his motives, but at present, we don't know enough to say why," Grace answered.

"Dr. Reuben, do you know where Lauren was going to spend the weekend?" Karen asked.

"No. She didn't usually tell me things like that."

"She told me she was going to Savannah on Wednesday with a friend," Shira interrupted.

"Did she say who the friend was?"

"Only that he was a friend at the College."

"I am going to be on your necks until you catch this killer. This serial killing has gone on long enough," Dr. Reuben said in obvious pain.

"I understand, Dr. Reuben. We are doing all that we can to catch him."

"Apparently your efforts are not enough."

"I apologize. Under the circumstances, we are doing the best we can. We will keep you informed."

"My sister was a little wild at times, but she didn't deserve this."

"I know, Shira. No one deserves this."

"Dr. Reuben, I will contact you as soon as we have anything I can share with you concerning Lauren," Karen offered.

"That's the least you can do," Dr. Reuben snapped.

Back at the station, Karen approached Susan in the break room.

"It was heartbreaking to see the family. Even though Lauren had an independent streak, she was much loved by her family," Karen said.

"Did he know where she was spending the week?"

"No, but his daughter Shira knew. She went to Savannah. More fun, more excitement there. Her sister said she was going with a friend. She couldn't tell me who he was."

"This guy is not going to stop," Susan complained.

"We have to stop him, but we're still at a dead end. Without the code being broken, we do not have much to go on. The code is our hope," Karen said.

"What do we do now?"

"Susan, honestly, I don't know. No one sees or hears anything. We have been asking the same, old questions for years now. Why does the killer want us to identify the women easily? Is it just to satisfy his ego? Is it a way of saying, 'See how powerful I am. You'll never catch me'."

"I hate to state the obvious, but we only have one letter, now another similar murder, and no leads. Karen, there just isn't any evidence we can find other than his profile gifts. If he doesn't slip up otherwise, we will continue to fail."

"I know, Susan. Moreover, we are not fully equipped to solve the code. Don and I may be able break it sometime, but I'm afraid the press and citizens will not tolerate the wait."

"I hope we aren't dealing with a copycat," said Grace as she entered the room.

"What made you think of that?" Susan asked.

"No second letter," Grace answered.

"That is true, but the deaths are sophisticated; I doubt a copycat knows that technique. In the meantime, Grace, you will have to attend Lauren's autopsy. Please be on time. Gordon becomes grumpy when he's delayed."

"What time did he schedule it?"

"He said it would start promptly at 9:30 tomorrow."

"He's an eminent guy, but at times he is such a pain," said Grace.

"Have Gordon send us the results as soon as he can. I want to know if there was any evidence that shows he forcibly raped her. If she was, that fact makes this murder different.

"Susan, please review the records to find if any of the murdered women were HIV positive. My suspicion is that Mendosa was not. I am not sure that Reuben will test negative. She seems to have had a host of lovers," Karen said.

"Why are you concerned with that?"

"It bothers me that this guy doesn't seem to worry that he could get a disease from prostitutes. Of course, what rapist does? What could be the reason? I'm wondering if he is HIV positive himself; maybe he just doesn't care," Karen replied.

"He isn't the typical kind of rapist. He does not batter his victims, even those he kills. The women willingly have sex with him. So, is it the sex; is it the killing; is it both desires that drive this guy?" Grace asked.

"If everything else about his MO is the same for Lauren, there is probably another semen sample for profiling. This killer is collecting trophies of his kills. He takes their underwear, that's not very original," Karen added.

"I almost forgot, Karen, Chief told me to tell you that he

has assigned three detectives from Vice to assist us in interviewing Lauren's friends."

"That is a help. We can use them to find out who may have seen her last. Have them obtain cheek swabs if the people they interview are willing. Otherwise, for now, we will have to assume that her acquaintances will not match the profile we have. Time will tell if that assumption is wrong."

"We should try to pressure her male friends to give us swabs, just to exclude them," Grace said.

"Grace, we can't just require people to give us their samples. You know. It's Fifth Amendment stuff."

"I think that anyone who refuses to give a swab, we should ask them to submit to a lie detector test."

"Okay, Grace. Moreover, if they refuse, you are back to the Fifth problem. No sense going there until we have more proof."

"It doesn't mean they're not suspects, though."

"Grace, please. You are not listening. We cannot require them to do anything unless you arrest them. That is just plain silly. The DA or a judge isn't going to support that."

"Do you have any saner ideas?" Grace asked.

"Right now, no, but I know we can't do that."

* * *

Karen went to her office. As she sorted through various items, an envelope addressed to her lay on the bottom of her 'In' basket. It bore a return address from Savannah. For reasons that Karen did not understand, simply handling the envelope made the hair on her neck stand up. When she turned it over, she found nothing of significance on the backside. The mailing address and the return address were hand written. Karen was nearly at the decision point of sending it to the mailroom to be x-rayed. With the powder scares of late, some nut could be sending her a biological present or something else.

Overcoming her feelings, she carefully slit open the envelope, half expecting the letter to blow up in her face, and gently slipped the letter from the envelope. The sinister content was instantly recognizable.

March 18th 2011

Major Karen Hunter,

No doubt, you have found my latest present for you. I told you in my first letter that you were too simple to figure out my code, so I am giving you another chance. All the clues you will need are in my other letter; but, of course, you and your team are incompetent.

I gave you my name last time and now I give my name again in the last lines. See if you can do a little better this time. Catch me if you can. It does not matter; I know that I will be victorious. I am the worst stalker you will ever know. I have given clues to solving this code, not that it will do you or your team any good.

I know where you live and play. You have always been so much fun to play with.

Your admirer from a distance –

JEJNBDIB TACJBYSN UACOVHOW IICKAHAN HARJGEEB
YRXJFQTN YNNNBIAC HEJEFDOC KTNKAIIA HOWEFJEJ
IACABDRR KKGUQQBTBZWNKZELOXE

38636321479039593841491578222820
93691574039572410246039292743153
63963016536905413201386413902969
58914382584988574369840409444300
56526573618591185987121805036158
69186585768502693460455183536219
88675661382932148593103269626307
44159997087323974745747663940790
50235149399438802849596258444743
85930294727588476307020976425434
93699811305388274097086555076874
67050494623579939886740484626528
16331324436856158054179284458358
43483792688464138359910545103194

After reading it, Karen reached for her phone to call Tate.

"Chief, another letter has arrived from the killer. I am going to call the Unit together and show it to them. I'll send you a copy."

"Thanks, Karen. Keep me posted. I guess we'll have to share this with the Committee."

"Grace, please have Susan and Don come to the conference room. I have something you all need to see."

After rereading the letter, Karen grabbed the corner of

her desk to steady herself. She could not afford to have her staff see the impact this letter was having on her. Bracing herself, she left the office heading for the conference room.

My God, why is this so personal? This killer is definitely stalking me. Why is he doing this? Why does he want to kill me? What does he mean by 'where I live and play'?

"Look at this," she said when the staff arrived moments later.

"We knew this guy wasn't done; worse we have barely scratched the cipher problem. He just sent this letter. What's worse; we have more cipher lines to work on."

"This guy is incredible. I can't say for sure at this point, but maybe it's good that we have more code lines to look at," Don said.

"You may be right, Don."

"Karen, unless we can spot anything unusual with this latest cipher; I need to concentrate on the Mendosa letter," Don cautioned.

"Don, you and I will meet again after this meeting to decide how we handle this letter. How is the work progressing?" Karen asked.

"I'm forging ahead as well as I can. Marcus told me he is not able to work on it just now. His chief has pulled him off it to work another case, which is a priority for Atlanta."

"Well, continue with your work. I'll call his boss to see if we can set some sort of priority in view of this latest murder."

"I feel I'm making some progress."

"I know, Don. You are a hard worker. We have to meet again for any updates I can present to the Committee."

"Can you let me have another day or so? I have an idea that has been rattling around in my brain. My idea is to release it to the crypto world. See if they can crack it."

"We have to tread carefully with that. We will need a buy-in from the DA. It is evidence, after all."

"Let's set a meeting for Thursday morning at nine. Is that okay with your schedule?" Grace asked.

"It's fine with me."

"Karen, I'll have an intriguing cipher to show you," Don said.

"What do you have new?"

"After our last talk together, I believe I know what cipher system the killer used."

"That is good news."

"If I am right, it will still be a difficult cipher to break. I did mention that idea to Marcus. He thinks we may be on to something."

"That's great, Don."

"I think we are closing in on the answers. It will still take time." Don cautioned again.

"Let's talk more at our meeting in the morning. I'm not feeling well today," said Karen.

Karen awoke the next morning sick to her stomach. She had missed her period in February. Now for the second month, it did not arrive. She had been feeling somewhat nauseous, especially mornings. An unfamiliar heaviness in her breasts drove her to read some literature describing early pregnancy symptoms. She bought a test kit. The little tester confirmed her suspicion.

What will Bill think about our marriage now? He is going to be a father! I have to tell him. We have always wanted a baby.

Karen hoped the baby would bring new life to her marriage. Bill needed to know. She would not tell Joe she was pregnant. The baby was not his, after all.

However, could she talk to Joe, at least? Maybe he could be a friend in a platonic way. For some reason, he seems to be the only one to whom I can bare my soul. We were very close one time and he was always there for me. Now things have changed between us. Sex always changes things. I am not going to be involved with him anymore, but he is a person with whom I do feel safe. Well, I do somewhat. On Saint Patrick's Day this year, I knew he wanted to take it further, but it is only sex that drives him to me. No, it will not happen again. I need to repair my marriage, but I would still like to talk with him. Can I tell him my secret? Should I tell him?

She thought that her behavior this past week was deplorable. She had too many uncontrollable feelings, too many things to change within her, too many things she did not want to change. There were too many complications to sort out.

Karen dialed Joe's cell phone.

"Hi, Joe, how are you doing? I am calling to apologize. I am not sure why I reacted as strongly as I did on Thursday. I didn't need to be cruel to you, but I know that you realize I can't have an affair with you."

"I understand. I know the cases are bothering you and our fling in February, but there seems to be something else. Is there?"

"You have to understand the conflict in my mind. I cannot believe I cheated on Bill. It was very wrong of me, of us. The guilt is almost overwhelming."

"Karen, you have to make your own decisions. I can't help you much there. Listen to my advice. You need to see someone. I am the cause of your latest anxiety. You need professional guidance."

"I know you are right. I feel weak, vulnerable right now. I want a strong support system. I do not know how to find it. Shrinks do not accomplish much. I know it from my experience. It only pushes back the problem. It does not solve it. They are not gods, only human. It is we who have unrealistic expectations of their abilities."

"I understand, Karen."

"Joe, I'm nervous. You remember what happened this week. I now believe it was the killer stalking me. We have found another body on the highway. The woman is the daughter of Dr. Reuben. The family is devastated, but there is more. I have been putting on a strong face with the Unit here. This creep is out to kill me. None of us can figure out why."

"I heard he sent another letter."

How does he know that? Who is talking in the group?

"Yes, he sent a letter. It says similar things as the first letter, but he refers to the Mendosa letter for clues. I am pissed that he keeps focusing on me. How did you know about the letter?"

"By the grapevine, I have my sources. With all of this bedlam, you are making me nervous, Karen. I am asking myself why I pulled you back into my life. You nearly drove me over the edge years ago. Now the pain is back."

"I know, Joe. I am sorry."

"You know, 'sorry' doesn't always cut it."

"Wait a minute, Joe; you're the one that seduced me. However, like it or not, you are the only one I can talk to right now."

"Do we have to play the blame game? It seems that you weren't unwilling."

"It was a mistake that I sincerely regret; don't be angry with me. We both made the mistake."

"I'm not angry. I am having a tough time being wound up every other day or so. You don't know what it's doing to me."

"Joe, I need to share something I have never been able to tell anyone. It goes to the depth of my soul. It goes to the heart of my problem. It affects how I cope with my life. I cannot tell you on the phone. We must meet face-to-face in order for me to say it. I have never told Bill this. I do not want you to think badly of me. I know he would. Can we meet in some safe, but quiet place?"

"I don't know. I don't feel comfortable coming to your home or you at mine until you solve your situation with Bill."

"Let me be the judge of that. I can think clearly enough to sense if it is reasonable or not. It has to be platonic. I will not go to bed with you again. I just want to talk."

"I'm not making any promises."

After a pause, Karen said, "Joe, you do need to promise me that. Is that acceptable to you or not?"

"Okay. Where do you suggest we meet?"

"Don't think the wrong thing, Joe. Your home is the right place."

"Karen I think you are wrong."

"I promise to be strong for both of us."

"When do you want to meet?"

"If possible, tonight, Bill is out again this week."

"So Karen, the only thing we do tonight is to discuss your secret?"

"I promise. After I tell you, you probably would never want to talk to me again anyway. It is four o'clock now; I can be in Atlanta by six."

"Okay, I'll make a light dinner for us. How do fried hot peppers and sausage with acini di pepe sound? I'll throw together a light salad to cleanse the palate."

"I remember those meals. We're both Italian, but something less spicy would be better for me with my nerves these days."

"Interesting, I always thought that was one of the reasons we would be a compatible, married couple."

"See you around six."

The drive to Atlanta was slow. Karen's nerve was beginning to fray, and she began to dread reaching Joe's home as each mile evaporated.

Should I tell him? How will he react? When we went together years ago, I did not tell him. I was afraid I would lose him. He is only a friend now. So, why am I doing this? I need to get this off my chest. The pain of it has never gone away. Well, I am committed now.

"Come in, Karen."

The two ate their dinner nearly in silence. Both were reluctant to speak fearing that words would spoil the aura.

"That was a delicious meal, Joe."

After dinner, they went to the living room, and Karen began her story.

"Joe, do you remember I told you one time that I had an older brother who died?"

"I remember that you mentioned it; it was never an important part of our conversations as I recall."

"That's true. All my life I have been unable to confide this to anyone. I did come close to telling you when we were in love."

"That was a long time ago. Why is it so important now to tell me?"

"After tonight you may wish I hadn't told you. You are really the only person I can tell. I do not know why. For some reason, I think you will understand, but…."

"Karen, I am not sure that I can help you with your secret. My caring for you long ago was real. You threw it away; I know we made a terrible mistake in January."

"I know. I am ashamed how I am treating you now and back when we went together. This is very painful for me. I have to trust you, Joe. I do not understand why I need to tell you, but I do. Of the few men I was intimately involved with, you affected me the most. You had my heart. Maybe that is why I feel I can trust telling you. I need to cleanse my soul."

"You can't rely on me that much, Karen. You're feeling pain now, but do you realize what you did to me?"

"Maybe this was another bad idea I have; perhaps I should just leave."

"You came this far. Why don't you get it off your chest although it's not clear how telling it to me will help you?"

"Let me be the judge of that, Joe."

"It's your call, Karen."

"I'll start my story with the tragic day it happened. He died by his own hand. He shot himself."

"When did this happen?"

"Joe, please let me tell you in my own way. Please just listen. Let me tell it without any questions. This is extremely difficult for me. I do not know if I can do it without crying. As I said before, I have never told anyone this. My parents were innocently part of the horror.

"My family moved to Middlefield when I was thirteen.

My brother was fourteen at the time. He did not move with us. By then he was dead.

"My father owned LoPorti's Italian Bakery in the north section of Boston. He sold all sorts of Italian desserts. His business was popular, and it did very well. We were comfortable as a family. My mother started working there to help my father out after my brother and I began school.

"The mess all started when I was eleven years old. As I said, both my parents worked during the day. After school let out each day, we spent the afternoons doing our homework as my father demanded.

"Mind you, I loved my parents. They were patient with us both. What I tell you now is no reflection on them. They did their best as parents for us. They were kind. They worked hard for what they provided us.

"What happened later devastated them. They were never the same afterward. It tore up our lives. They blamed themselves. They were innocent.

"As I said, Subby and I were latchkey kids. His real name was Sebastian. At thirteen, my brother began to have thoughts; urges—sexual urges. It was not long before he began to talk to me concerning the urges. The folks certainly had never mentioned sex, out of embarrassment, I suppose, like most parents. He found some books with pictures. We educated ourselves. It was a dangerous education for a couple of Catholic kids.

"At the time, I looked a little older than eleven, but not by much. I was not at puberty at that point. I had not even heard the word. The longer we talked, the more intrigued we became to understand how people did it.

"One afternoon we tried it. It was painful for me. We were both embarrassed. I bled a bit, but the bleeding stopped. I was scared, but eventually I calmed down. Joe, this is difficult for me to admit.

"Well, after that Subby made sure he didn't hurt me. The feelings I had doing it were mixed with pleasure and guilt. He was my brother. There was no harm done, right? It was our secret. We kept the secret from our parents. We both began to look forward to our afternoons. It happened regularly. We sinned continually for nearly a year. Joe, this is so embarrassing.

"One spring morning, I had my first period. I panicked, thinking that I was going to bleed to death. I ran to my mother, crying. In my panic, I told her what Subby had done to me. I thought God was punishing me. In catechism, the nun warned us that it was sinful; she told us that sex was dirty. I knew that God was definitely punishing us.

"My mother calmed me down, but she was incensed. She did not scream at me. She raged at Subby. My father was getting ready for work. When he heard the commotion, he asked my mother what was wrong. She told him. He had always been so calm, gentle with us.

"I had never seen him that angry. He became violent. He started yelling at Subby that he was going to kill him when he got his hands on him. Subby ran to my parents' bedroom locking the door. My father kept a .38 in his nightstand for family protection. Subby knew it was there, and grabbed it while my father screamed for him to come out.

“Subby began wailing from the bedroom. It was the pathetic cry of an animal in pain. My father was yelling and pounding on the door. Subby was crying so loudly that he could not answer my father. He must have been so scared.

“Then it was over. The terrible, loud explosion of sound came from the bedroom. We were all stunned. My father broke into the room. Subby lay there on the bed, his blood and brains on the wall. Blood stained the bed covers. My father fell to his knees crying ‘Subby, Subby’. My mother called the police.

“The loss of their child was unbearable. Subby was the carrier of the family name into the future. Now it was all gone. My parents never admitted to the police why Subby was depressed enough to kill himself.

“My parents were inconsolable and never recovered from it. The family was shattered. I was physically devastated. There was no way to ease my conscience or theirs. I felt life was over for me.

“If I hadn’t been such a sinner, or they hadn’t let tempers rule the moment, perhaps we all could have somehow gotten through the nightmare. I thought we might become whole, pure again.

“Of course, it was only a twelve-year-old’s impossible wish. You cannot go home again. They never mentioned Sebastian’s death. They mourned in silence for both of us.

“I know they loved me, but I could feel their disgust that

their daughter was a whore, a puttana, never to be trusted. I was a twelve-year-old whore.

"A year after my brother's death, they sold out of Boston. They moved to Middlefield where no one knew us, or more importantly, about us. Here we could pretend it never happened. However, life was one dreary day after another.

"There was no joy left in any of our lives. My father's pain lasted until he passed away. I was fifteen. He died of lung cancer, but I think the stress of the last years gave him the cancer.

"My mother died a year later, much too young. She loved me throughout her life. After my father died, she constantly told me that she loved me. That God would forgive all of us.

"People said she must have died from a broken heart. My father's death and my sins had shortened both their lives.

"My only relatives lived in Italy; I had never met them. There was no one left here for me. I was an orphan at sixteen years of age. I had killed my family.

"The state of Georgia placed me in a foster home where I lived for two years. My foster parents were kind. They accepted me as their own daughter. I felt I had no right to their kindness. I wanted to love them, but I knew I was unworthy of their love. I would only hurt them.

"I went to a psychiatrist for two years, paid for by the state of Georgia. It did not help. I never told the psychiatrist anything related to having sex with Sebastian. He knew that Sebastian had died violently at a young age. He assumed it was a suicide. He had no idea of my part in it.

"At sixteen, I began to date, thinking boys were my ticket out. It was always the same push from boyfriends, sex, sex, sex. I understood the drive boys have. In the end, it was always easier to go all the way than to fight about it. There were very few of them, Joe. I did not enjoy it. There was always the threat of pregnancy.

"The boys were not careful, nor was I. You understand what comes next. I could not tell my foster parents that I was pregnant at eighteen. A baby was the last thing I needed in my life. State had accepted me, and I was ready to start another part of my life in college.

"When you and I met, I had so much baggage that I was afraid to let you know of anything in my past. You had asked to meet my parents; I took you to meet my foster parents.

"As far as you knew, I had been orphaned when my parents were killed in an auto accident.

"Our relationship in those days was a gigantic lie. The stories I told you were not the truth. I said my parents did not raise a daughter to screw around. That was a lie. They did not even know that their son and daughter were doing it. They were gone during my teen years when I needed them the most. I had killed them. I am so ashamed.

"Maybe I left you because I felt you were the only decent, considerate man that I had ever met. I could not let you marry a person who was so worthless. I was running away from you.

"Even back then, I wasn't sure I loved Bill, but I thought he had more potential for the life I wanted. You see how callous I can be. There is nothing left to tell. Please do not hate me, Joe. You were the only bright spot in my life. That is now ruined."

"Karen, I'm astounded that happened to you, but it is not my place to judge you. It is not my right to decide your worth. Only you can do that."

"It's kind of you to say that, Joe. I feel certain it comes from your heart."

"Karen, had I known your story before our thing in January, I probably wouldn't have pushed you into bed."

"I didn't tell you this to burden you, Joe. I wanted to free my soul from the guilt I've carried over the years."

"Karen, I never would have suspected you went through such an ordeal. I realize that people put up tremendous fronts to hide pains they have endured, especially early in their lives. Occasionally it creates monsters. In most cases, people overcome it. They go on to lead successful lives."

"Joe, I had to do something good with my life, or I would have become one of the hopeless."

"Karen, our breakup overwhelmed me. I do know that you hurt me very much."

Is everything always about you, Joe?

"I have no right to say this, Joe, but I'd like us to stay on friendly terms. I need to be able to share my thoughts with someone. It will not be often. Bill does not seem to care, so he is not an outlet for me. You are a person I feel I can trust to listen."

"Bill is your husband. I am feeling guilty for having had his wife."

"I betrayed him. It was only one time with you. It will be the last. We did not do anything in Savannah. I did not know you were going to be there. After I met you at the bar, I began to weaken. Now I am ashamed of what I was thinking. I thought I wanted to be unfaithful to Bill with you again. It was wrong."

"You didn't let your early life push you down. I admire that."

"When we were a couple, back in college days, you opened your heart. You told me of your early life. I could say the same to you. In spite of what happened to you, you became a success."

"Yes, it seems that way."

"I should be going. Think of me. I will be thinking of you. Thank you, Joe. Goodnight."

"Goodnight, Karen."

As Karen drove back home, she felt a calmness for the first time in many years. She had faced the past, as she had never done before. Joe, she was sure, would look down on her. How could he not? She had hurt him for the last time.

What was it Doctor Henry Adams said? The killer considers women in terms of Madonna or whore. Joe must surely think of me now as the whore.

In a way, I think I will always have strong feelings for him. How could he ever love me, now that he knows of my sordid life? I will not call him again. My 'friend question' was just to ease the tension tonight. I have to move on; I can't depend on Joe for emotional support. I have to believe in myself. I still have my work. I still have a serial killer to catch. I will catch the son-of-a-bitch. How dare he threaten me? I will put him in the ground.

* * *

The next morning at work, Karen called Denise Lee.

"Morning, Denise. This is Karen at PD. I have some news for you per our agreement, but a few items need to be unpublished. I will share with you all the information I have concerning the woman found March 18. There was another letter, but I am asking you not to print anything regarding that for now.

"We want to have this person thinking that we did not receive it. We think it infuriates him. The letter does have a code in it, which we are close to solving. Come to the Red Rooster Grill this evening for your scoop."

"Thank you, Karen. I will keep my word."

Karen sat at her desk pondering her next steps.

I need to tell Bill that we are having a baby. I can't wait much longer to contact a prenatal doctor. I have to decide whom to call. Tomorrow will be soon enough. Now, kid, prepare the package for Tate's Committee meeting.

Chapter Eleven

Standing afar off for the fear of her torment, saying Alas, alas that great city Babylon, that mighty city, for in one hour is thy judgment come. Revelation 18:10

"Don, come to the conference now. Have Grace and Susan come with you. I want to have our cipher meeting now instead of Thursday."

"I 'm not quite ready to give the presentation, yet"

"We meet at nine in the conference room. I want to share the information we talked about yesterday."

"Okay. I will do my best."

"Don, our best in this case is not enough. We have a serial killer. We have to do better than our best. We have to nail him. He is smart, but we are smarter than he is. Be prepared for nine."

"Grace, this is Don. Can you have your stuff ready for a meeting at nine this morning? Just received a call from Karen and she is ripping. In all my time here, I haven't ever seen her this way."

"I'll do my best, Don"

"Uh, don't use that phrase with Karen, she will kick your butt."

"Something is different here. I wonder what's up."

Karen opened the meeting with a stiffness that the MCU had not expected.

"Okay, Folks. Don, start us off with what we've decided for the ciphers."

"All right, Karen. First, can I ask if anyone solved the

cipher from the last meeting?"

"I didn't have time. Other stuff took priority," Betty said.

"I tried. I must have made a mistake somewhere. I only decrypted gibberish," Grace said.

"That leaves you, Susan."

"I deciphered it. It was the first part of the Gettysburg address," Susan said with some smugness in her voice.

"Congratulations. See me later for the ten bucks."

"Wow, another budding crypto person. Don, please continue."

"Okay. I mentioned earlier that there is a general class of ciphers called Nihilist. We will discuss other Nihilist cipher types as necessary. Today, I will focus on the fundamentals of the system. Later I will explain some variants along with other derivatives of the Nihilist system. I need to describe it this way because it helps to identify the cipher type that we think the killer uses.

"The Russian Nihilists developed a cipher system in the 1880s to employ terrorism against the tsarist regime. It was successful at the time. The general encryption method was to construct a Polybius square having a scrambled alphabet. The Nihilist type I showed the other day had the alphabet unscrambled.

"The Polybius square enciphers a plaintext message to a series of two digit numbers by a numerical keyword. By adding plaintext digits to keyword digits, the ciphertext is prepared. If the plaintext is longer than the keyword, the keyword digits are repeated as necessary to cover the full extent of the plaintext."

"Can we please move on with it, Don?"

"We need to be patient, here, Grace," said Karen.

"You're right. Excuse me."

"I am not trying to be cute or insensitive with the next example. It fits with our killer. I am going to prepare a Polybius square with the keyword **RAPED**. R becomes 11, A is 12, P is 13, E is 14, and D is 15 from the square.

	1	2	3	4	5
1	R	A	P	E	D
2	S	B	C	F	G
3	H	I	K	L	M
4	N	O	P	T	U
5	V	W	X	Y	Z

"Now, suppose the plaintext is:

I LIKE TO KILL YOUNG WOMEN

"We would add the keyword to the plaintext digits to get the ciphertext as I show here:

	I	L	I	K	E	T	O	K	I	L	L	Y	O	U	N	G	W	O	M	E	N
Plaintext	32	34	32	33	14	44	42	33	32	34	34	54	42	45	41	25	52	42	35	14	41
Keyword	11	12	13	14	15	11	12	13	14	15	11	12	13	14	15	11	12	13	14	15	11
Ciphertext	43	46	45	47	29	55	54	46	46	49	45	66	55	59	56	36	64	55	49	29	52

"The two digit numbers can be smooshed together to hide the message even further."

“Smooshed? Where did that come from?”

“Sorry, Grace. Leave out the spacing between the pairs, so the first two digit pairs, 43 46, becomes 4346.”

“She’s just teasing, Don, keep going,” said Karen.

“As I said at the last meeting, I will explain some of the later variants of this cipher system.”

“How much time will you need to complete this?” Karen asked.

“I can use an hour or so. That should wrap it up.”

“Don’t misunderstand me, Don. These meetings are very important for the team. The cipher meetings you and I have every day are getting us closer to solving these ciphers, but there are other matters I have to address right now.”

I understand, Karen,” Don said.

“I need to have Grace, Susan, and Betty on board every step of the way, which is why I insist on having these meeting with them. But we have a lot of regular police work to do with the Reuben murder, notwithstanding the last letter we’ve gotten,” Karen explained.

“Karen, I want to talk with you later; I have some thoughts that came to mind after our meeting yesterday morning.” Don said.

“Can you see me later today? Please continue, Don.”

“As I said earlier, the Nihilist cipher is essentially a number version of the alpha character-based Vigenère cipher. Therefore, it is possible we can break the cipher by using similar methods used to decipher the Vigenère.”

"How will that help us, Don?" asked Susan.

"The killer left us Vigenère ciphers, which may give us clues to the other ciphers."

"Please continue, Don," Karen pushed.

"The real improvement in ciphers utilized something called a straddling keyboard versus the Polybius square to convert the plaintext to numbers. This method also slightly compressed the plaintext allowing faster transmission of the ciphertext. By appending an additive to the method by non-carrying addition, that is, modulo 10, a truly subtle ciphertext is possible. I will explain modulo 10 in a minute.

"This system made the ciphertext uniform in its appearance, so that it wouldn't leak as much of the plaintext information. In the Russian Nihilists' variance of the Nihilist cipher, the keywords used were often quotes from the Bible, other books, et cetera. The Russian Nihilists then converted these words to numbers.

"This type of cipher was generally secure. The proof of my statement is that generally their messages were not successfully deciphered."

"Is this what our killer used?" asked Grace.

"That's close, but not exactly. The Russians also developed something called the **VICTOR** cipher, which is another, more advanced type. Used during the 1950s, its general classification is within the Nihilist family. I believe this type is the one our killer used."

"Don, from our off-line discussions, I am convinced we have the right idea. The killer knows that cipher system is incredibly tough to decrypt. Please continue."

"As a hand-operated cipher it is not terribly complex to use. Field spies used it frequently. Its cipher complexity comes from having the modulo chain addition I spoke about earlier. For keywords, a spy could use mathematical concepts such as a Fibonacci generator."

"Why would that be used?" Susan asked.

"It's a formula that generates a sequence of false random digits, which makes the keyword more secure," said Don.

"How does that foil the decipherer?" Grace asked.

"Well, regardless how you encipher, you don't want non-random repeating digits in your ciphertext that can leak away information. Therefore, you want secure keywords.

"The system utilizes a straddling keyboard, which by its nature has a disrupted transposition. People once thought that using double transposition was the most complex cipher field spies could use."

"It turns out that that concept has limitations," Karen added.

"Yes. With the **VICTOR** cipher, that impression is not necessarily true. Moving on, I have an example of a straddling keyboard.

	0	1	2	3	4	5	6	7	8	9
	E	T		A	O	N		R	I	S
2	B	C	D	F	G	H	J	K	L	M
6	P	Q	#	U	V	W	&	X	Y	Z

"Notice that the top row has two blank spaces. In the bottom row, two characters are symbols. The keyboard I have shown here can be arranged in any way. The system users need to know how the keyboard is arranged, so they can communicate. To encipher a plaintext from this keyboard, you can see that the first row is straightforward, where A is 3, N is 5, et cetera. For the second row, G would be 24, for example."

"From our discussions, Don, one nagging question is the third row order. We haven't decided if the killer places the symbols under the blank columns of the first row, or some other arrangement," Karen added.

"Karen, a more critical concern is that he may have scrambled the alphabetical sequences of the third and second rows."

"Yes, that would make deciphering incredibly difficult," said Karen.

"I'm not sure why that would be," Susan said.

"Don, please plan to explain permutations at a later meeting," Karen directed.

Grace interrupted, "In the third row, would W be 65?"

"That is correct. To continue the process of enciphering, a spy would prepare a plaintext message he wanted to send. Then he would convert each letter of the plaintext into a number.

Here's the example we used in the Nihilist method. Using the keyboard, I showed earlier, we would get:

Plaintext	I	L	I	K	E	T	O	K	I	L	L	W	O	M	E	N
Keyboard	8	28	8	27	0	1	4	27	8	28	28	65	4	29	0	5

"Now, this cipher can be sent directly by smooshing the numbers together, sorry. By eliminating the spaces, the ciphertext would be **826827014278282865429 05**. If our spy wanted to confuse someone further, the ciphertext could be re-enciphered using another keyword converted to a number. As an example, let us use Karen's birth year. Would that be 1950?"

"Watch it, Buster."

"That's apparently not a good idea. Sorry. We will add some year; say 1984, as a keyword.

"First, transform the raw cipher into single digits. Then add the keyword, 1984, to obtain the (PT Cipher + the Keyword), **C+K** values I have shown in the next table. Then subtract 10 from any **C+K** digit that is greater than 9, which is the process of modulo 10.

"Any **C+K** digit that is less than 10, use it as it is. Thus:

PT Cipher	8	2	8	8	2	7	0	1	4	2	7	8	2	8	2	8	6	5	4	2	9	0	5
Keyword	1	9	8	4	1	9	8	4	1	9	8	4	1	9	8	4	1	9	8	4	1	9	8
C+K	9	11	16	12	3	16	8	5	5	11	15	12	3	17	10	12	7	14	12	6	10	9	13
Mod 10 (–)	10	10	10	10	10	10	10	10	10	10	10	10	10	10	10	10	10	10	10	10	10	10	10
Let. Cipher	9	1	6	2	3	6	8	5	5	1	5	2	3	7	0	2	7	4	2	6	0	9	3

"The row, **Let. Cipher,** is the resultant ciphertext a spy would send. If he wanted to be more confusing to an enemy, he could take the **Let. Cipher**, and convert it back to letter characters using the same straddling keyboard."

Raw Cipher	9	1	62	3	68	5	5	1	5	23	7	0	27	4	26	0	9	3
Convert back	S	T	#	A	Y	N	N	T	N	F	R	E	K	R	B	E	S	A

"How does all this help us to nail our killer?" asked Grace.

"Karen and I believe our killer used a Nihilist cipher of this type. If we are correct, it narrows the world we have to probe."

"Why do you think it's a **VICTOR** cipher?" Susan asked.

"In the Mendosa letter he made a statement, 'I will be **victorious**?' Why would he write that? Why not write 'I will win?' His statement was over the top to Don and me. One day, when we were looking at the letter, the word stood out. Suddenly, it was a Eureka moment," Karen explained.

"What are you saying?" Grace asked.

"Let me write it this way: 'I will be ***victor***ious.' "

"You amaze me; great sleuthing, you two," Grace said.

"Karen and I have deliberated this idea for some time. We believe he wants us to have as many clues as possible to show he is smart, but he does not want it to be easy for us to decipher the lines with his name," Don added.

"Terrific. Can we attack it now?" asked Susan.

"I don't intend to be unfeeling, Folks. Have you been listening? The **VICTOR** cipher is a bear to decipher. It may require years to do it."

"This is hopeless. How the hell are we ever going to break this code?" Grace asked.

"One way would be to smear the cipher parts of the two letters across all News outlets. We could also send them to any cryptanalysis organizations. There are some smart people in this world. A challenge such as this might just provide the answer."

"I think we might do that, Don. The DA has given us her blessing. Otherwise, you and I need to keep working this," Karen said.

"I agree. In the meantime, Marcus and I are getting together some other thoughts to solve the ciphers. With your permission, Karen, we will send out our clues along with the ciphers to see if that helps."

"Push forward with our work. Bring in any resources you can," Karen ordered.

"Is there any way we can we offer a reward for their solutions?" asked Don.

"Maybe GBI has some extra cash. Don, check this with Marcus. See if he has a GBI name I can contact to work for the reward," Karen said.

"I will, Karen. I see our time is up. I will get back to work," Don suggested.

"Yes. Susan, please continue with the background checks. Grace, can I see the case summaries for the 2009 and 2010 murders? I've been concentrating so much on the damn ciphers I'm losing touch with the personality of this killer," Karen said.

"Let me gather up some information on some thoughts I have. Gordon told me yesterday that he sent a semen sample for testing from the Reuben slaying. That result won't be back until next week," Grace said.

Later, Grace and Karen met to continue a discussion.

"All right, Grace. We agreed some time ago to drop the FBI profiler and use GBI instead. Have you tried to get something from them? I know Don's opinion was that character profiling is not something that we can base our case investigations on, but I don't want to abandon any possible help."

"I'll follow up on that as soon as I can," Grace said.

"You told me a while back that we may be able to do some DNA testing that could tell us what race Mr. X is," Karen probed.

"Karen, let me explain what that type of DNA testing entails. I have had a lot of experience in the DNA world, but I am no expert. I spoke with Dr. Louis Loomis who is a DNA geneticist at UGA. When you asked me to investigate this topic a while ago, I took the liberty of finding out as much as I could. Loomis volunteered to come here to enlighten us, if we wish."

"We may need his expertise if we ever find out who this guy is. I do remember courses in DNA forensics I took; nevertheless, it's been so long that I could use a discussion as a refresher. Can you explain more?" Karen pushed.

"Yes, I had to spend some late nights getting ready for

this meeting. I had forgotten a lot. Guess I wasn't paying as much attention as I should have when I had those courses."

"Our libidos were governing us more than we thought. Do you think that was the gift from feminism? But I digress," Karen teased.

"I'll quickly review some essential ideas of DNA. Scientists have done much testing in the past few years; there have been many advances in this area. The Human Genome Project has been completed. It turns out that 99.9% of human DNA sequences are the same in every person."

"That's remarkable, but we all look so different."

"True. Loomis did mention some theories concerning current human DNA dogma. One was the 'genetic bottleneck' idea that theoretically happened 70,000 years ago. Some think the last explosion of the volcano, Toba, wiped the human population to nearly 10,000 individuals.

"Successive generations of humans then developed from a small genetic pool. Another idea is that coalescence of the genetic pool is a long, naturally occurring event. So the belief is that long or short bottlenecks could be responsible for DNA similarity."

"Grace, this is getting pretty theoretical. We do look quite different from one another."

"I know, but Dr. Loomis assures me that because enough differences in DNA exist, it allows us to tell one individual from another. He mentioned an exception, which I cannot parrot back right now. I remember that he said we would only have to be concerned with that in a particular instance. I'll let that rest for now."

"Be sure you thank him. Also, be sure to record that exception idea into our case file for the future," Karen ordered.

"I will do that. There is one last thing concerning DNA profiling that I want to mention. The profiling process uses sequences called 'variable number tandem repeats', or 'VNTRs'. Testing is focused on something called 'short tandem repeats', again abbreviated to 'STRs'. I'm sorry, Karen, these acronyms are aggravating to me. I feel out of my depth in these areas of science."

"I understand. They grate on my nerves too, but we use acronyms all the time around here, so I guess I can't bitch too much if other fields want to simplify their work."

"This topic as a whole is pretty complex. I am not doing it justice in my explanation for you."

"That's why we have these eggheads to figure it out for us. We will use whatever time they can spare us. You do know their egos are huge. You must massage them."

"Yeah, many things need massaging," teased Grace.

You never give up, do you?

"All right, Gutter Girl, move on."

"I'm going to tell you what was done to our semen samples. When we are able to get results from the Reuben murder, we will finish comparing them all. I am going to skip the details of what was done for the tests on our samples for now. We may have to discuss that at some point. The pros know what they are doing, so we will trust to that."

"Trust, yeah. Do not lose sight of our role to push them in the direction we need. We have to stop this guy."

"Since we know we are dealing with a male; the samples were subjected to Y-chromosome analysis called 'Y-STR'. Since the Y-chromosome only appears in males, it is passed from father to son.

"As we both remember; mitochondrial DNA is passed from the mother to her children of both sexes. Only females pass it on to future generations. The current belief is that the male DNA is not mixed with the mitochondrial DNA at conception of the individual."

"What does this Y-STR test tell us?" asked Karen.

"Since it is paternally inherited, it serves to identify males who are paternally related. The markers are identical for all the profiles of our murders so far. That test tells us who did these murders. Lauren Reuben's killer's DNA will clinch it."

"Well, hell, didn't we already know that once we received the 2003 test results from the Atlanta murder?" Karen pushed.

"It was only when we were given the 2003 profile that we realized we were dealing with a serial murderer who was operating beyond our area. The profiles of our cases confirmed that the killer was one man."

"Please continue with the DNA testing ideas."

"These tests are quite expensive, so I suggest we don't have mitochondrial testing done, unless we need it for the future. Hindsight is revealing, but at the time of the 2008 murder, we only had the three semen profiles obtained from the women. There was no match in the state or national databases."

"I'm sorry, Grace. We know that. I do not want to insult you, but pressure is building; focus on what we need to do next."

"That's okay. I understand."

"Has any of the semen sample from the 2003 murder been saved, so we can test it also?"

"No, unfortunately the sample wasn't stored properly, so it degraded. Apparently someone decided to throw it out."

"Ouch. I hope that person has been disciplined."

"Don't know. You originally asked if we could tell the race of this murderer. It is not as effortless as you see on TV. We do have samples from all our murders; we could choose one, say Mendosa's, and have a mitochondrial DNA test done. If it is viable, then we may be able to determine something concerning the ancestry of this person."

"Why are we just picking the Mendosa profile?"

"We could also do the same test for the Reuben profile, but again, this type of testing is quite expensive. Therefore, it is best to limit the number of tests. Also by his own admission, the 2008 letter ties him directly to her murder.

If we can pin this down to him, we have a winnable case against him. At that point, the DA should prosecute."

"How does the mitochondrial DNA testing provide information we need?"

"Well, another term is necessary for us to understand. As you know, a person's genetic information is in their Y-DNA along with their mitochondrial DNA. Scientists have done extensive work with new DNA tests such that they can sort test results into something called haplogroups

"Haplogroups could be loosely called clans, if that fits. Not to be too confusing, a haplogroup consists of similar haplotypes. The Y line haplogroups are different from the mitochondrial line haplogroups. They may represent, in a general way, populations of major regions, e.g., Africa, Middle Europe, etc. There may be markers in both types that point to, say, Britain, since those populations today exhibit similar haplogroup information. The belief today is that human DNA started in Africa.

"Anthropologists believe that populations migrated out of Africa spreading throughout the world. Most of the DNA along their migration paths did not change over long periods. That's why we have vast similarities in our DNA."

"So, we are sisters."

"No doubt about it. The small mutations in DNA for each generation create the slight differences in our DNA. That allows us to differentiate populations. Many geneticists believe that the mitochondrial DNA is stripped off the sperm when it penetrates the ovum. That means the mitochondrial DNA from the father does not combine with the mother's DNA to form the child's DNA profile. Further, Y-DNA as well as mitochondrial DNA alters only by chance mutation at each generation. This theory supports the 'Adam and Eve' lineage."

"So, Grace, what I understand from our review is this: we may not be able to identify exactly what this perp looks like, but we can say with some probability that he is one race or another because of his ancestral line."

"That's probably safe to say. Race as a label is becoming less certain as a definition of individuals."

"Where are you going with this idea?"

"Look at our group, for example. Susan is what we call Hispanic – not truly a race; Don is what we call black; we call ourselves white. These labels are wacky because the DNA in each of us is 99.9% the same. We can see outward differences, but I ask; is Don truly a different race from us? I think that someday we will not describe people as different races, but as members of different cultures. Cultures can contain people of all 'races'. They would live by cultural rules as an amalgamated population. Okay. I am off my soapbox."

"So let me paraphrase what you have said. Y-DNA, as well as, mitochondrial DNA provides information defining haplogroups. Haplogroups can point to a geographical area where a person's ancestry is derived. Very interesting. Thanks for giving me a truly eye opening presentation. Thank you again."

"You're welcome, Karen."

"Grace, I'll ask the Chief to ante up some bucks for the mitochondrial DNA test. Someone is going to ask me why we are spending this money for another test."

"We have enough of the necessary facts we need at this point to justify the testing. Karen, I have already talked to the Chief. He says that we have a fund for extraordinary expenditures. I have to let him know the ballpark amount needed. I wanted to check with you to see if you had any problems with it," said Grace.

* * *

Grace went to her office to review recent events, which had occurred in the Unit.

What is happening to Karen? She is edgy these days. I understand the pressure is building to have Lauren Reuben's murder solved. As we all know, the daughter of a well-known couple will receive special treatment in the press. I can understand that. Karen is receiving calls from the Chief, the Mayor, and the press daily. She is short tempered, as my mother used to say. I guess I am also, but still…

Is she strong enough for the work? She always has been. I know the Bill and Joe triangle is not going well. Nor should it be. Karen, I <u>told</u> you not to get involved with Joe again. Who am I to talk? I was never faithful as a wife. It cost me my first marriage, and I have not found anyone to replace him. Marriage number two isn't going well either. People expect cops to be upright, honest in

their personal lives–most are, some are not, like me. As they say, you don't know what you have until it is gone.

I am going through another divorce. I am lonely. Any guy I date only wants to hit on me. Slam, bam, thank you Ma'am. It is not much fun these days.

Then why do you fall in bed with every man you date?

Grace, you are a mess. Well, you made your bed, now lie in it. Enough of me. What is it with Karen? I have too many years left to work. She needs to pull herself together. Push this team back on track. She has to stop bullying us. She needs to treat us as vital to the resolution of these murders.

Karen's voice pulled Grace out of her reverie.

"How is the reward process coming for the code stuff?"

"I thought you were going to check with the GBI."

"I haven't had time. Check with Don. See if he's made any progress with the code kooks."

"Karen, with all due respect, these 'code kooks' may be our lifeline to solving these cases."

"Grace, I don't need any lectures from you. Have an update to me by noon."

"Will do, boss."

Grace went to see Don.

"Don, do you have any updates on the code process to the outside world?"

"In fact I do. I was going to call Karen with some news."

"She's in a foul mood this morning. It had better be superior news. She took my head off after I gave her a rundown on the DNA stuff."

"Oh. Sorry I missed your presentation. Wasn't invited, I guess."

"I thought it strange you weren't there. She is in no mood to tolerate any push back, so I moved on with it. She's not pulling us together as a team well these days."

"Let's go see her before she loses all of her mojo," suggested Don.

"Karen, do you have a minute?" asked Grace.

"What's it now?"

"Don needs to update you on the code stuff."

"I can't now, that's why I told him afternoon. The Chief wants to see me. I need a report ready for that."

Grace and Don headed back to his office.

"I guess she wants us to work through lunch time. You notice she isn't coming in to work until nine?" asked Grace.

"I hadn't noticed, but then your office is near hers."

"I'm thinking it is not the usual Karen. She used to be right on time in everything."

"Now that you mention it, I guess I have noticed a difference, especially her short fuse. She chewed me out the other day because I asked her if she had checked with the GBI. Didn't she say she would do that?"

"Enough of her. Can you bring me the latest status of the code reward to date?" asked Grace.

"Sure. I did check with GBI for any funds. The best they can do is $5000, which I told them is generous. They will have the money as soon as we need it. Will it be okay to advertise it?"

"Wow! That is great news. She needs to approve it though."

"Here's my update. I have the ad ready for the papers along with all the brochures ready to send out to the cryptanalysis groups across the country. My hope is that interest in solving ciphers will yield some results for us."

"What happens if no one comes through with any solutions? You have to face that possibility. If not, what will you do?"

"I think Karen and I will make progress even if we have no luck with anyone collecting the reward. We will have to solve them. Karen knows ciphers; I have come to realize that."

"She has been a tremendous help with the cipher discussions, but I pray it isn't fully on your shoulders."

"I hope so too, Grace."

"You both are under stress, which is not helping you personally or the group."

"I know, Grace, I know. Kim is pushing me to take some time off. I am neglecting her and the kids."

Chapter Twelve

Nevertheless I have *somewhat* against thee, because thou hast left thy first love. Revelation 2:4

After Karen's meeting with Chief Tate to confirm funding of the DNA tests, Karen met with the MCU.

"Let me tell you how my meeting went with the Chief. The death of Lauren Reuben has gotten the attention of the city. Four prostitutes and a graduate student do not. Dr. Reuben is well respected. His family is angry with us for not solving the murder. They are starting to go to the papers, which is only going to increase the misery of our investigations."

"We're doing the best we can at this point," Grace pointed out.

"Not good enough. The Chief is threatening to pull some 'high power' folks in here. Our weekly updates to the Citizens' Committee are not doing what we hoped. Of course, we knew they wouldn't. The city is losing confidence in us. The Mayor is shouting from the rooftops. I don't need to tell you that, you see the news."

The meeting with Karen was tense. She picked apart each suggestion anyone presented.

"Grace, update us on what you've been doing."

"That's fine. The first DNA test is due in a week from the cell lab. With that information, we will be able to fit our murderer roughly into a 'clan.' We may be able to classify him as a descendant of a region of the world in terms of his ancestry. A reasonable guess as to his race will be insightful. Karen, do you remember what I said earlier regarding the problem with the idea of race? Since there are no eyewitnesses, our perp could be a light skinned black or a dark skinned white, or any other combination you can think of."

"Hard to see how that benefits our work. When you have results, spend some time with them. I want a solid report out of you."

"You know I will, Karen."

"Karen, are you planning to have Grace update us on the testing she is doing?" Susan asked.

"She has already explained her work to me. Grace, please set up a meeting with Don and Susan to explain what you have been doing."

"I will."

"Don, what do you have to say?" Karen pushed.

"The reward ads for the papers went out late this morning. I hope the reward will inspire people to solve the cipher."

"I hope that also."

"Keep me posted. I mean it. The GBI is out on a limb approving that amount of money. Any developments I want to know about immediately. Is that understood?"

"Yes, Karen. I will."

"How are the ciphers coming along?"

"Karen, I've been trying my hand at deciphering using various keywords the murderer says he gave as hints," Don added.

"Good. At our meeting tomorrow, please explain more," Karen said.

"I will have some ideas for you," Don replied.

"Susan, what are you working on now?"

"I am collating all the dribs from the cases into binders, so that when we know who our perpetrator is; we will have something to deliver to DA Waters. I am also working the background checks you asked for. By the way, I looked at your request to find out where all the bodies were found on I–16. We found all the women along the eastbound lanes, even Mendosa. That's odd, because Mendosa and Reuben were supposedly in Savannah. You might expect the killer to dump them as quickly as possible."

"Do you suppose the killings are happening north of Middlefield, and the killer is just trying to throw us off track?" Susan asked.

"It is only a gut feeling; I think the killer is from the Atlanta area," said Karen.

"The problem is we don't have witnesses who saw anything at the drop off places," Grace added.

"In fact, we don't have any witnesses. Eyewitnesses are generally poor for a case anyway; I'm not optimistic concerning that. It is going to be forensic evidence or the breaking of the code, which will be our decisive factor. It is not going to help us to speculate," cautioned Karen.

"Yeah, I agree."

"All right, everybody back to work. You need to keep me updated," said Karen.

"I will keep you posted."

"Same here," added Don.

* * *

After the meeting, Grace huddled with Don to strategize a plan to maintain the case rolling to solution, but it soon turned to gossip.

"It's a miracle she approved the advertising. I don't know how you feel, but she is getting on my nerves," said Grace.

"What is wrong with her?"

"I don't know for sure, Don. Karen is wearing down physically. She is putting on some weight. She is tired all the time. Maybe she is not sleeping well. I can't blame her for that. The killer is out to murder her. This case is enough to drive anyone batty."

"Let's hope we can be successful. We have to solve this nightmare before the killer strikes again. I'm not sure I can deal with the pressure or her moods much longer. I am just being selfish right now. I need a break."

"Don, don't you get any ideas about leaving. She needs us even if she can't see that right now. I am not going to roll over because of her changing moods."

"Do you have any ideas why she is acting differently?"

"I hate to gossip. I think it does have something to do with her affair; a person at Tech, I understand. He is an old flame who is still pursuing her. Not good. Her husband suspects what happened. Obviously, he isn't happy knowing she is unfaithful."

"It would bother me a lot. I am not the jealous type; if Kim ever did run around behind my back, I might feel differently."

"I'm sure she won't. Now, I need to get back to work."

* * *

Karen left work early for home. Feeling depressed, she went directly to her comfortable couch. Sleep did not come. The cases were always present on her mind. She had not had a full night's sleep in nearly a week.

Thoughts rolled through her head.

I am tearing my group apart. They will hate me. I am starting to hate myself. Moreover, I have this other problem. I have to tell Bill tonight when he comes home. In the meantime, sleep.

That evening Bill returned from his trip.

Pouring himself a drink, he relaxed in his favorite chair.

"Where's the newspaper?" he asked.

"It's on the counter. I will bring it in right away, but I have something to tell you first–I am pregnant! I'm so happy!"

"You're what?" Bill screamed.

"I know; I am as surprised as you are. I thought we would never have a baby."

"Who's the father?" Bill asked with a sneer.

"You are, of course."

"Not likely. That is not likely at all. Do you know why you never became pregnant all these years?"

"No, I thought it was just the way it was. Some couples

cannot conceive. They can be too tense; I read that somewhere."

"Let me tell you why, kiddo. I had a vasectomy before we were married. I did not want kids, ever."

"What? Bill you can't be serious. You never told me that!"

"Well, I'm telling you now. Now you've gone off and gotten yourself knocked-up. I should have known you couldn't keep your panties on."

"You are a son-of-a-bitch, Bill. I would have never married you if I had known that. I wanted kids, a white picket fence, and a loving husband.

"What did I get? I married a liar and a cheat! All this time you have been lying to me. Maybe it will happen, you said many times. You knew all along that it was a massive lie to me. I will never forgive you," Karen screamed back.

"Now there's no doubt you've been screwing around. Is it pretty boy Romano?"

"I hate you, Bill. I'm going to a lawyer in the morning."

"What are you going to tell him? You are pregnant with Romano's or some other road tramp's baby. How long has this been going on?"

"It was a one-time mistake of weakness. I have always cared for him, but not in that way since we have been married. I was always faithful to you. If anyone is wrong, it is you."

"Yeah, but I don't have a package in the oven. How is this going to look to your friends at the department? Right, our boss is a whore. That'll have everybody respect you."

"How would they know if you've had a vasectomy? For all they know it is your baby."

"Grace knows. She was a good time for a while. You never knew that, did you? Screwing the boss's husband and enjoying it. She knows."

"I knew she sometimes was slutty. I never thought she would betray me."

"Well, she did. She enjoyed it."

"I knew you'd been screwing around on me for years, but I had no proof. You are no one to talk. Why is it okay for you, but not for me? I received a call from one of your girlfriends last week. She thought I would not be here. She thought I was an old girlfriend you were trying to dump. Apparently, you told her you were not even married. She told me a lot. I set her straight. I bet you did not have any rolls in the hay after that call. Do not play the injured husband with me. You are scum in my book. I have given you the best years of my life. You did not appreciate it. I cannot believe that you have lied to me all these years. See you in court."

"You finally understand; I am not going to support Romano's bastard child."

"I want a divorce; I don't care how it looks to the world. I am ashamed. Now I understand that you made this a marriage to suit you. You have made a fool out of me in front of my staff. I will never forgive you for that. I will decide what I do next."

"You screwed yourself into this. Now find a way out."

"Bill, you are cruel, but I did not realize just how cruel. You will not see this child if I have it."

"Oh, maybe an abortion? Will Joey boy go along with that? I will bet when he finds out; he will dump you like the pile of dung you are. I never want to see what you two cooked up. Have a good life. I am out of here tonight."

"You are so hateful. Goodbye, you bastard."

"Look who's using the word bastard. That kid of yours will be one."

I will not break down. I am strong. Oh, God, why did this have to happen?

After Bill packed and left, Karen dialed Joe at home.

"Joe, this is Karen."

"Hi, Karen."

"I have something to tell you."

"What's up?"

"Joe, I'm pregnant."

"Wow, when did you find out? Bill must be ecstatic."

"I just found out. He is not. We have just had a major fight. He's moved out."

"Why, Karen? You have wanted a child for years. I thought that's what you both wanted."

"It's certainly been my dream, but not Bill's."

"Well, what are you going to do?"

"Joe, Bill had a vasectomy before we were married. I did not know that. The baby is not his."

"Whose is it?"

"Well, Joe…."

"Are you saying it's mine?"

"Joe, I have been faithful to Bill all my married life except for the one time with you two months ago."

"Christ, Karen. We only did it one time. How did you become pregnant?"

"Are you that dense? Of course, it can happen the one time. We always used protection when we were dating, as I am sure you remember. You did not worry about it this time because I was married. Yeah?"

"Karen, that's kind of cruel. I didn't exactly plot for it to happen."

"Sure you did, Joe. Remember saying, 'Stop by my house, I have something to show you'. Now I know what you wanted to show me. It must have been my fertile time. Fertile women are sometimes weak. I could not resist that night. I had not intended for it to happen, but you did. That wasn't the purpose of my seeing you that day."

"What are you going to do?"

"Well, I will never live with Bill again. We are going to divorce. Of course, there is always the option of an abortion, or I have it and let the world think its Bill's baby. That is a bit of cruel feminine justice. I'm heading for divorce with Bill whether I want it or not."

"What will you do?"

"I really don't know. A baby should have a mother and a father."

"Whew. I have to think; what do you want me to do?"

"You've told me many times in the past that you care for me. What do you think I may be thinking?"

"I need time to calm down and think."

"Bill said you would dump me once you found out. It looks as though he was right."

"Karen, slow down. I did not say that. Don't do anything foolish. Allow me a little time to plan. I said I cared for you."

"You've said a lot of things to me. I loved you once, Joe. I don't know if saying I loved you is real, or am I just saying it because I am in a fix."

"I have no idea if what I think is real either. Again, allow me some time. I will call you on Friday."

"Joe. I do feel a little better. Still, this whole mess is so depressing."

"Wait for my call on Friday evening. I promise I'll call back."

He is right, no abortion. I killed my baby once. I vowed I would never do that again. Perhaps I should resign; move to another state. Appears that is the LoPorti way of solving problems. Joe is not going to want to marry me. How could he trust me after all I have done to him? I cannot hurt him again. I am not lucky for people who love me. I will go in tomorrow to see Grace. It is time she 'fesses up. Since she KNOWS, it will be bittersweet to let her understand that I KNOW. Now go to sleep.

Arriving at her office the next morning, Karen immediately called Grace.

"Grace, can I see you a minute?"

"Be right there, boss."

"Grace, I'm pregnant. What do you think of that?"

"What? I am so delighted for you. I know you have wanted a baby for a long time."

"That's bullshit, Grace. Bill told me everything last night. He also told me about you two. I don't know how could you do that to me–a friend, or so I thought. Was Bill's fertility the reason you cautioned me to be careful with Romano? You did not want 'ole' Karen to chance it and slip up. Don't get pregnant because old Bill might find out? Apparently, you had a number of tumbles in the hay with Bill, or so he says. He says it was such a wonderful time with you. Was it fun knowing that you were screwing your boss's husband while all the time pretending you were such a caring friend to poor, old, uninteresting Karen? I know I am an emotional wreck right now."

"Karen, that's unfair."

"Unfair? You disgust me. It will never be the same again between us as friends or co-workers. It is you or I in this department. Transfer out, or I will find a way to fire you."

"Karen, I am sorry. I have made mistakes that I understand you cannot ever forgive me for doing. I have hurt you. I feel terrible."

"Why is that? Is it because I found out?"

"I guess so. I will transfer out, but I have a request if you can see your way to do it."

"What is it? I do not have much time to talk to you. I am

going to see the Chief."

"What are you going to tell him?"

"I'm going to tell him that you are thinking of leaving the group to pursue something else. I will say that you let me know this morning."

"Will you hear what I am asking before you do that?"

"What is it?"

"I have too much invested in these cases to simply walk out on them. I would ask you to delay my leaving until we have solved the cases. I understand it is asking a lot. We are a team. We are pushing closer to the solution. If your cipher efforts pan out, we could be finishing this soon. I know you hate me. I will stay out of your way as much as possible. Let me have that chance, at least."

"I don't hate you, Grace. I know I cannot work with you knowing what I know now. I can never be your friend again. I do not hate you. I will agree to your scheme on one condition."

"What is that?"

"You will shut your mouth about me. As far as anyone else is concerned, a baby could not save my marriage to Bill. Got it? I am not going to contest the divorce, nor will he. I do not know what I will do with this pregnancy. You have all the information now. Shut your mouth about my personal life."

"Thank you, Karen. Again, I am so sorry."

"Get out of my office. Now get back to work."

At that moment, Don came to Karen's office.

"Hi, Karen. I have some exciting news. Our little effort at deciphering may let us read the first two lines of the cipher. It isn't easy, though."

"Tell me what you've found. Better yet, get the rest of the Unit together, so that everybody is on board," Karen demanded.

Twenty minutes later, the Unit assembled in the conference room.

"Don, give us your latest news."

"Yes, Karen. You remember that last week we agreed the cipher used was the **VICTOR** cipher. I am more convinced than ever. When I showed a common straddling keyboard, I said, the keyboard letters could be configured in many ways. From my last meeting with you, Karen, my thought is that he used an uncomplicated version of the straddling keyboard that anyone can find on the internet."

	0	1	2	3	4	5	6	7	8	9
	E	T	R	A	O		N		I	S
5	B	C	D	F	G	H	J	K	L	M
7	P	Q	U	V	W	#	X	&	Y	Z

"The killer hinted that the alpha character ciphers would allow us to solve the numeric ciphers. From that clue, the killer gave us these five sets of Vigenère ciphers:

MIRHCAHTVZ XZNVJABY KKNPOWHZ MKNYKWBY KKGUQQBTBZWNKZELOXE.

"Karen suggested that I show you the 26 by 26 matrix as you see below. Let me show how it's done to encipher.

		PLAINTEXT LETTER																								
		A	**B**	**C**	**D**	**E**	**F**	**G**	**H**	**I**	**J**	**K**	**L**	**M**	**N**	**O**	**P**	**Q**	**R**	**S**	**T**	**U**	**V**	**W**	**X**	**Y**	**Z**
	A	A	B	C	D	E	F	G	H	I	J	K	L	M	N	O	P	Q	R	S	T	U	V	W	X	Y	Z
	B	B	C	D	E	F	G	H	I	J	K	L	M	N	O	P	Q	R	S	T	U	V	W	X	Y	Z	A
	C	C	D	E	F	G	H	I	J	K	L	M	N	O	P	Q	R	S	T	U	V	W	X	Y	Z	A	B
	D	D	E	F	G	H	I	J	K	L	M	N	O	P	Q	R	S	T	U	V	W	X	Y	Z	A	B	C
K	**E**	E	F	G	H	I	J	K	L	M	N	O	P	Q	R	S	T	U	V	W	X	Y	Z	A	B	C	D
E	**F**	F	G	H	I	J	K	L	M	N	O	P	Q	R	S	T	U	V	W	X	Y	Z	A	B	C	D	E
Y	**G**	G	H	I	J	K	L	M	N	O	P	Q	R	S	T	U	V	W	X	Y	Z	A	B	C	D	E	F
W	**H**	H	I	J	K	L	M	N	O	P	Q	R	S	T	U	V	W	X	Y	Z	A	B	C	D	E	F	G
O	**I**	I	J	K	L	M	N	O	P	Q	R	S	T	U	V	W	X	Y	Z	A	B	C	D	E	F	G	H
R	**J**	J	K	L	M	N	O	P	Q	R	S	T	U	V	W	X	Y	Z	A	B	C	D	E	F	G	H	I
D	**K**	K	L	M	N	O	P	Q	R	S	T	U	V	W	X	Y	Z	A	B	C	D	E	F	G	H	I	J
	L	L	M	N	O	P	Q	R	S	T	U	V	W	X	Y	Z	A	B	C	D	E	F	G	H	I	J	K
L	**M**	M	N	O	P	Q	R	S	T	U	V	W	X	Y	Z	A	B	C	D	E	F	G	H	I	J	K	L
E	**N**	N	O	P	Q	R	S	T	U	V	W	X	Y	Z	A	B	C	D	E	F	G	H	I	J	K	L	M
T	**O**	O	P	Q	R	S	T	U	V	W	X	Y	Z	A	B	C	D	E	F	G	H	I	J	K	L	M	N
T	**P**	P	Q	R	S	T	U	V	W	X	Y	Z	A	B	C	D	E	F	G	H	I	J	K	L	M	N	O
E	**Q**	Q	R	S	T	U	V	W	X	Y	Z	A	B	C	D	E	F	G	H	I	J	K	L	M	N	O	P
R	**R**	R	S	T	U	V	W	X	Y	Z	A	B	C	D	E	F	G	H	I	J	K	L	M	N	O	P	Q
	S	S	T	U	V	W	X	Y	Z	A	B	C	D	E	F	G	H	I	J	K	L	M	N	O	P	Q	R
	T	T	U	V	W	X	Y	Z	A	B	C	D	E	F	G	H	I	J	K	L	M	N	O	P	Q	R	S
	U	U	V	W	X	Y	Z	A	B	C	D	E	F	G	H	I	J	K	L	M	N	O	P	Q	R	S	T
	V	V	W	X	Y	Z	A	B	C	D	E	F	G	H	I	J	K	L	M	N	O	P	Q	R	S	T	U
	W	W	X	Y	Z	A	B	C	D	E	F	G	H	I	J	K	L	M	N	O	P	Q	R	S	T	U	V
	X	X	Y	Z	A	B	C	D	E	F	G	H	I	J	K	L	M	N	O	P	Q	R	S	T	U	V	W
	Y	Y	Z	A	B	C	D	E	F	G	H	I	J	K	L	M	N	O	P	Q	R	S	T	U	V	W	X
	Z	Z	A	B	C	D	E	F	G	H	I	J	K	L	M	N	O	P	Q	R	S	T	U	V	W	X	Y

"When enciphering, the columns are the plaintext letters and the rows are the keyword letters. The intersection point is the ciphertext letter to use when encoding."

"We still have to find the Vigenère keyword from the clues in the letter before we can try to decipher."

"I would very much like to see that, Don," Susan said.

"Please continue, Don. I'm familiar with the Vigenère systems, but an explanation will help us all," Karen said.

"For a plaintext of '**MARTINELLI**' and a keyword of '**TODAY**', set up a matrix as follows:

M	A	R	T	I	N	E	L	L	I
T	O	D	A	Y	T	O	D	A	Y

"Then, using the Vigenère matrix, select 'M' in the plaintext letter column and 'T' in the keyword letter row. The intersection point in the Vigenère matrix gives 'F' as the first enciphered letter. Continue this process for each plaintext letter to get:

'FOUTGGSOLG'

"To decipher, you would reverse the process."

"Let me see if I have it. First I would go to row 'T' of the keyword letters on the left-hand side of the matrix; then I would go over to the letter 'F' and read up the column to the letter 'M' of the plaintext columns," Susan said, smiling.

"That is absolutely correct, Susan," Karen said.

"Have you been able to decipher any of the Vigenère ciphers yet?" Grace asked.

"I haven't broken them because I haven't found the right keyword. If I spend some more time, I think I may be able to get them. My thought is the decrypted Vigenère will give us the <u>first row</u> of the straddling keyboards, if he meant what he said. Karen and I think that the last Vigenère of the four relates to the keyboard for the last two lines. It's just a guess at this point."

"I agree. The alpha ciphers are too short to describe a full keyboard," Karen asserted.

"Don, what will we do with the two last lines?" Susan

asked.

"I will keep working on them. The good thing is that I am receiving questions from the crypto world concerning the ciphers."

"Is that helping?"

"Not so far. Just questions, no answers."

"Let's try to decipher the first Vigenère cipher he gave us. I will use **KAREN** as a keyword to see what that gives for the first row of the straddling keyboard.

M	I	R	H	C	A	H	T	V	Z
K	A	R	E	N	K	A	R	E	N

"Use the 'K' column and look up the 'M' row to get 'W'. Using this process, we get **'WIILPKHKZM'**.

"Obviously, I have the wrong keyword. You see what has to be done, though. I am going back to work. We really have to crack these ciphers."

"Thanks, Don. Please meet with me tomorrow morning. I have a few more ideas that we could look at. In the meantime, the rest of us have to work these cases as we would any murder case," Karen said.

"Once we break his ciphers, it may tell us how she died. The only signs of stress for her were the light ligature marks on her wrists. There were no signs of strangulation," Grace said.

"I hope. Didn't Gordon say he discovered a needle mark on her arm during the autopsy? Since Mendosa was not known to use drugs, that needle mark may have something to do with her death. However, the toxicology tests found nothing suspicious. Then, we don't know what to test for. The person disabled her somehow; raped her; then killed her."

"Susan, all we can say is he has a method that kills them without any visible violence. We have his DNA, and we have his ciphers. Other than that, we don't have much."

"In 2008, we sent people to Savannah to question all the shop keepers. No one noticed anything out of the ordinary. You know what a zoo River Street is before and after the parade. We also checked on Bay Street with similar results–nothing. We pasted fliers throughout Savannah. No one came forward with any information," Karen reminded Grace.

"Why we are assuming the killer only goes to Savannah rather than Atlanta for his victims?" asked Susan.

"Mendosa and Reuben were supposedly in Savannah when they disappeared, so we've blindly assumed all the women were from Savannah. That may be a foolish assumption. For all we know, the four prostitutes were picked up in Atlanta," Grace said.

"We have to break the ciphers. I think it's our only hope," Karen pushed.

"Don, thank you for all the work you've done. I understand it puts a huge strain on you. I also want to thank Grace and Susan for all they are doing. It is a difficult time, I know. I have to run. I have a meeting the Tate."

"I will move along also. I need to sort our reports for these cases, so they're in some reasonable order," said Grace.

Grace followed Don back to his office. "I know why Karen has been so upset recently," she whispered.

"What is it?"

"She's pregnant! It's not Bill's baby. She became angry with me for guessing she has gotten into trouble. She told me to transfer out of the department, or she would fire me. She is going to let me complete these murder cases. Do not say anything. Keep this under your hat."

"What? Why would she do that to you?

"I don't know. She may be jealous of me for some crazy reason."

"You need to talk to the Chief, Grace."

"I can't go the Chief yet. I want to finish these cases we are working on."

"Who's the father?"

"I don't know for sure. It may be Dr. Romano from Tech."

"Whew, now I understand why she's been so nasty at times."

"Yeah, I need to get back to work. Do not say anything to anybody. Please keep this between us."

Chapter Thirteen

For her sins have reached unto heaven, and God hath remembered her iniquities. Revelation 18:5

For Karen, the days dragged by. She spent much time arguing with herself over the idea of terminating her child. The guilt she suffered by her aborting her baby long ago was always with her. She had purposely taken a human life to avoid embarrassment. She had taken an innocent life. Could she ever do that again?

It was one night, one mistake. It was not just a mistake; it was your mistake, Lady. You made the decision to let him. He did not force you. Oh, Karen, what are you thinking? Get on your knees. Pray to God for help.

She asked for a sign from God, but none appeared.

Karen remembered something that had happened to her when she was at church long ago. The nuns in catechism had told her that when the priest raised the "Host" during mass, you must bow your head.

One Sunday, she had looked up when the priest raised the Host above his head. She saw an intense white light coming from the Host. It was so bright it hurt her eyes. Karen looked around to see if anyone else saw it, but all heads were bowed. Was this a sign she was forgiven, or was it just an illusion?

This vision had happened just after the loss of her baby boy–her abortion.

Was this a sign that God had forgiven me, or was it a

warning? Would he forgive me again?

Karen went to St. Mary's Catholic Church the next Sunday. During the Mass, she had looked up as the priest raised the Host. There was no light. She knew that she would not be forgiven this time.

Karen sat back in her chair fully understanding what she had just done. There would be no termination. She would carry this baby to birth and rear it herself.

On Wednesday, Karen dialed up her OB/GYN clinic in Atlanta.

"Good afternoon. Adelphi Clinic, how may I direct your call?"

"Good afternoon. This is Karen Hunter. I'm calling to make an appointment for an obstetrics visit."

"Just a moment, let me look up your record. Computer is a bit slow. Hmm, I do not see you listed. When was your last visit?"

"Over four years ago."

"Your old records have not been entered into our computer base. What is the reason for your visit?"

"Prenatal."

"How far along are you?"

"I think a couple of months."

"Do you have a preference for a day or time?"

"Afternoon times are better for me."

"Dr. Terrance has an opening at 3:15 on Wednesday, April the 20th. Will that be convenient for you?"

"Dr. Terrance? What has happened to Dr. Culver?"

"Both Dr. Culver and his brother retired over three years ago. Dr. Terrance bought the clinic from them."

"I guess I missed the announcement," Karen replied.

"He is a fine doctor, Mrs. Hunter."

"I'm sure he is. Is his first name Sean?

"It is; do you know him?"

"I think I do. Could you have him call me when he has a chance?"

"He is pretty busy, but I will ask him."

"Thank you."

"Do you want to confirm your appointment?"

"No, I will wait to talk with Dr. Terrance, thank you."

"Goodbye."

Karen's phone rang an hour after she hung up.

"This is Dr. Terrance calling. I am trying to reach Karen Hunter."

"Hello, Sean, this is Karen Hunter."

"Hello, Karen. It has been a long time, too long. What have you been up to?"

"Well, you know, I met someone; married him; I moved on with my life. I feel a little strange calling you. I had not heard that Dr. Culver retired. I just learned you're associated with the Adelphi Clinic."

"Yes, when they retired, I bought the clinic."

"Congratulations. I called this morning because I need to setup prenatal visits. Since Dr. Culver was my gynecologist for many years, I called your clinic. When I found out that Dr. Culver retired, I became concerned having you as my doctor, since we seriously dated years ago. I'm not sure I can handle this idea."

Karen had met Sean during her college days. She had a serious romance with him that had ended rather suddenly. She had met Joe Romano and tossed Sean aside.

"Karen, we're old friends even though we haven't seen each other for a dog's age. That doesn't matter, does it?"

"Well, we were lovers, so it is a bit unnerving to have you as a doctor."

"If you're not embarrassed, then I won't be. It was a long time ago. This is strictly professional. My RN would be with us the entire time."

"You're making me feel a little more comfortable. Our past relationship would have prevented me from having you as my gynecologist. Now I need to deal with someone I can trust because I am pregnant; I need pre-natal services. This is my first one. I am not sure; I don't feel right, so I thought I should be checked."

Will he be able to tell if I was pregnant before? I hope not.

"If you are still uncomfortable having me as your doctor, I have an associate who handles the mornings here. I have hospital rounds in the mornings, so afternoons are when I see patients."

"I guess it will be you, Sean. Mornings are impossible for me to get away from the station. I will confirm an afternoon appointment with you. If I feel comfortable with you, I'll set up more appointments."

"That's good. Is there anything else?"

"I'll need to schedule much later in the afternoon, if possible. We are working on some tough cases. I need to be in the office as much as possible. The demands during the day can be overwhelming."

"I understand, Karen"

"Not to bring up an old issue, but I remember your mom didn't care much for me. The split was my fault, as you know. I prayed you would forgive me."

"It hurt quite a bit. I'll never forget that last night together."

"I heard you were married shortly after we separated. That was a surprise to me. I didn't know you had someone in the background."

"Jean had been an 'on and off' affair. When I went with you, it was 'off.' "

"It was a surprise when you invited me to your wedding. I knew I could not attend. It was your bride's day. My presence would have spoiled it for her. You must not have cleared it with her."

"No I didn't, but I was happy when you didn't attend; it would have been a disaster. I was silly for inviting you. I admit it was tough when you left me. My mother was happy. I moved on, though, as you know."

"I think how I must have hurt you. I've always felt pain that I acted that way; it haunts me often."

"I think about it at times too, but I've been happily married for fifteen years. We have two wonderful kids.

One of each. Both in their teens, but they are not a handful so far. They are making excellent school grades. Thank the Lord; they stay out of trouble. I have to run. I will connect you with my assistant, Barbara. She will schedule you in here as soon as I have an opening. If you have a problem with the date, let me know."

"Thanks again, Sean."

Karen kept her appointment for the following week. After completing the long 'who are you' medical forms reserved for new or returning patients, Karen's weight and blood pressure were taken.

Karen sat in an examining room for several minutes before Sean and his Registered Nurse, Doris, entered the room.

"Hello, Karen. I am so glad you could make it."

"Hello, Sean. Good to see you."

"Since this is your first pregnancy, we are going to do a thorough physical including a pelvic exam. Also, let's get a blood test to ensure everything is okay. If anything shows up with the blood test, I will have Doris call you. You need to give a urine sample. Okay?"

After the exam was completed, Karen dressed and waited for Dr. Terrance to return to the examining room.

"Is everything all right?" Karen asked.

"Everything looks fine at this point, Karen. From your information, I would say you are close to being ten weeks pregnant. Does that sound right to you?"

"I would say that is probably right. End of January."

"I think you will be due in early November or slightly sooner."

"Maybe it'll be a Halloween Baby. That would be fun."

"It's possible. First pregnancies are often a bit longer than expected. Let's hope not. Otherwise, everything looks good, Karen. You are healthy. Your pregnancy should go well for you. Are you sleeping well?"

"Most nights, although lately I have some dreams that disturb me."

"I advise you to refrain from any sleeping pills. At this stage of pregnancy, it is not advisable for the developing baby."

"Okay."

"I'll have a diet for you. Try to maintain your weight. Post-baby flab can be tough to get rid of."

"Thank you, Sean."

Karen went to reception area. Sean soon came out with her diet instructions of 'dos and don'ts'.

"Sean, is it possible to bend your ear a moment? I have something bothering me."

"Come to my office. What do you need, Karen?"

Karen briefly shared her story of her problems in her marriage to Bill. She did not tell Sean of her affair with Joe Romano. She didn't expect that Sean could do anything; his quiet understanding was what she needed.

"Thank you for listening and not judging me, Sean."

"I'm not here to judge anyone, Karen. I hope it works out for you and Bill. If you have nothing else, please see

Barbara in the front office to set up monthly visits. If anything changes, call me right away."

"Thanks, Sean. Take care."

Karen spent the next week on a mental roller coaster. It was all her fault; it was none of her fault.

Will Joe be emotional support for me? In my heart, I do think I care for him, but it is not love. I need to see if he wants to be a part of this baby's life. If he does not, the baby and I will carry on without him. Nevertheless, it is time to get this sorry mess straightened out.

Friday came, but Joe did not call. Thoughts raced through her mind.

I will not call him. He promised. That is so typical of men. I guess Bill was right. His 'love' for me was just the lust of a bachelor. The 'old fool me once…' Wait, Karen, you hurt him deeply before. Maybe he has a resentment that will not go away. He says he still cares for me, hah.

Screwing up her courage, Karen dialed Joe's number.

"Hello Joe, this is Karen."

"Hello, Karen."

"Joe, you didn't call me, so I'm calling you. I need to see you, or you need to come to see me. We need to meet face-to-face. We need to settle this. The last time we talked on the phone it was unsatisfying for a matter this critical."

"I was tied up. Just didn't have a chance."

"Doesn't a promise to call mean anything to you?"

"I told you. Something came up."

"Joe, I need to understand if you plan to be a part of this

baby's life or not."

"I'm sorry, Karen. I have been doing a lot of thinking. You hurt me a lot a long time ago. I'm not sure I want to go through that again."

"Wah, wah, Joe. How do you think I feel? Why did we do it? I am pregnant. I am so angry with us. These are only a few of my emotions."

"Please calm down, Karen. I understand that I sound wimpy. I have been reaching some solid decisions. Can you come to Atlanta this coming weekend? Let's spend some time; make some plans regarding the baby, if you're agreeable. Come to my home on Saturday morning."

"Why does it have to be Saturday morning?"

"On Saturday, I have a grad student completing his research work. I want to review his thesis defense with him this week. I will have to see him early on Saturday, but I should be free around 10:30. I will leave the key under the front mat. I do want to talk with you, Karen, see you then. Sometimes I miss you."

"Okay, Joe. See you Saturday."

He says that sometimes he misses me. I am carrying his baby! I would like him to be a father to it. I cannot push him, though, or he might just walk away. This is the oldest problem women face. Become pregnant. Watch men scatter like geese from a lake. We will see what happens Saturday. Now back to business.

Karen dialed Grace's phone.

"Grace, come to my office."

"Be right there."

Grace entered Karen's office.

"Grace, have you had a chance to correlate other states' murder MOs that match ours?"

"We are trying. We have nothing so far."

"So, do we conclude that the murders are local to us? Why they only happen in March is an unsettling mystery. Moreover, I still do not understand the directed threat toward me. Another thing is bothering me. I can't put my finger on it, but I feel that something important is staring me in the face with these six murder cases. I just can't see it. I guess I'm pulling at any straw I can find," Karen said.

"We know that the six killings all occurred around the same time in March–during Saint Patrick's celebrations. Interestingly, you've said most of your lover break-ups were during those times," Grace added.

"Does the killer think he's safe by letting time pass between murders?"

"I have no idea what drives this guy," Grace said.

"I wish I could get over a strange feeling concerning my past."

"Karen, are you saying that the timing definitely points to one of your old beaus?"

"Not necessarily. When I was a rookie, I made mistakes handling cases. Not murder cases, but drug arrests, etc."

"The problem with that idea is it opens up a huge door, Karen."

"Well, they are potential avenues. We cannot afford to

let anything go without scrutiny. Susan is continuing to check on my early records. I appeared in court a number of times. Lennox had me handling anything the old-timers didn't want, so checking those records may be vital."

"Yeah, I know, Karen," retorted Grace.

"I need you to put aside the personal stuff we had last week. If we can't do that, we should stop right here."

"I'm with you, Karen. I will try setting it aside. It still bothers me that you want me to leave, though."

"Once we can solve these cases, you must leave the MCU. I can never trust you again. I am not forgiving you. Nevertheless, we are professionals. We should act that way. I was angry, but I am over that. In the long run, though, it is better for you to find another position."

"I've made mistakes in my personal life, too. I am sorry; I will work with you, Karen. Let us just improve our business relationship until this is over. We have a killer to catch. It makes me sick to think he might escape his punishment."

"All right, move on."

"Karen, any luck with your mental recollection of someone who may be pissed enough to want to hurt you?"

"Other than old boy friends, or some of the run-ins with an arrest or two in my early cop years; I can't remember anything that stands out at this point," Karen answered.

"This case never gives us answers," Grace moaned.

"You need to get back to the DNA process you started," Karen ordered.

After Grace left, Karen called Don.

"Have you had any responses to our ads?"

"I've had a few e-mails in response to the fliers we put out. Most ask questions concern the cipher or the reward."

"Any worthwhile for follow-up? Any other news?"

"I did receive a somewhat suspicious e-mail asking questions that I feel are a little too inquisitive. The person wants to know what information we have to identify the killer. The person sent the e-mail with an anonymous user name. Therefore, I do not have a name to go with it. The problem is that anyone can set up an e-mail address as 'anonymous'."

"What are you going to do with it?"

"It will take time to find out who it is. The trouble is it may turn out to be nothing. I will try to track down the person, but it pulls me away from the cipher work. The e-mail services don't generally give out the user's real name as a matter of policy."

"Yeah, but we are the police; we should be able to ask for that info," said Karen disdainfully.

"We have to get a court order signed, but that doesn't always work for international companies," Don noted.

"Don, try the soft way first. I am just curious why the person is asking to see the progress of the cases. It reminds me of Romano's interest years ago."

"I'll try to get the person's identity from the mail source. If they refuse, we will have to decide if it is worth pursuing legally. Anything else I need to do?"

"No, carry on with that and, of course, the ciphers."

"Oh, I almost forgot. Chief asked me to have you call him this morning when you have a chance."

"I wonder what he wants now. See you later. Update me on your progress, immediately if things change."

Karen called Chief Tate.

"Hello, Chief. I heard you wanted to see me. What can I do for you?"

"If you have a few minutes, come to my office."

"Be right there. What's going on?"

"Just come on over to the office, I will explain."

Hmm. When there are issues related to how the MCU works murder investigations, Chief Tate is always the arbitrator. Beyond that, the argument the other day with Grace was not his concern. Well, maybe it is nothing.

"Come in, Karen. Please close the door. Have a seat. As I told you in the past, I am very pleased with your group. The work you have done over the past years is commendable. I knew when I hired you that you were the right person for this role."

"That's nice of you to tell me, Chief."

"You told me at the time that you were uncomfortable if I was promoting you because you're a woman. For sure, the City Council was pushing me to promote women within the force. However, I wanted a qualified person. I felt that you were it."

"Is that the reason we are meeting? You wanted to tell me that?"

"No. I wanted to see you because I have heard rumblings in the brush that there may be problems in the group. I wanted to give you a chance to give me your side."

"What have you heard?"

"I have heard that you are going to fire Grace. Is that true?"

"I did tell her that I would fire her if we couldn't work out some issues."

"You understand, of course, that I always have the last word on firing someone. Tell me what issues have come up."

" It's a personal issue between us."

"While we are working high profile murder cases, there are no personal issues that I will tolerate."

"It is too embarrassing to explain, Chief."

"Okay, but it must be resolved today. I do not want either you or Grace leaving the department at this critical time. I know I threatened to pull in some power folks, but that was to please the Mayor. I need you two to keep doing what you are doing to solve these cases. Both of you will come to my office tomorrow morning. You two will update me on this issue you have. It must be resolved. I don't want anything that reflects on the honor or integrity of the Department."

"Grace and I are both professionals. We will resolve it today."

"Tomorrow morning in my office at 9:30," ordered Chief Tate.

Karen stopped by Grace's office.

"Well, I guess we've done it this time. I verbally slapped you around and you blabbed. We are both close to losing our positions here if we can't reach an agreement."

"I didn't blab to anyone, Karen."

"Well, I don't understand how Tate found out then. He is pissed. We have to go to his office tomorrow morning to tell him all is fine."

"Karen, at our last discussion you said I could stay until we solved these cases. Then I would move on. I say we tell him that we have buried the hatchet. We will work smoothly together from this point on. I'll do my best to make it work."

"I'll also do mine. But Grace, stop talking about our issues."

"I told you, I didn't blab."

"Let's move forward. We have to meet with Tate tomorrow."

In the morning, Karen and Grace went to Tate's office.

"Good morning, y'all," said Chief Tate in his best folksy way. "Where are we with this issue, Karen?"

"We've realized that our issue was not worthy of two professionals. There will not be a problem in the future," said Karen.

"I agree with Karen," echoed Grace.

"How will you settle this with the troops?" asked Tate.

"We are calling the Unit together this morning to quell any rumors. That should settle it."

Chapter Fourteen

I know thy works, and charity, and service, and faith, and thy patience, and thy works; and the last *to be* more than the first. Revelation 2:19

It was Saturday. The drive to Joe's condominium was slow with the weekend traffic stretching the capacity of Interstate 75 into the city. It did give Karen time to reflect whether there was a future relationship with Joe. The thoughts were not comforting. Resolution of the relationship impasse was in serious doubt. The baby she was carrying was most vital to her. How to turn a difficult situation into something less dire seemed impossible. Joe had been cool to her after the baby announcement. She would give this meeting with Joe one last try.

As Karen parked her car, Joe opened his front door.

"Karen, come in. I am so glad you came up."

"Hi, Joe, I'm glad to be here. It was a long drive."

"Was the traffic slow?"

"Not too disagreeable," she lied.

"That's good. It can be brutal driving into town on Saturday."

"Did you get your grad student squared away?"

"I did."

Karen noticed that Joe appeared flustered by her presence.

"Our foolishness has brought me a lot of pain. I see that it hasn't calmed your nerves either," said Karen.

"I hope we can settle this problem between us today. I'd

like some resolution that works for both of us," offered Joe.

"I do too, Joe. This situation is embarrassing as well as career threatening for me."

"I understand embarrassing. Why career threatening?" asked Joe.

"Let me settle down first. Then I'll explain."

"Let me pour you a coffee or tea in the meantime," said Joe.

"No, it makes me nauseous these days."

"Anything else I can get you?"

"You mean besides knocking me up? Sorry, that just slipped out. No. Joe, we need to discuss the situation we're in, so we can figure out what we are going to do," Karen said angrily.

"Well, we are adults. We should be able to resolve what we should do," said Joe, trying to pacify Karen.

"Don't patronize me."

"Please Karen; I'm not trying to do that."

Hearing the anger in Karen's voice, Joe retreated into his own thoughts sitting quietly.

I pushed her when she was vulnerable. Wasn't that my plan that night? Didn't I give her enough wine to lower her resistance? Face it. I wanted her, at least one last time.

Karen waited for Joe's return to the conversation. She did not want a threatening situation. Her nerves exploded with anger at Joe.

"Apparently we won't find a reasonable resolution to

this, Joe."

"I've been doing a lot of thinking also. Can you share your ideas first?" Joe asked finally.

"I have many conflicting thoughts. I am distressed, so I do not think I am always rational. My mind pushes in one direction, then another toward decisions that I cannot make alone. You must be part of those decisions, but I don't want you to decide for me."

"Karen, I'll attempt to understand."

"I'm not sure how much I care for you, Joe. I thought I did. Now I am not sure that you care for me. You told me you loved me at the time we had sex. That was probably just lust. That is not the reason we are talking today. I need to find out what you want for a relationship with your baby."

"I know. We need to work on the issues facing us. I want to fix whatever we need to fix."

That is so typical of men. Fix things. Let emotions go to hell.

"Grace has opened her mouth to someone at the office, so the rumor mill is alive and living well. Grace knew the situation with Bill's sterility, so I'm sure you are part of the rumors."

"How did Grace know about Bill?"

"She had an affair with him. Let me be clear, Joe–she was fucking him."

"Wow, when did you find that out?"

"Bill told me that little piece of news in our argument;

that's when I threw him out. I confronted Grace; she admitted it. She figured it had to be you as the father. There hasn't been anyone else."

"I thought there probably wasn't anyone else with you."

"You know damn well there wasn't anyone else. How dare you insinuate there may have been?"

"Strictly speaking, Karen, how would I positively know that? You are miles away. We only did it once. As far as I know, there may have been someone else. There's a probability it is not me."

"Well, Einstein, we could have a paternity test done, so you could be sure that you're it."

"Karen, you just told me that you don't love me. How do we start a relationship with that?"

"I wouldn't be talking a relationship. I would be asking what your involvement with the baby will be."

"What is it you want from me?"

"You know; you men are all the same. Knock a woman up, and then run like a scared rabbit. Oh, she is going to expect something from me. She's 'gonna' tie me down. She's 'gonna' rob me of my money. You're pathetic."

"You haven't heard what I was thinking. Perhaps it would be logical if you terminated this pregnancy. I will pay for it. It would make it easier for you at work. It would give us time get our acts together."

"How can you even say that? I bared my soul to you one time. This would be my second abortion. I believe in God. I believe I will have to answer for my sins someday. To have killed two innocent children, I could never explain or live with. God will not forgive me for that."

"Come on, Karen. We are pedestrian Catholics. We believe many of the tenets to obey, disregard others. What's the big deal?"

"Joe, a life is a life. What is the difference between a child in the womb slain or the poor women we have found murdered by their spouses, boyfriends or kooks? You are being callous. Some people regard the death penalty as a violation of someone's rights, while the killers have no respect or compassion for the people they torture and kill. Killing a baby is no problem for them. Do not ever kill a convicted murderer, though. What jerks they are."

"I'm just trying to make it easier for both of us."

"I suppose it makes it easier on the baby too. Can you pour a glass of water for me? This discussion is wearing me out. I can't bear much more."

Joe returned with the water.

"Here, Karen. I am sorry it turned out this way. It isn't the way I wanted it."

"I'm sure you didn't want any of this. It was cheap one-night stand. That is all you cared; get into my pants one more time."

"Now who's being callous?"

"We've accomplished nothing today. This conversation is at an end. I was not sure how it would play out. I am now aware of your feelings for me. I said at the start of our conversation today that I was not sure I cared for you. I said that to let you off the hook. You did not disappoint me there. I will decide myself what my baby's future will be. I do not need you for that. Keep your money. Keep your freedom. Keep your stupid ideas. Goodbye, Joe."

"I'm sorry."

You sure are.

"Goodbye, Karen."

The drive back to Middlefield was long and torturous. Karen had not expected Joe to be so uncaring.

What should I do now? Abortion is out. I will not do that.

She knew that Joe did not love her. He had been putting on an act since "that night." He had said that the breakup many years ago was sad for him. He had moved on with his life.

I wonder if that is true.

She had been cruel to him, though, dropping him for Bill with no warning.

Could it be revenge? Wow, she thought, revenge. Has he planned this all along? He told me about his terrible early life, but look–he overcame it. He has become a successful chemist. He is not the type to mope about the past. Still, could he be the pervert stalking me? What a horrible thought. The idea that I still can't flush out of my mind is how he is acting. It is almost as if he wants me to suffer. Did he know that Bill had a vasectomy?

Was that the reason he pushed to seduce me that night? An opportunity he could not pass up for revenge.

I have a low opinion of someone I let into my pants not so long ago. It's time to go home and rest.

Home, yes. After eight years renting, Bill and Karen had saved up for the dream house they wanted. Their careers had expanded. Bill's MS degree in biology fit perfectly with American Pharmaceutical.

With his success as a sales representative, Bill was promoted to national sales manager. He was grossing over two hundred fifty thousand dollars a year. Karen's MS in criminal justice had given her the edge over others. She had been promoted to Captain in the homicide division at the Middlefield Police Department with a seventy-thousand-dollar salary. They were a "Dual Income No Kids" couple savoring the good life.

The home they had built was large, with five bedrooms for the kids they were going to have. Guests, oh yes, room for them. Karen had been rather selfish in choosing a design. The result was a spacious antebellum architecture.

From the front of the house, the Greek style columns were the most riveting feature with the grand balcony having a covered porch that extended from the front along the two sides of the structure. They had the home designed by an architect that Bill had known in college.

Although the design was in the style of the old plantation owners' homes, it had been scaled down in size to five thousand square feet. Even at that, the house had cost them over six hundred thousand, including the building lot. In a city where the average house cost was barely two hundred thousand, this house was almost ostentatious.

The house sat on a five acre wooded parcel. A large section had been cleared of southern yellow pines to prepare room for the house. Neighbors were within hearing distance, if not by sight.

Neighbors looked upon the couple as rather pretentious. Nonetheless, they were accepted in spite of it. Both had responsible positions. They clearly had income to support such a home.

Karen had furnished the inside of the house with expensive furniture of the colonial period. The windows, of which there many, had drapery treatments with matching valences, carefully selected by Karen.

Every Christmas she had wreaths placed on the exterior of the eight front windows. The central front door had, in place of the obnoxious doorbell, a large brass knocker to announce visitors.

The outside of the house had been landscaped tastefully with trees of the area. The Bermuda grass lawn stretched along the one hundred foot curved driveway. Flowerbeds flourished where space permitted.

As Karen turned into her driveway, she realized that soon she would have to be moving from a home she loved. Bill was gone. With a divorce, she would not be able to support the mortgage alone. Bill would give her nothing.

* * *

On Monday morning, Karen called an attorney to make

an appointment. It was time to get on with the divorce. Then she called Grace to her office.

"Come in, Grace."

"Morning, Karen."

"When you called earlier; saying you had the Y-DNA results already, I was surprised."

"GBI found a lab in Toronto, Canada that specializes in ancestry research using Y-DNA. It was routine. For them it was quick turn-around. It still took a little while, though."

"I hope there are no mistakes here. We cannot afford any issues to come up around this testing, if we ever find the killer. Have you set up a conference call with the lab?" Karen asked.

"Not yet. I'll let you know when it is set."

"Is there any value for us going through the results since we are not experts?" asked Karen.

"Let's at least look at what I understand so far. We did the ancestral testing to give us some date to determine this person's race. Our last race conversation left us with the idea that, if the person's ancestry is northern European, the person could be white looking. He may be swarthy or even dark skinned. Without going into deadly detail, the genetic markers in our killer's Y-DNA indicate that his ancestry is most likely the western part of Sicily. Our killer may be swarthy looking with dark brown eyes or may be lighter skinned with blue eyes–you just can't tell from that alone."

"My family history is from Siracusa, Sicily. My parents came from that city. If I recall, Romano said his parents emigrated from Italy before he was born," said Karen.

"An awful lot of solid people came from Sicily to the US. That includes your folks. They had a fine daughter."

"Save it, Grace."

"Look, Karen. I have apologized to you. I cannot change anything now. I want to work with you to solve this case. Can't we put this behind us for a while?"

"It isn't pleasant for me right now, Grace, but I will let go of our differences for now."

"Thank you, Karen."

"I was just thinking, Grace. Based on what you have said, our killer may have an Italian surname. That is not necessarily true. He could have been adopted. He could have any surname."

"The more information we get, the more unanswered questions pop up, and the more uncertain everything is. What a mess to sort through."

"Grace, we have to stay positive around this. I'm of the opinion that this guy will slip up somehow."

"Yeah, but if he only kills once a year, that proposes waiting until next year. That is unacceptable for us. The community will call for our heads. I know Don and you are working as furiously as you can on the ciphers. Don is here on the weekend. I don't know how long Kim will put up with that," Grace said.

"I've been so wrapped up with my own issues; I haven't noticed that Don is doing that. I need to insist that he throttle back," Karen said.

"I agree. He is special to this group."

"Yes, we need to crack these ciphers, but I don't want him killing himself or ruining his marriage. Thanks for the update, Grace. I'm going to call Don now to limit his overtime hours."

Karen's phone rang.

"Hi Karen, Don here."

"Don, I was just going to call you. What's up?"

"I don't know how to tell you this."

"Spit it out. What is it?"

"I was lucky in finding out who the anonymous guy is."

"So it's a guy? Are you going to tell me or not?

"It is Dr. Joseph Romano."

"Whaaat? Are you sure it's him?"

"Positive. I found out his home number."

"What? I can't believe that."

"I'm sorry, Karen. It's true."

"Let me think. I know he has an interest in codes. He said that in years past, he has coded some of his best ideas in some simple code."

"What do you want me to do?"

"Ignore his email. Let him stew," Karen directed.

"Will do, Karen."

"Well, let me follow up with him, Don. I'll find out how invested he is in this. By the way, I understand you are putting in long hours on weekends even when it is not your duty weekend. Stop it. Your wife needs you."

"I'm too involved, Karen. I cannot just shut it off. If I'm

not working on the case, my nerves won't let me settle down."

"I want you to have a week off. Can I suggest taking your family to Disney World? I won't accept no for an answer."

"I'll do it, but my mind will be here."

"Look, Don, the most precious thing in your life is your family. Your work comes second to them, always. Now go. Tell Kim your plans for vacation."

Don knew Karen was right. Over the past few months, he had become a workaholic. Karen understood the difficulties they faced to break the ciphers, but his unrelenting drive was not fair to Kim or the children. It was consuming his every waking moment.

There was no doubt there. Kim deserved more. She had given him two children. The six years they have been married were the happiest of his life. It was all that a man could ask for in a wife.

He had met pretty Kim Smith his last year at Fort Valley State University. Kim was the product of a tight-knit family whose values revolved around dedication to God and country. She was not shy, but she was unwilling to commit to a serious relationship until she had completed her degree in biology. Being in college meant work.

No time for parties or intense boyfriend relationships, that dragged one from one's work. She believed that it was foolish to delay college for marriage. That part of life could always come later. First, earn the degree!

Her mother, Anna, had delayed college for her father. She was never able to go back to finish it.

Anna was a loving mother to her five children, but changing mountains of diapers or washing the kitchen floor was not her idea of fulfillment. Anna had insisted that Kim, as the only girl of her five children, attend college. Make something of herself. Kim had listened well, promising herself that she would not be led into that type of domestic situation before finishing her degree.

For Kim, her children had come too quickly to launch her career. She did not regret that. Once the children were in school, Don had promised Kim that she would start her career in science. He would be there to support her.

Don would honor it. He had to give proper time to his family. Karen was right. Disney World was a good start.

Chapter Fifteen

Fear none of those things, which thou shalt suffer: behold, the devil shall cast *some* of you into prison, that ye may be tried; and ye shall have tribulation ten days: be thou faithful unto death, and I will give thee a crown of life. Revelation 2:10

In the morning Karen met with Grace to review the few facts they had, hoping to create a profile they could possibly use to identify the killer.

"I brought in a white board to list what we need for this exercise. When we are done, we will summarize our thoughts. We will start with some essential characteristics. That means we have to justify any suggestion we come up with. Even if the characteristic is obvious, we still have to hash it out. So no 'Not Invented Here' stuff," Karen directed.

"I agree. For a starter, this perp is intelligent. This person is well educated. He probably has a Masters or even a Ph.D."

"Possibly, Grace."

"The language of the two letters says he is educated. Maybe a BS education is fine for our profile."

"I am backtracking here a bit. Let us just say the person is educated. The level of education for this profile may not be meaningful."

"Another characteristic is that this guy is reasonably well versed in code writing. Don and I agree that the killer has selected a sophisticated paper/pen system so the need for a computer is not required."

"Good point, Karen. I was not thinking in those terms. Good at codes doesn't necessarily mean a high degree in education."

"That's another item for our list. The DNA test you had done shows the heritage of our killer may be Italian. That seems to fit with one of our suspects."

"Karen, I just had an ugly thought."

"What's that?"

"We've been thinking that our guy only strikes each year. The only things we check the databases for are MOs similar to our perp's methods. What if: he kills more frequently than we suspect; or he changes his method of operation? Those alone would throw us off track."

"Grace, you may be correct, but we have to continue with what we know now, which unfortunately, isn't much."

"I have a feeling that he is professional type who can travel without notice. His profession lends itself to travel."

"Sure, sales, academic types, medical folks, etc."

"Those careers may not limit our perp to be single, married, or otherwise attached to another person. If he does have a Significant Other, his travels would not be suspect at all. Let's go back to my earlier point. This guy may be killing on a scale greater than we imagine."

"You may be right. We always have to apply Occam's razor here; otherwise, we will go around in circles. We will not accomplish anything. In some ways, I am getting discouraged. We have done this exercise several times already. It isn't getting us any closer to our perp," said Karen.

"First, let's assume our guy is single," Grace suggested.

"If our killings are local, he may live somewhere in the area. He may reside within a reasonable driving distance from Middlefield. With that thought, it could be Atlanta."

"Karen, let's summarize our assumptions so far:"

- **Single**
  - **Rationale: Needs freedom to travel without undue concern by spouse or co-workers.**
  - **May be a loner. Unfortunately, does not rule out having a spouse.**
- **White male, probably Italian descent, Sicilian, perhaps**
  - **Rationale: Y-chromosome tests, haplogroup analysis**
- **Professional, academic type or well educated**
  - **Rationale: Our kill pattern indicates perp is a frequent traveler, maybe a sales rep, for example. Local person?**
- **Education in science, or medical (RN, etc.)**
  - **Rationale: The MEs findings for all our murder victims cannot explain the deaths.**
  - **Single syringe punctures on the left inner arm of each of our women. Knowledge of toxins, etc.**
- **Hobby – Cryptanalysis**
  - **Rationale: May not be an expert. Is well versed in the subject.**
- **Murders were premeditated**
  - **Rationale: A typed note was left at the first murder/body dumpsite. The first murder**

may be unrelated to our murders. No way of knowing for certain even though, DNA profiles were the same for all. There may be other letters besides the ones we received, but they are unknown at this point.

- **Personality traits**
    - **Inflated Ego**
    - **Rationale: Taunting of police to solve cases. Brazen gift of name in the ciphers assuming we cannot ever decipher it.**
    - **Vendetta against women**
    - **Rationale: Only kills women.**
    - **Maybe acting out a death wish against mother, lover, or some woman who deeply hurt him.**
    - **Sexual predator**
    - **Rationale: Women may have submitted to sex. No evidence of forced sex. The fact that sex is always involved with the murder. Why? Power, control, hatred?**

"I suggest that we are done here with this, but we haven't considered what possible reasons he may have for these killings. We know from the letters; he hates you, Karen. Why would that lead him to kill innocent women he may or may not know?"

"Let's move on. Let's try to identify possible motives for his killings. There is nothing scientific with our choosing these reasons, but if it helps to focus our thinking, it may serve a purpose."

Suggestions from the group were expressed rapidly.

- **Motivation (our best guess)**
    - **May have been sexually abused as a child**

- **May not have had a father figure**
- **May have deep resentment toward mother.**
- **May have been jilted by a woman he strongly loved.**
- **May have grown up in an orphanage, foster home, or other relatives' homes.**
- **May now be an abuser himself from his early life experience.**

"Anything else we can put on our dream sheet?" asked Grace.

"I can't think of anything else."

"I can't either. I guess this is as far as we can go for now."

"Should we start lining up possible suspects who may match the profile we've developed?" Karen asked.

"I'm not sure our profile really means anything. I honestly don't think it helps that much."

"There is nothing solid enough to even accuse someone. If the killer has put his name in the letters, we have to decipher them. We have failed to catch a serial killer in our own community. The GBI gives us help, but they are just as baffled. They don't have any more answers than what we can come up with," Grace complained.

"We've had six murders from 2006 to 2011 plus the murder in 2003 in Atlanta. We have two letters. We have the same semen profiles found in all seven. As good as the DNA sounds, we are no closer to nabbing this guy than we were when it first started," Karen said.

"In Gordon's examination of the women, he believed he had evidence that someone had injected each of them using a medical syringe. However, the four prostitutes had so many syringe marks from drug use; he could only assume his belief was correct. We do not have a single, viable suspect. I would call that a failure at this point. Denise Lee with the other bozos of the press may be right. It's sure looking as if we are incompetent. So what we are going to do?"

"Slow down, Grace. We need to step back. We know from the letters that this person has a lot of my personal information. The one person who is very familiar with me is Romano. I think I need to face up to that. It's painful, but…"

"Well, now that you to mention it, Romano's habits do match some of our profile. I do not know him, but I can't imagine him being the killer. He has a good position at Tech. What could possibly drive him to murder?"

"It seems farfetched to me also, but you never really know another person."

"Karen, did Romano ever share any of his early life with you?"

"He did. I swore to him I would not reveal it to anyone."

"Did Green ever get a DNA sample from him? We could rule him out if we could compare his profile."

"No, I don't think it came to that. He wasn't really a suspect at the time."

"I think we should ask him."

"And if he refuses?"

"We should find a way to get a sample."

"What do you want me to do? Go to Atlanta to make love to him?"

"That's one avenue."

"That's funny, Grace. You should be doing stand-up comedy."

"I was just kidding. Relax."

"If he is willing, I will ask the Atlanta police to send a criminalist to get a cheek swab. I'll give him a call."

"Karen, I'm not suggesting that Romano is the killer. However, he is not off the hook here, either. He could have written that letter as easily as anyone else."

"I know, Grace. I just don't want it to be him."

"Karen, you're carrying Romano's baby. How can you remain objective? And that's not considering the huge legal issues."

"That's why I suggested we run this investigation together."

"You're not listening. If he is the person, we can send him to trial. Then his defense attorneys will moot this case because you're physically involved with a murderer," Grace nearly yelled.

"This whole conversation may be silly. Let me find a way to get his DNA sampled."

Karen dialed Joe's cell phone.

"Joe Romano."

"Joe, don't hang up. This is Karen. A profile of our killer

has been prepared. We are going to a few people to obtain swabs. Would you be willing to give a sample?"

"Are you saying I'm a suspect?"

"No, you are no more a suspect than anyone else I can name. I want to be able to show that you are not in any way involved. I want an airtight case that proves it can't be you."

"This is insulting."

"Joe, I'm a cop. I have to tie up any loose ends that a lawyer could use to confuse a jury. When we catch the killer, our case has to be clean."

"Karen, 'the transparent'; call if you need to arrest me."

"Joe. I believe you are innocent of this. I want to prove it. Work with me. I believe in you."

"I am not involved. Send someone to do a sample."

"I have no doubt in my mind, but to have the proof will be so sweet."

"Trust is a two-way street. Right now, I have no trust in you or your goons."

"Joe, please. That is not helping you."

"Goodbye, Karen."

Karen turned to Grace.

"Did you get the gist of that conversation? He is willing to give us a sample."

"Well, that's positive. He doesn't sound as if he's very happy, though."

"He isn't, but no one likes to be considered a suspect. I want to believe it will rule him out. Let's hope."

“So, your message that you believe he isn’t involved is a lie,” needled Grace.

“At times, you have to put out a little honey to attract the flies.”

“I guess that is something all women understand intuitively.”

“We need to get cracking, no pun intended, Grace. Don is due back from vacation tomorrow. I need to sit with him and go over some more cipher ideas that I have. I was able to make some headway on them. I want you to continue to focus on the Reuben murder.”

“Right, I’m going investigate Lauren’s last contacts. I hope I can come up with something.”

“Thanks Grace. I do appreciate how difficult it is for us. I just want you to know.”

“It is okay, Karen. We’ll find our way through it somehow.”

Chapter Sixteen

And there were voices, and thunders, and lightening; and there was a great earthquake, such as was not since men were upon the earth, so mighty an earthquake, *and* so great. Revelation 16:18

"Good morning, Don. How was vacation?" asked Karen.

"The kids loved Disney World. The place is made for them. We enjoyed spending time with them. It was nice relaxing with each other. A little difficult with us all sleeping in the same room, but we managed. Thanks for the time off. I wouldn't have asked for it."

"You are welcome. How was the drive to Orlando?"

"I-75 is crazy as usual. I think some drivers believe speed limit signs are only a suggestion. Seventy miles per hour is not fast enough for some drivers. How was your week?"

"We spent a harrowing week racking our brains over these murders. We did come up with another round of profile characteristics, for all the good that will do. We spent a fair amount of time noodling the bombshell you threw at us before you left."

"What was that again?"

"You said that it was Romano asking questions by a blind e-mail address. We can back off Romano for the moment. He is going to submit a sample to profile."

"Wow, how did you manage that?"

"Feminine wiles, Don, feminine wiles."

"I came directly here from my office. I did notice that there was a call note from Marcus on my desk. I will call him now. I'll let you know what he wants."

"Good. Let me explain some progress I have made this week with the ciphers. When we are done, prepare another meeting to let the group know where we stand in breaking the ciphers. I am excited over the progress we've made so far."

Karen and Don worked well together. His abilities complemented her abilities. He was sharp; he knew his business of being a detective. He had the demeanor that draws people to want to associate with him. Call it charisma or anything else you wish. It is a valuable asset for a person. Karen wished she had a department full of Dons. If that were true, she felt that they would have solved these cases by now.

As Don sat working on the cipher presentation, his phone rang.

"Hello Don. This is Marcus. How are you?"

"Hello, Marcus. I am okay. How are you?"

"I am well. I would like to come to Middlefield as soon as possible. The boss wants me to find out how you are progressing. I do know you have been making real strides. Which letter are you putting your focus on?"

"The Mendosa letter. If this person is true to form, he probably did similar things in the second letter, so I will let that one rest for now. I am preparing an update for the Unit."

“Don, the main reason for my visit is that I have some things I want to share with your team.”

“Can you come tomorrow around nine? You can tell us your news. I will check with Karen to confirm the time. I’ll text you if we can’t all meet.”

The following morning Marcus arrived promptly on time. All five met in the conference room. Don made the introductions, as Marcus had never met the Unit members.

“Marcus, I’ve invited Chief Tate to sit in with us today. He cannot come here until ten. Is that okay?” Karen asked.

“That’s fine with me. I assume you keep him informed of developments. I have some interesting news concerning your mysterious deaths, which is the reason I wanted to see you. I will need to return to the office directly after we meet today, but I want to hear about your progress first.”

Using her laptop, Karen projected her presentation on the wall.

“I am going to recap the cipher work progress at this point. It interests me that the last pair of cipher lines is the same in both letters. I now really believe that he put his name in those lines. I plan to concentrate on the final cipher lines of the Mendosa letter. That is my main goal. Remember the alpha codes he gave us?”

MIRHCAHTVZ XZNVJABY KKNPOWHZ MKNYKWBY KKGUQQBTBZWNKZELOXE

“Notice that the first of the Vigenère ciphers has ten characters, the second, third, and fourth ciphers each have eight. The fifth one has nineteen.”

“What’s the significance of that?”

"In the fifth case, we believe he is trying to hide the arrangement of the straddling board characters by adding nonsense characters. The first cipher with ten characters I'll explain in a moment."

"From the readable part of Mendosa letter, Don and I tried many words from the letter as possible passwords. Finally, we found the following series of letters from the Vigenère ciphers: **TCEAGRONIS**, **ETAONRIS**, and **REAISNOT** using the keyword, **HUNTER.**

"We found the fifth alpha cipher using the keyword **HUNTER** to give us **RETNUHINOSAERTRESOL**. The fourth Vigenère cipher was a repeat of the first Vigenère cipher without the two extra letters. I'll show you it in a moment."

"It was more than luck to find a word as the keyword. We had to grind through nearly every word until we made a hit," Karen said.

"We thank you for your perseverance, Don and Karen. I understand that this problem is frustrating for you," Marcus said.

"Right, we tried to think as our killer does, so we put the letters we found into a straddling keyboard. When Don described straddling keyboards at the last MCU meeting, he said that we thought that the second row was fixed alphabetically. With the third row, we think he kept the alphabetical sequence of letters, but shifted the symbols in accordance with the blank spaces in the first row.

"Here's how we found the first row of the straddling keyboard. Using the ciphertext, **MIRHCAHTVZ**, the keyword,

HUNTER, and the Vigenère matrix, she worked a solution:

H	U	N	T	E	R	H	U	N	T
M	I	R	H	C	A	H	T	V	Z

		KEYWORD LETTER																									
		A	**B**	**C**	**D**	**E**	**F**	**G**	**H**	**I**	**J**	**K**	**L**	**M**	**N**	**O**	**P**	**Q**	**R**	**S**	**T**	**U**	**V**	**W**	**X**	**Y**	**Z**
	A	A	B	C	D	E	F	G	H	I	J	K	L	M	N	O	P	Q	R	S	T	U	V	W	X	Y	Z
	B	B	C	D	E	F	G	H	I	J	K	L	M	N	O	P	Q	R	S	T	U	V	W	X	Y	Z	A
	C	C	D	E	F	G	H	I	J	K	L	M	N	O	P	Q	R	S	T	U	V	W	X	Y	Z	A	B
	D	D	E	F	G	H	I	J	K	L	M	N	O	P	Q	R	S	T	U	V	W	X	Y	Z	A	B	C
C	**E**	E	F	G	H	I	J	K	L	M	N	O	P	Q	R	S	T	U	V	W	X	Y	Z	A	B	C	D
I	**F**	F	G	H	I	J	K	L	M	N	O	P	Q	R	S	T	U	V	W	X	Y	Z	A	B	C	D	E
P	**G**	G	H	I	J	K	L	M	N	O	P	Q	R	S	T	U	V	W	X	Y	Z	A	B	C	D	E	F
H	**H**	H	I	J	K	L	M	N	O	P	Q	R	S	T	U	V	W	X	Y	Z	A	B	C	D	E	F	G
E	**I**	I	J	K	L	M	N	O	P	Q	R	S	T	U	V	W	X	Y	Z	A	B	C	D	E	F	G	H
R	**J**	J	K	L	M	N	O	P	Q	R	S	T	U	V	W	X	Y	Z	A	B	C	D	E	F	G	H	I
T	**K**	K	L	M	N	O	P	Q	R	S	T	U	V	W	X	Y	Z	A	B	C	D	E	F	G	H	I	J
E	**L**	L	M	N	O	P	Q	R	S	T	U	V	W	X	Y	Z	A	B	C	D	E	F	G	H	I	J	K
X	**M**	M	N	O	P	Q	R	S	T	U	V	W	X	Y	Z	A	B	C	D	E	F	G	H	I	J	K	L
T	**N**	N	O	P	Q	R	S	T	U	V	W	X	Y	Z	A	B	C	D	E	F	G	H	I	J	K	L	M
	O	O	P	Q	R	S	T	U	V	W	X	Y	Z	A	B	C	D	E	F	G	H	I	J	K	L	M	N
L	**P**	P	Q	R	S	T	U	V	W	X	Y	Z	A	B	C	D	E	F	G	H	I	J	K	L	M	N	O
E	**Q**	Q	R	S	T	U	V	W	X	Y	Z	A	B	C	D	E	F	G	H	I	J	K	L	M	N	O	P
T	**R**	R	S	T	U	V	W	X	Y	Z	A	B	C	D	E	F	G	H	I	J	K	L	M	N	O	P	Q
T	**S**	S	T	U	V	W	X	Y	Z	A	B	C	D	E	F	G	H	I	J	K	L	M	N	O	P	Q	R
E	**T**	T	U	V	W	X	Y	Z	A	B	C	D	E	F	G	H	I	J	K	L	M	N	O	P	Q	R	S
R	**U**	U	V	W	X	Y	Z	A	B	C	D	E	F	G	H	I	J	K	L	M	N	O	P	Q	R	S	T
	V	V	W	X	Y	Z	A	B	C	D	E	F	G	H	I	J	K	L	M	N	O	P	Q	R	S	T	U
	W	W	X	Y	Z	A	B	C	D	E	F	G	H	I	J	K	L	M	N	O	P	Q	R	S	T	U	V
	X	X	Y	Z	A	B	C	D	E	F	G	H	I	J	K	L	M	N	O	P	Q	R	S	T	U	V	W
	Y	Y	Z	A	B	C	D	E	F	G	H	I	J	K	L	M	N	O	P	Q	R	S	T	U	V	W	X
	Z	Z	A	B	C	D	E	F	G	H	I	J	K	L	M	N	O	P	Q	R	S	T	U	V	W	X	Y

- She deciphered the Vigenère matrix using the columns for the keyword letters and the rows for the ciphertext letters.

- Using the **H** column and the **M** row, she found where they intersect. That gave **T** as the first letter of the keyboard. She continued this process for each letter of the keyword and ciphertext.

The full result gave her:

	0	1	2	3	4	5	6	7	8	9
	T	C	E	A	G	R	O	N	I	S
1	B	C	D	F	G	H	J	K	L	M
4	P	#	Q	U	&	V	W	X	Y	Z

"If you look at the first row, the letters "C" and "G" don't belong there, if he is using a conventional keyboard. He is telling us where the spaces are. If you pull those letters out, it becomes **T_EA_RONIS** for the first row of the keyboard. By adjusting the third row for the two spaces, I believe the keyboard is this:

	0	1	2	3	4	5	6	7	8	9
	T		E	A		R	O	N	I	S
1	B	C	D	F	G	H	J	K	L	M
4	P	#	Q	U	&	V	W	X	Y	Z

"In this case, we just placed the hashtag, #, and the ampersand, &, symbols in row three under the spaces in row one."

"We do understand why he would want to do that. We

do not think it is a mistake. Without this clue, we would have a very difficult, if not impossible, task to decipher the numerical ciphers. He wants us to read part of the ciphers," Don added.

"Maybe he's not as smart as we have thought. Perhaps, the keyboards for the lines he says contain his name will be as easy as these," Grace said.

"For some reason, Grace, I doubt it. This killer is no dummy. I will bet that he made the keyboards and keywords as difficult as possible for us, that is, if he isn't lying over his name being in those lines," Karen said.

Karen continued, "For the second Vigenère, we have this next keyboard. He did not add extra characters.

	0	1	2	3	4	5	6	7	8	9
	E	T	A	O	N	R	I	S		
8	B	C	D	F	G	H	J	K	L	M
9	P	Q	U	V	W	X	Y	Z	#	&

"The third one was achieved by the same method."

	0	1	2	3	4	5	6	7	8	9
	R	E	A	I	S	N	O	T		
8	B	C	D	F	G	H	J	K	L	M
9	P	Q	U	V	W	X	Y	Z	#	&

"We have assumed that the order of the characters in both of the first rows is what he wanted us to know."

"Can you explain how you worked with the first

straddling keyboard to solve the first numerical cipher line?" Susan asked.

"Since we knew how the first straddling keyboard was configured, we tried some numerical keywords."

"How did you figure out the keyword?" Susan asked.

"We tried to find a couple of 'promising' clues in the letter, which might be keywords. When we tried 2008 as a keyword, for the first keyboard, it worked."

"Why do you say it worked?" Grace asked.

"I still don't understand how the reverse process works to decipher back to the plaintext," said Susan.

"Don, why don't you take it from here," Karen said.

"Okay, Karen. In one sense, it is a relatively simple process. Remember, this system design is such that any reasonably educated person can use it. The spy networks throughout the world have smart and not so smart spies. You have to plan systems that the lowest capable spies can use or their information is useless. Worse, improper use could compromise the whole system. Let me show you how to use it.

"The killer gave us this series of numbers for the first numerical cipher:

5190912413873946383849027819281

"I'll show you how he enciphered his message in the line, and then I'll show how Karen deciphered it.

"In the table below, the label, **Let. Cipher,** are the digits the killer put in the letter to us. The **PT Cipher** label is for the plaintext digits the killer used by converting his message to numbers using the **T_EA_RONIS** straddling keyboard."

"Please, what is the **C+K** row again?" Grace asked.

"That is the addition of the **Keyword** numbers to the **PT Cipher** numbers."

"Again, the killer developed the **PT Cipher** by using the straddling keyboard to convert each letter of his plaintext into numbers. Notice that in the first row of this straddling keyboard that positions **1** and **4** are blanks, so anytime I see a number **1** or **4**, I know that the next number completes a plaintext letter. For example, **A = 3, 19 = M, 2 = E, 42 = Q**, etc. An example, 'I am here' would be **8 3 19 15 2 5 2**.

	0	1	2	3	4	5	6	7	8	9
	T		E	A		R	O	N	I	S
1	B	C	D	F	G	H	J	K	L	M
4	P	#	Q	U	&	V	W	X	Y	Z

"Once the killer converted his plaintext to numbers, he then added the keyword, **2008**, to the **PT Cipher** to obtain the **C+K** line as I show in the following table.

PT Cipher	3	1	9	2	7	1	2	6	9	3	8	9	1	9	4	8
Keyword	2	0	0	8	2	0	0	8	2	0	0	8	2	0	0	8
C + K	5	1	9	10	9	1	2	14	11	3	8	17	3	9	4	16
Mod 10 (–)	10	10	10	10	10	10	10	10	10	10	10	10	10	10	10	10
Let. Cipher	5	1	9	0	9	1	2	4	1	3	8	7	3	9	4	6
Plaintext	A		M	E	N		D	O	S	A	I	S		M		Y

“Next, he subtracted 10 (modulo ten function) from any number in the **C+K** row greater than 9, to give the **Let Cipher** digits. These numbers were put into the Mendosa letter as his first half of the first cipher line. The killer used this process for each cipher line of his plaintext.

“In the following table, I’ll show the second half of the first cipher line, ***3838490278192817***, he gave us:

PT Cipher	1	8	3	0	2	9	0	4	5	8	1	1	0	8	1	9
Keyword	2	0	0	8	2	0	0	8	2	0	0	8	2	0	0	8
C + K	3	8	3	8	4	9	0	12	7	8	1	9	2	8	1	17
Mod 10 (–)	10	10	10	10	10	10	10	10	10	10	10	10	10	10	10	10
Let. Cipher	3	8	3	8	4	9	0	2	7	8	1	9	2	8	1	7
Plaintext		L	A	T	E	S	T		V	I		C	T	I		M

“When you want to <u>decipher</u>, take the **Letter Cipher** digits and subtract the keyword digits from them to obtain the **Let Cipher–Key** numbers as I show next.

“Again I show the process in two tables:

Letter Cipher	5	1	9	0	9	1	2	4	1	3	8	7	3	9	4	6
Key	2	0	0	8	2	0	0	8	2	0	0	8	2	0	0	8
Let. Cipher–Key	3	1	9	-8	7	1	2	-4	-1	3	8	-1	1	9	4	-2
Mod 10 (+)	10	10	10	10	10	10	10	10	10	10	10	10	10	10	10	10
Plaintext Cipher	3	1	9	2	7	1	2	6	9	3	8	9	1	9	4	8
Plain Text	A		M	E	N		D	O	S	A	I	S		M		Y

“Whenever the **Let Cipher–Key** number is negative; you add 10 to each one to ensure positive number results. That number in the **Plaintext Cipher** row is now used with the straddling keyboard to revert the numbers to the plaintext.

Letter Cipher	3	8	3	8	4	9	0	2	7	8	1	9	2	8	1	7
Key	2	0	0	8	2	0	0	8	2	0	0	8	2	0	0	8
Let. Cipher–Key	1	8	3	0	2	9	0	-6	5	8	1	1	0	8	1	-1
Mod 10 (+)	10	10	10	10	10	10	10	10	10	10	10	10	10	10	10	10
Plaintext Cipher	1	8	3	0	2	9	0	4	5	8	1	1	0	8	1	9
Plain Text		L	A	T	E	S	T		V	I		C	T	I		M

"Once you see it, it is quite simple, no?"

"It does look pretty easy," Grace said.

"The problem is that none of the three keyboards work for lines seven and eight," Karen said.

"How will you and Karen decide how the straddling keyboards for lines seven and eight look?" asked Susan.

"The fifth Vigenère alpha cipher is a mess. That cipher we believe gives us the straddling keyboard for the last two lines. We will need more time to solve that."

"That's unfortunate, if the fifth cipher is the clue to solving the seventh numerical line, we'll have his name," said Marcus.

"I've asked Don to focus his time on that fifth cipher. I will try to sort out where the spaces in the two keyboards are. If successful, Don and I will work on the numerical code lines. At this point, we don't fully understand how he used the keyboards with respect to each numerical cipher line," Karen advised.

"Since there are only three keyboards for six lines, could

he have doubled up on lines?" Grace asked.

"Perhaps, I'm trying to put myself in our killer's mind. If I were him, how would I plan a cipher message that I hoped someone would be able to decipher, but would not be able to decipher the lines with my name? Don asked hypothetically.

"For some reason I can't explain, I think our killer's first six line messages are not as significant as we think they may be," Karen said.

"Why do you say that, Karen?"

"Again, it is just a gut feeling I have. We saw from the readable part of the letter that he thinks he is superman. They first lines may just be to waste our time. The messages may be just bragging. He could be lying; perhaps he hasn't given his name in the message. He just has to show us how smart he is compared to us."

"With all the immense possibilities, it wouldn't have been possible to decipher any of this in a reasonable time. If it were not for our killer's distorted sense of fairness by giving us the Vigenère ciphers, it would have been nearly impossible for us to find the right keyboards."

"Explain that further for them, Don," Karen said.

"Sure. It is a matter of permutations. In permutations, the order of objects in a group is essential. If you ask how many ways ten different objects selected eight at a time without repetition could be arranged, it would be ten factorial divided by 2 factorial. The possible arrangements would be over 1.8 million."

"Well, that's like trying to find a needle in a haystack," Susan said.

"That's a good way to look at it," Don replied.

"Obviously, it's not possible for us to try them in a reasonable length of time. However, because of his generosity, the killer may have given us a way to select the right keyboards. He's not as clever as he thinks he is," Karen said.

"Again, Don, how did you and Karen know which keyboards he used with each numerical line?" repeated Grace.

"Patience, Grace. I will show the keyboards with their solutions for the first six lines."

"There are algorithms written to produce a list of permutations. Marcus provided us a printout of the possible permutations of the first row of the keyboard. The print out is extensive. We are zoning in on a few of the possibilities for the last two lines.

"As Karen said earlier, our work is focused to understand the last Vigenère cipher he gave us. It is longer than the others are. He is playing with us again. I still think it tells us the sequence of letters in the top row of the keyboard, but we don't have any proof."

"It will take us awhile to get there, but we are making good progress," Karen added.

"The result we found was **RETNUHINOSAERTRESOL**. In looking over the possibilities, we are convinced that this killer chose letter combinations spelling a word for row one of the straddling keyboard. That keyboard we think is the solution for lines seven and eight on the numeric cipher. It would fit his ego. Remember for lines one through six, the letter sequence spelled no logical words," Don added.

"Again, this guy is not as clever as he thinks, unless his motive with the **VICTOR** ciphers is to give us a chance to solve them. Notice that the second and third rows of all the straddling keyboards are treated the same by the killer. It's always **BCDFGHJKLM** for the second row. For the third row, he moves the ampersand and pound symbols under the blank spaces in the first row. Our assumption was right. We had to concentrate on the first row only. It is lucky for us; he did not re-arrange the order of the second and third row letters of the keyboards. If he had, that would have made the deciphering nearly impossible," Karen said.

"Once we had the sequence of letters and spaces of the first row of the keyboard, we began looking for possible keywords for the **VICTOR** cipher," Don added.

At that point, Chief Tate entered the room.

"As I was saying, we deciphered the plaintext for the first three lines from the following three keyboards:

	0	1	2	3	4	5	6	7	8	9
	T		E	A		R	O	N	I	S
1	B	C	D	F	G	H	J	K	L	M
4	P	#	Q	U	&	V	W	X	Y	Z

A MENDOSA IS MY LATEST VICTIM

“For line two, he used the following keyboard with the result using the keyboard shown next:

	0	1	2	3	4	5	6	7	8	9
	E	T		A	O	N		R	I	S
2	B	C	D	F	G	H	J	K	L	M
6	P	Q	#	U	V	W	&	X	Y	Z

I AM COMING FOR YOU SOON

“And finally, for line three, the keyboard gave:

	0	1	2	3	4	5	6	7	8	9
	R	E	A		I	S	N	O		T
3	B	C	D	F	G	H	J	K	L	M
8	P	Q	U	#	V	W	X	Y	&	Z

I HAVE WATCHED YOUR ACT FOR

“Did the killer use the same straddling keyboard for lines four through six?” Marcus asked.

“He did. For the first three lines, he used the three different keyboards I’ve shown,” answered Don.

“But, perhaps, he showed a weakness by repeating the keyboards for lines four through six. The killer used the same keyword, 2008, for the first six lines, maybe all of them. I can’t tell the last two, yet,” Karen added.

“Were you able to read the next three lines, Don?”

“Yes, we were. Using the three keyboards in the same

order as the first three lines yielded:

"Line four reads:

<u>YEARS YOU HAD IT GOOD WHILE</u>

"Line five gave:

<u>I SUFFERED YOU WILL DIE A</u>

"Line six:

<u>TERRIBLE DEATH I PROMISE THAT</u>

"He used three different keyboards for lines one through three in the Mendosa letter. He repeated them for lines four through six. For the last two lines, we know he did not use those keyboards. We have tried them. They don't work."

"Don and I have agreed that we will only work the Mendosa ciphers for now," Karen said.

"Marcus, would you be willing to work some lines of the Reuben letter?" Don asked.

"Time permitting, I will. Work at headquarters is crazy right now," Marcus answered.

"This guy is a creature of habit, so he may not have changed all the keyboards. I have received a couple of suggestions from the public. I haven't had time to share them with you, Marcus."

"Do they look worthwhile?"

"I haven't had time to review them. I'll turn them over to you to evaluate."

"All right, Don."

Don continued, "For the second letter, the killer may simply be switching keyboards he applies to the cipher lines. It saves him work and confuses us. Again, I'll leave the Reuben letter for now to concentrate on the Mendosa letter's last two lines."

"Marcus, I can't express how grateful I am to you for all your effort in this case," Karen said.

"Thank you. Now, I have some important news for you. Gordon called me yesterday. He said he is able to determine definitely how Lauren Reuben died. Has he talked to you, Karen?" asked Marcus.

"He called me. We are going to talk more tomorrow. What changed his mind?" asked Karen"

"He's been distressed over the cause of death of all six killings. He acted on a hunch in the Reuben autopsy. He had Reuben's brain tested for succinic acid. The test confirmed the presence a large quantity of succinic acid in her brain."

"What's special about that?" Karen asked.

"It was discovered some time ago that succinic acid is a metabolite of a compound called succinylcholine. In biological systems, it dissipates rapidly and converts to succinic acid. In such cases, succinic acid remains in unusual quantities in the brain of a dead person exposed to succinylcholine.

"Normally, the quantity of succinic acid in a human brain is relatively small. Doctors use dilute solutions of the dichloride as a muscle relaxant during certain surgeries. In the hands of an anesthesiologist, it is safe. In the hands of a killer, an injection of succinylcholine will kill a person rapidly. The LD50 dose is 0.45 mg/kg of body mass. It doesn't take a great amount to kill someone."

"What is LD50?" Susan asked.

"LD50 is a system to determine toxicity of drugs. A dosage given to lab rats, which results in 50% of them dying, is the LD50 value," Karen answered.

"The killer alluded to a terrifying death of Mendosa," Grace voiced.

"It is a terrible death because the person injected is totally aware of things, but the person cannot move any muscles and slowly asphyxiates. It was believed for some time to be the ideal poison because of detection problems."

"That is cruel," Susan said.

"It is. Gordon told me of a murder report he had read some years ago, but had forgotten it until recently. A husband killed his wife using succinylcholine. Dr. Carl Coppolino murdered her because of a love triangle. He had been having an affair for years."

"Did his wife know of the affair?"

"Apparently, she did not know. The story goes that in 1996, his mistress's husband suddenly died. In 1997, Coppolino's wife also died suddenly. The coroner ruled her death as cardiac arrest. However, as with most killers, he made a silly mistake. Dr. Coppolino quickly remarried, but not to his mistress. As a result, she went to the police claiming Coppolino killed her husband because of their affair. She became a witness for the prosecution in Coppolino's subsequent murder trial of her husband, but he was acquitted."

"You said earlier that Coppolino murdered his wife. How did the police know that?" Grace asked.

"The police did not give up concerning Coppolino's wife. When police became aware of the succinic acid connection to succinylcholine, they exhumed her body and tested her brain for succinic acid. The tests revealed that she had a large quantity of succinic acid in her brain. Coppolino went to trial for her death and the jury found him guilty. It is interesting that routine toxicology screens did not catch Coppolino. The tip-off came from his jilted mistress."

"Marcus, that is a strange story," Karen said.

"There is more. Gordon wants permission to exhume the bodies of our five early victims to test for succinic acid. He is not sure the succinic acid will still be there, but he feels he has to try. That will be a major undertaking. Sorry, no pun intended. I've already told Gordon, but let me know if the GBI can assist in any way," Marcus said.

"Thank you, Marcus."

"Pardon me, but why has it taken so long for us to come to understand this?" asked Grace.

"Our murders occurred approximately a year apart. Four of the women were prostitutes with histories of drug use. They had many needle marks on their bodies. Dr. Gordon would not have noticed any particular one. Mendosa and Reuben were not druggies," Karen said.

"That's right, Karen. It was the death of Lauren Reuben, which drove Dr. Gordon to attempt to resolve this. Lauren

Reuben was not a drug user, so he did notice the puncture wound. That sent him back to the books. The rest you understand. We never connected the dots before, as they say," said Marcus.

"If we believe we failed to connect dots, I say we didn't even know we had any dots to connect," Grace said

"If it was succinylcholine, how does the drug kill a person?" Susan asked.

"I've been talking to the medical folks at Mercer. All these deaths over the past few years have the same signs. No outward cause of death except their systems shut down, including the ability to breathe. A person injected with this drug dies from asphyxia. They will be wide-awake while this occurs because succinylcholine causes muscular paralysis. It is not a sedative. The scary part is that the victim is alert during the death throes as their systems fail. They know they are dying, but they can't move a muscle," explained Marcus.

"But it makes sense now why we never found the drug that killed them. We had no idea what to look for," Karen said.

"It's worse than that, Karen. Because succinylcholine dissipates rapidly, unless you test a person shortly before or after their death, it is no longer there. Therefore, it is not seen in routine toxicology tests. Many times, you would not be looking for it, anyway. Now, of course, we will be looking for the metabolite succinic acid," Marcus added.

"Aren't these drugs regulated?" asked Grace.

"Well, many of them are on the EPA TOSCA list. Those in the medical profession or science community can get them for medical or research uses."

"What is the TOSCA list?" Karen asked.

"It is a list of dangerous chemicals that the EPA maintains. Any institution having those chemicals must maintain as well as report the quantities on hand. They even have to show where the areas of storage in that institution are."

"I can't believe it. It could be someone in the medical or science professions. God, can't we trust anyone these days?" Karen exploded.

"It is becoming difficult. Sorry, I must head back to Atlanta. I hope your work on the ciphers pays off. Please keep me updated. I have some ideas that I will be working on for the second letter," said Marcus.

"Marcus, thank you again for all you've done," said Karen.

"Glad to assist. These killings are creating a lot of heat at headquarters, so it's to our mutual benefit."

"And that's not saying anything of the public's concerns with a serial killer on the loose," Karen added.

After Marcus had left, Karen's staff huddled for a last minute of strategy talk.

"Don, keep up your excellent work on code. Grace, you follow up with Atlanta to get Romano's sample. Susan, please keep working on the background checks."

Chapter Seventeen

And I looked, and behold a pale horse: and his name that sat on him was Death, and Hell followed with him.
Revelation 6:8

"Morning, Karen. I have some unsettling news."

"Morning Grace. Come on in. What's the news?"

"Romano is now refusing to give a DNA sample. He says if you want it, get a court order, or arrest him. He is sick of you treating him as though he is a suspect," Grace informed her.

"Well, until I can prove differently, he is a suspect."

"What do we do now?"

"If he is the guy, we should watch him closely. I have some thoughts about that, but I have to see the Chief first."

"Unless he varies his method of operation, we have a little bit of time. His next murder won't be until next year."

"Grace, we have to make something happen before then."

"I know, but you have to watch your step. The Chief thinks we should have someone watch your house."

"Grace, I'll be okay."

"Do you have any suggestions for handling Romano's refusal?" Grace asked.

"No. It would be waste at this point to arrest him. We have no proof he has done anything. We have to rely on finishing the last ciphers to get our answers. I'll continue to work with Romano to get the DNA sample."

"What is this idea you mentioned?"

"I am going to talk to the Chief. I have been thinking that we need to set up a sting to force Romano out in the open. Since I'm bait for this guy, why not exploit it?"

"That could be very dangerous for you. Would you mind if I went with you to see the Chief?"

"Come along."

Karen called Tate and agreed on a time to meet.

"Come in, folks."

"Chief, I really want to set up an operation to settle the Joe Romano situation. He has reneged on his promise to give us a cheek swab. I am beginning to believe that he is the guy we've been looking for."

"Why do you suspect him?" Tate asked.

"He is acting guilty. Plus, there are details I know of his life that lead me to believe it."

"What do you mean?"

"It's a mixed bag, but you have to know. Romano and I were very serious lovers before I met and married Bill. We had plans to be married. I did something that I am not proud of. I met Bill and dumped Romano. I know it hurt him very badly. I was not sure at the time if he would forgive me. He became violent, but never hit me or anything like that. I felt he stalked me for a while. It stopped after I married Bill. Now I believe he never let the thing go. It fits that Romano may hold a hatred for me. He talks a good line and doesn't exhibit any ill feelings toward me, but…"

"How do you know that? Have you been associating with him?"

You have to tell him about that night.

"I'm ashamed to admit something to you, Chief. I went to see him a couple of months ago. Grace is aware of it. Something happened that should not have happened."

"Are you saying you slept with him?"

"I did. I am so ashamed."

"Karen, for Christ's sake, you're a police officer! Do you realize what this does to a case if he is the guy?"

"I do. It is a mess, but I think we have to play every card we can to nail him. If Don and I can break the cipher with his name, we have him for the Mendosa and Reuben murders. Whether or not I had sex with him should become moot. He's hanging himself with his codes."

"So that was the embarrassing thing you couldn't tell me? Grace, why didn't you stop this, or at least let me know?"

"I should have come to see you, but I'm with Karen on this. She did a stupid thing, no doubt. She is a good leader, and I believe she is the force that will break the ciphers. We need to back her. Now isn't the time to ostracize her for a mistake."

"So the Unit knows this tidbit?"

"Yes, I opened my mouth when I shouldn't have," Grace admitted.

"Okay, you two. What a mess! Therefore, this is only a guess on your part, Karen. We should expend the resources for what you are suggesting on a whim?"

"Well, I don't want to sit around for his next killing.

Maybe I can force him into action," replied Karen.

"Neither do I. What do I need to do?" Tate challenged.

"I want you to ask the Atlanta PD to post a surveillance on Romano for the next thirty days. If something solid develops, we arrest him. If you find nothing, I want to set up a meeting with Romano to discuss some issues we have. I could use 'that night' as the excuse to meet him."

"So you really think after all these years, he wants to kill you?"

"Again, I'm not sure he has ever gotten over our breakup. It's my strong feeling that he's the guy."

"If nothing happens from your meeting, then what? You still won't be able to tell if he's the killer or not."

"No, but there may be other things we could do."

"What do you want me to do?"

"Set up the surveillance with the Atlanta PD. I will set up a meeting next month with Romano. Have the Atlanta PD be there in case something goes wrong."

"You are taking a huge chance if he is the killer," said Tate.

"I know. This whole thing is wearing me down. I want to clear this, at least. It will feel like some progress."

"Okay but you stay close to me through this thing."

Later, Don came to Karen's office.

"Hi Don. What's up?" she asked.

"I've looked at the last cipher lines again in the Mendosa and Reuben letters. Lines seven and thirteen are identical in both letters. Lines eight and fourteen are also identical.

That says the same straddling keyboard and key are used for the line pairs."

"Yes, Don, I noticed that awhile back. It reinforces my belief that he is not lying; his name is in the ciphers."

"Karen, it still may be that he is toying with us. I worry that he may be giving us a phony name. If so, he will have wasted a great deal of our time."

"I know, Don. Obviously, we cannot be certain until we decipher them. As we dig deeper into the letters, he may have given us other simple keywords clues related to me as crazy as that sounds."

"Well, it is a constant worry for me."

"Don, I have suggestion. Arrange the first row of a keyboard to form a word. We know from the Mendosa letter that he feels I betrayed him. The first rows of the keyboards we found for the first six lines did not have any particular sequence. They formed no words."

"I agree, Karen. I believe his ego demands that. I believe the first row of the keyboard he used for the last two cipher lines needs to spell a word important to him."

"How will you decide what the word is?" asked Karen.

"As a start, I will use Marcus's extensive list. I can whittle it down to include possible words for that first keyboard row. When I have better ideas concerning keywords, I will come back to share that with you. Mind you, if we are up the wrong tree, we are wasting a lot of time. Worse, it is only our guess that he needed a word. He may have done something different."

"I think that's a good plan, Don."

"I'll get started on it right away."

"Don, I do not have any particular insight into the clues for keywords he may have left us in the letter. What are your thoughts?"

"Karen, I think my first job now is to identify keyboards having a first row that spell words appealing to our killer. His ego thing may help us. Once I have that, I can concentrate on keywords."

"After that, what will you do to find the keywords?" asked Karen.

"In the letter, the killer said a clue was that "a mathematician" may have written the ciphers. I have been spending some time thinking. I talked to a math professor at the College. He says there are obviously many possibilities to consider, but for his money, he would look at prime numbers or maybe even the Fibonacci series."

"That's seems a reasonable idea. I know this is not a trivial task. Each keyword and keyboard have to be tested," Karen said.

"Do you agree with my strategy?" asked Don.

"Yes, Don. Forge ahead. And thank you."

"Thanks for the support, Karen. I do appreciate it."

"Don, at this point our options are severely limited. The idea may work or it may not. We have had so many false leads. It is worth the effort you are putting in. Keep pushing. I believe we will beat this," said Karen.

"If there is nothing else, I will go back to my office."

After Don left, Karen's phone rang.

"Karen, your old beau list; can we discuss it a bit more?" asked Susan.

"What do you need?"

"I'm following up on the background checks, but I have a feeling the list is not complete."

"Why do you say that?"

"I don't know, Karen. I have a feeling."

"If I can remember any pseudo romances that didn't end well for the guy, it may provide some clues," said Karen.

"Were there many?" asked Susan.

"I've told you that there were a few teen ones. In those cases, the boys just wanted out. They had what they wanted and said goodbye. My overall recklessness during those years drove my foster parents crazy. I cannot think of anything during that time to have someone hate me. There was the one terrible mistake in my teen years. That boy could not leave town fast enough. I will need to think more of the early college years. I only had a few romances before Romano. Those all ended amicably, I thought. If I think of anyone I've left out, I'll call you."

"I'll leave you to it, Karen."

Karen opened the lowest drawer of her desk, put her feet on as if it were an ottoman, then sank into her office chair, began to think.

What possessed me to become involved with Romano again? What is going on with his 'I'll give you DNA for testing' and then 'I've decided not to give DNA?' Hey,

Buster you gave me plenty of DNA! That is why I am in the shape I am in. Wake up Karen; no one will nominate you for princess of the year. You let your libido take over that night. I could blame it all on Sebastian. He killed himself for his lust. The folks could not live with any of it. We broke their hearts. My life spiraled out of control after that.

Is Joe the killer? It is too painful to think I am carrying a baby of a serial killer. I have to move on. Joe remains a question mark, but I don't want to believe it.

Karen's phone rang several times before she realized it; pulling her out of her reverie. It was an outside call.

"This is Detective Hunter speaking."

"I'm calling about something I saw a couple of weeks ago on I–16," said the voice.

"Can you tell me your name?"

"Can I stay anonymous?"

"I don't know what you have to tell me yet. It is important that I realize who I am speaking to."

"My name is John Spelling. I drive a service van for a bread company. I do not want to say what company. Can you hold that information?"

"I'll do the best I can. I cannot promise you that. I will tell you that I will not give it to the press."

"Okay. I was driving west along I–16 on the morning the young girl was found beside the road."

"Which girl is that?"

"It is the Reuben girl."

"What time was that?"

"It was 6:30. I checked my watch. You see, I deliver to food stores in Atlanta. My route has many stops, so I have to get moving early from the bakery in Macon."

"What did you notice?"

"I saw an old Oldsmobile Cutlass in the breakdown lane. I slowed down a bit to get a better look. It was a Gray 1996 Cutlass Ciera. I know this because I am a car buff. That was the last year they made the Ciera. I did not get the tag number, sorry. I was too interested in the car."

"Can you tell me what you saw other than the car?"

"It wasn't fully light yet, so I couldn't see that clearly. When my lights flashed on the car, there was a man struggling to lift something in the trunk of the car. It was wrapped in a blanket or something that appeared to be too heavy for the man to carry. I almost stopped, but I had my deliveries to complete. It scared me, to be honest. Sorry."

"Can you describe the man?"

"He appeared to be a white guy. He was bending over, so I could not tell how tall he was. His hair looked to be gray. It could have been any dark color. There was not enough light, so I can't say. Unusual thing is I read she was found on the eastbound lane of I–16. I don't understand that."

"Is there anything else you can say about this?"

"When the guy saw me, he stopped, and let the thing fall back into the trunk."

"Is there anything else?"

"No. It happened so fast. Sorry."

"Please don't be sorry. Thank you for the call. Can you give me a number where I can reach you if we need?"

"I'm in the phone book. I live in Dublin. It's the only 'Spelling' there, no pun."

"Thank you. I may be calling you back sometime in the future."

Karen reflected on the call.

We don't have much to go on. At least, if he is the killer, we may know what type of car he has. We can start looking for that, at least.

"Grace, can you come to my office?"

"What do you need boss?"

"Please do a search for any Gray 1996 Cutlass Ciera autos in Middlefield or surrounding towns, including Atlanta. We may have our first real lead in these murders. I just received a call from a potential witness who saw our killer dumping the Reuben woman along I–16."

"Karen, that's good news. I hope it pans out. I'll check back when I have something."

"Grace, I'm pinning my hope on the cipher stuff, and this witness's news. Success for either one may give us a name."

After Grace left, Karen pushed back in her chair trying to believe that this nightmare could be nearing solution.

If we can tie the car or decipher his name he so stupidly left for us, we have him. It is a huge if, though. So far, he has outwitted us.

Karen's phone rang.

"Karen, we just ran a check with DMV. There are seventy-five 1996 Cutlass Cieras in the Atlanta Metro area alone. Fifteen are in Middlefield. I found only twelve registered having the gray color. All are in the Atlanta area."

"Let's get uniformed officers out there and check each one out. I will contact the Atlanta police to ask for their help. I will have Tate send some support from Middlefield."

"Grace, you will need to send the APD the information to tell them what we are looking for. Also, it would be nice if we can get the owners' permission to search the vehicles' trunks."

Karen then called to confirm her prenatal appointment for May thirteenth.

Chapter Eighteen

After this I looked, and behold, a door *was* opened in heaven: and the first voice which I heard *was* as it were of a trumpet talking with me; which said, Come hither, and I will shew thee things which must be hereafter.

Revelation 4:1

The stress of the investigation was seriously wearing on Karen's nerves. Her sleep was fitful. Often nights would pass; blending into the day. Nights when she was able to drift off became an additional worry. Recurring nightmares awoke her. She was grateful to be in her bed safe, but horrified by the violence of the dreams.

Her nightmares followed the same theme. She was alone in a darkened room that was unfamiliar to her. The air was ice cold. She heard footsteps behind her, and terror gripped her. Every step she tried to take was blocked. Everything she touched was slimy. Unable to run, she watched as a man grabbed her arm and injected something into her with a huge syringe. His face was horribly deformed and the stench of his breath made her retch.

"What do you want? Why are you doing this to me?"

"You have destroyed me, and you will die in a terrible way."

The injection took effect. It froze her muscles making it impossible to resist his moves. She needed to scream, but no sound came out.

As she watched, he began to amputate her fingers. The pain was excruciating, but she did not faint.

He sliced off her hands, her arms, and her legs. Then he began to slice her belly to take her tiny baby. At last, when he began to slice at her neck, she awoke.

Knowing that it was only a nightmare did not restore Karen. She had survived physically, but that was all. The horror was complete. Her muscles shook violently. Her helplessness terrorized her most. There was no way to protect her baby.

The nightmare returned several times a week. The dread of them often prevented sleep at all. She read books; she sewed; she wrote in her diary until overpowered by exhaustion, she nodded off.

Sometimes, the man in her dreams had faces Karen recognized. It would be Joe, Sean, or Danny or, God forbid, even Bill. Each one had told her she had destroyed his life. She had to die a horrible death. The ending was always the same.

However, one night, Karen's dream was very different. In this dream, she found herself in a brightly lit room. The air was warm with the sun shining through a large window. There was an aroma of fresh cut flowers. At first, she did not recognize where she was. For some reason, it was comforting. Suddenly, Karen realized it was her parents' home. ***Where is everybody? What am I doing here?***

There was a large doorway leading from the room. The door was closed, but Karen felt an impulse to open it. Moving toward the door, she suddenly felt terror. What would happen if she opened the door? Would she be letting in the killer? Would he kill her baby?

Karen's curiosity overcame her fear. Gripping the doorknob, she slowly turned it. Through the doorway, she saw a man with his back to her. A large German shepherd sat by his side.

Karen cautiously moved through the doorway. As she walked toward the man, he slowly turned to face her.

At first, she did not recognize the face. Images passed through Karen's mind.

"Sebastian, it's you."

"I HAVE COME TO WARN YOU."

"But you're dead."

"WE ARE ALL DEAD IN ONE WAY OR ANOTHER."

"Why have you come to me?"

"I HAVE COME TO GIVE BACK WHAT I TOOK FROM YOU."

"Sebastian, what you took, you cannot give back."

"I CAN GIVE YOU BACK YOUR LIFE."

"I am alive. I am going to have a baby."

"I WILL TELL YOU THAT YOU WILL BE DEAD IN A WEEK, UNLESS YOU HEED WHAT I SAY."

"Sebastian, you are a ghost."

"YOU WILL BE DEAD IN A WEEK."

"We have a plan. We will catch the killer."

"YOUR PLAN WILL FAIL."

"What do I need to do?"

"BEWARE OF THE BROTHERS."

"I don't understand. You were my brother."

"AGAIN, I SAY, BEWARE OF THE BROTHERS."

"You need to tell me more."

"I HAVE TOLD YOU WHAT YOU NEED."

"That does not help me."

The shepherd slowly turned to face Karen. He opened his mouth. No sound came out.

"KAREN, NEVER TRUST..."

The sound of Karen's dog barking awakened her. The clock read 5:30. Daylight was beginning to break.

This can't be happening to me. Sebastian has been dead for twenty-five years. What he said makes no sense. Am I losing my mind?

The next day at work, Karen called Susan.

"Susan, do you have time to talk?"

"I do. What is up?"

"I can't do this over the phone. Can you come to my office?"

"I'll come right over. Do I need to have anything?"

"Just your patience."

When Susan arrived, Karen poured coffee, and began to share her demons.

"Susan, you realize I've been having a terrible time lately. My situation with Romano is becoming unbearable. I believe he is the killer. He is my baby's father, as you know. I have another life to worry about. I have told you some of my fears. I have not told you the extent of my paranoia. Lately, I feel as though I am losing my mind. It's incredibly stressful."

"Karen, slow down. Tell me what has happened."

"For the past weeks, I've been having horrible dreams, no nightmares, they are so terrible. I cannot completely describe them. They are sheer <u>horror</u>. I wake up shaking so much I feel my bones will break."

"How long have you had them?"

"For the past few weeks, I have not gotten a decent night's sleep because of them. I dread going to bed. It is affecting my ability to work. I know that you have noticed my temper. I feel so run-down."

"Karen, everyone here understands what stress you are under. We all are, in a way. Understand; we want to be there for you. We can provide only so much for support. We are one hundred percent with you in the ordeal. Don't ever forget that."

"Thank you, Susan. I am afraid you will think I have gone off the deep end if I tell you the details of a dream I had last night."

"You have stood up well considering what we are going through. Tell me. I will have your back. Trust me. I promise."

"Last night, I had a dream that was completely different from the nightmares. Please don't laugh.

"In my dream, I was in a room that was warm and inviting. It was my parents' house. A door beckoned me to open it. When I opened it, I saw a man standing in the distance with his back to me. I walked out to him. When he turned to face me, it was Sebastian, my brother–my dead brother."

"Go on."

"He said he had come to give me back what he had taken from me. He said he was giving me my life back. I told him

I am alive; that I'm going to have a baby. He said I would be dead within a week unless I listened to him."

"What did he tell you?"

"He told me to beware of the brothers. His words made no sense. I did not understand it then. I still do not know what he was saying. When I told him that, he only repeated it. Then I woke up."

"First of all, having this kind of dream is not that unusual. An aunt told me of a dream she once had. In her dream, her deceased husband, my uncle, had come to her. He told her he wanted to say that he loved her one more time. Of course, it was my aunt's brain trying to make sense of brain waves. For her, it was the man she loved all her life."

"I can understand that. I do not understand what this dream means. Is this dream just my mind imploding because of my fears? Do you believe I'm going crazy?"

"Karen, I don't think anything close to that idea. You subconsciously know something. It comes out this way. It is telling you something significant. But what it is, I have no idea."

"If he tried to help, it has only added oil to the fire."

"Again, it is your subconscious talking to you. What it means to you, I cannot say. Somehow, you are sensing that you understand more of this situation than your conscious self can admit. Do I sound as though I know what I'm talking about?"

"You're a smart woman, Susan. Just your giving some

feedback is comforting. Thank you for not laughing or calling in the white coats."

"We might spend some time trying to understand what your mind is telling us. The phrase 'Beware of the brothers' doesn't exactly ring any bells as far as I'm concerned."

"I've been thinking it over ever since I awoke this morning. I didn't tell you, when the dog turned to me in the dream, he opened his mouth. I expected him to snarl. No sound came out. I have no explanation for that."

"Well, maybe not everything has a meaning in dreams."

"True. Well, I'll be thinking about it."

"I will also."

Later that day, Karen began to relive the dream with Sebastian. ***What did it mean? What real message was he giving me?*** Susan was not much help. At least, she did not think I was losing my mind.

The phrase, "Beware of the brothers" repeated itself in her mind. The dream returned eleven nights.

It was always the same, and always the same warning.

* * *

On the twelfth night, another strange dream occurred.

Karen found herself at a door she did not recognize.

I can see that someone has replaced the door. The hinges and the door handle are shiny.

Suddenly, the door opened. The room was large, and brightly lit. Going through the doorway, she realized she had been here before.

There appeared many women slowly walking around

exposing only their faces in profile. They were all dressed in long, flowing gowns.

Karen vainly looked around the room hoping to see a face she knew. One of the women turned to her.

"Alejandra, is that you?"

"IT IS."

"What are you doing here?"

"THAT IS NOT THE RIGHT QUESTION."

"Tell me what I need to do."

The apparition pointed a finger at her saying, *"MY KILLER HAS WRITTEN ALL THE CLUES NEEDED TO BRING HIM TO JUSTICE. I AM WAITING TO WATCH HIM DIE. WHY ARE YOU BLIND TO HIS NAME?"*

"We have been trying to find out who he is."

"IT IS NOT GOOD ENOUGH. BEHOLD ALL THE OTHER WRETCHES NOW FACING YOU. THEY ARE SCREAMING FOR JUSTICE. LOOK AT THESE ROWS OF WOMEN. THEY ARE SCREAMING FOR YOU TO END THIS KILLING. YOU DO NOT KNOW THEM. THEY HAVE MET THE SAME FATE AS I DID. WE WILL HAUNT YOU UNTIL YOU CATCH HIM. WE CANNOT REST UNTIL THIS SCOURGE IS BEYOND EARTH'S BOUNDS. DO NOT JUDGE US. WE HAVE DONE NOTHING MORE THAT YOU HAVE DONE. YET, WE HAVE PAID WITH OUR LIVES. LOOK DEEPLY INTO YOUR PAST. YOU WILL UNDERSTAND WHO IT IS."

"Tell me who it is? WHO IS IT?"

Suddenly, a figure in a white coat came out from a door starring at Karen. His face was blurred.

"Show me your face," Karen screamed.

"THIS IS YOUR FATE; IT IS YOUR DESTINY, KAREN," the man said.

"Show me your face," Karen screamed again.

"YOU KNOW WHO I AM."

The man laughed. Suddenly, his mouth opened to a huge yawn. Karen felt herself drawn into it. She screamed.

Karen awoke in a sweat.

Am I to believe a dream? Do I subconsciously know who the killer is? What am I missing here? Is my subconscious telling me that the killer has taken the lives of many women and we haven't a clue who they are?

* * *

The next day, Karen decided not to share this dream with Susan. She feared Susan would believe she was losing her mind. Her resolve failed when Susan met her in the hall at work.

"Karen, you look terrible this morning."

"Thank you for the compliment."

"I am serious; you look dragged out. Have another nightmare?"

"It was different. Can you come to my office?"

The two sat to discuss the dream.

After hearing the details, Susan patiently said, "Your subconscious has information, but..."

"There's something in the letters the killer wrote that rattles around in my head. I just don't understand it."

"Maybe we should spend more time on the actual letters the killer wrote. There is something in the decrypted lines that we found in the Mendosa letter bothers me."

"Maybe there are clues we just haven't understood yet."

Chapter Nineteen

Remember therefore how thou hast received and heard, and hold fast, and repent. If therefore thou shalt not watch, I will come on thee as a thief, and thou shalt not know what hour I will come upon thee.

Revelation 3:3

Karen dialed Joe's phone number at home. Reaching Joe's voice mail, she left a message for him to call her back.

Her phone rang a few minutes later. It was Don. She could always count on Don's cup-half-full attitude of life. It was so refreshing to see this when the world was crumbling around her.

"Do you have a few minutes, Karen?"

"I do. Come to my office."

Don arrived with a sheaf of papers.

"Karen, I hope that we are on the right trail. I have not been able to spend as much time as I wanted. I have a start on the last cipher line. We agreed that I would test a couple of versions of the straddling keyboards for the two lines."

"Did you have any success there?"

"Somewhat, I have been thinking that the fact, actually our assumption, that our killer did not alter the order of the second two rows of the keyboard. That, I believe, is going to be his Achilles heel."

"Don, I believe that also. Let's forge ahead using this premise to decipher those two lines. Only time will tell if our assumption is valid. So the other bugaboo will be the keyword."

"Karen, that's going to be the painful part, I have to find the keyword. Marcus did send me a program that will try to match a keyword to the keyboard. I have my own method formatted on a spreadsheet. However, I actually have to push it. Marcus's program is self-looping. Once it's fired up, it runs to completion."

"What do you think concerning the keyword itself?"

"I believe our killer tried to give us a hint. I did test various dates on my three choices of keyboards. Those did not work. We have an algorithm that is running now. I am going to concentrate on the Fibonacci sequence. If that doesn't work, I will try prime numbers. I'll look up the first five hundred or a thousand prime numbers on the web."

"That sounds a bit daunting."

"It probably is. I'm worried that the killer may have used more than one keyword to create a cipher line. He may have used that cipher with another keyword to create the cipher line we saw in the letter. My plan is to use the cipher line he gave us, and then subtract whatever keyword I can come up with. Apply modulo 10 pushing that result back to letters. If the result is a readable, reasonable message, we have him. If not, I'll have to test other keywords. That's where it becomes mind-blowing."

"Thanks for the update, Don."

"Look, Karen. If you do not mind my saying this, I want to warn you again. This person is nuts, and is out to kill you. You don't appear to be that worried."

"Don, I'm trying not to show it. He may kill me, but I

will take a piece of him with me."

"Karen, you amaze me. Kim is afraid just thinking how you are handling what you are going through. You realize we will do anything to keep you safe. He threatens you, he threatens us, and we will not let that stand."

"Don, thank you for all you do."

Don went back to his office. Karen's phone rang.

"Detective Hunter speaking."

"Hi, Karen. Joe here. You called."

"Hi Joe. Thank you for calling back. I wanted to ask if I could stop by your place this Friday. I'm going to be in Atlanta that day."

"Why do you want to see me? What is the purpose? I thought we settled our differences."

"We didn't leave on good terms last time. I want to be friends."

"I'm not sure I do, Karen. I do not think we are good for each other. You have caused me so much pain. Your moods are tough. The baby just complicates it, whose ever it is."

"It's yours, Buster; you know it is. Have I asked you for anything? Have I said you have to pay child support? Can't we put that aside and see what we could do for a baby? I realize we will never be together, but we could do the right thing with the child, yours or not."

"Are you saying it may not be mine?"

"It is yours, Joe. I am only saying that I will decide what to do. I will raise the child myself or I will put it up for adoption, but I will not abort it. Got it?"

"Do you still want to collect the DNA stuff?"

"Oh, Joe, please."

"Karen, what time did you want to come by? I should check my calendar."

Karen was immediately on her guard.

He is not going to pin me down to a time. You have to check your calendar. What professor doesn't know his teaching schedule? Do you have a Friday afternoon class or not? I know the answer. You do not.

"I'm not certain what time my meeting ends. Would you be at your place mid-afternoon or so? Is that a reasonable time for you?" Karen probed.

"Let me see. Yes, I have an Organic Lab in the morning. Afternoon is free," said Joe.

Karen's thoughts continued.

I still do not trust you, Joe. Do you think I am a fool? Do you think we do not know your schedule? You are a suspect. We've been watching you for a while. We are going to catch you. I am the bait. I still can't figure out why you hate me so much. Was I such an uncaring person to you? Did I not comfort you when you had your stressful days?

Something made you different, Joe. Something evil. My decision to leave you cannot have been the reason. People come together and break-up all the time. They do not go on murderous rampages. Now that I think about it, you were a bit jealous of my friends, especially male, and your temper was short fused. I admit you never

behaved as though you carried a grudge, but I was probably wrong. I misjudged you, Joe.

"Yes, let's meet. Please, let's not have any scenes. We can have a relaxing glass of wine. Try to see if we can be friends. See you then."

"That sounds all right, Joe. Only one glass, though, you remember what happened last time we drank wine together. I am just kidding. I look forward to seeing you."

"That's not too funny, Karen. See you then, ciao."

Karen called her counterpart at the Atlanta Major Crimes Unit.

"Good afternoon, Detective Rose here."

"Hi, Tom, this is Karen Hunter. You've been doing much needed work for us by keeping a surveillance on this professor at Tech."

"Oh yes. Romano."

"On Friday, May 13th, we are going to spring our trap. This guy knows all our detectives, so we cannot use our people. Can you assign two detectives to Romano's condominium? We want them to be there at 3:00 p.m. I am going to meet Romano at his place around that time."

"Yes, the Chief set this up with your Chief Tate. We have been rotating two of our detectives at your request a month ago to shadow him. They are familiar with him and his place. I will assign Kelly and Hoffman."

"Once I am there, we will have a glass of wine. That was his idea when I set up the appointment with him."

"Chief Tate said you two were involved with each other

some years ago. Now you believe he's out to harm you?"

"Yes, that's the word–involved. His condominium is on the first floor. His living room is at the backside of the house. I'm going to ask him to open the sliding glass door to the patio.

"My excuse will be I'm not feeling well. Your people can be close enough to overhear our conversation, but be out of sight. We believe that Romano's method of operation is to first drug his victims before he kills them. I will only sip the wine. If I feel anything odd, I will drop the glass to the wooden floor. They can hear that easily. They should be prepared to crash in."

"You have our full support. Remember, we still have an unsolved murder similar to the ones you have. You can count on us, Karen."

"Thank you, Tom. You will receive full credit for this, I promise. Chief Tate is in full agreement with that."

"Having this guy off the street is reward enough, but we'll welcome the glory too. Did you know Chief Tate and I are related? He married a cousin of mine. Our families are close. We celebrate most holidays together, that is, when duty doesn't interfere."

"This is a small world. I had no idea."

"I told you this to let you understand that I consider this support is more than just a career consideration. Family is involved. That's important to me."

"Thank you, Tom. We have to stop this person. He has killed six women. Until we have a confession, we have no idea how many women he has killed. Why I am a target, I have no idea. I confess I am trying to be stoic, but it scares me. I am carrying a child. One of his murders was a young woman who was also pregnant. That didn't stop him. He has absolutely no qualms when it comes to killing unborn children."

"Karen, I go back a long way in law enforcement. I have seen the worst side of society, especially in a city of this size. Please do not fret. We will not let you down."

"Thank you so much, Tom. I guess we are set then. I will give you a call when I leave Middlefield that day."

"I'll wait to hear from you. I should be around for your call. Hoffman will be my backup, if I am away from my desk. Call him in that case. He will call me, guaranteed."

"By the way, Tom, has there been anything unusual with Romano's behavior?"

"There are none that we have been able to determine. We have covered him for nearly four weeks. The officers suspect that he may be aware of the surveillance. If that is true, he will not do anything to give himself away. Should we suspend the coverage of Romano until the 13th?"

"I would say yes. We feel strongly that he is our guy, though."

"Thanks again, Tom. See you soon."

Karen then called Susan to her office.

"Susan, have you been able to complete the background checks on the four names I gave you? I can't believe after being married this long to Bill, I still need to have you check on him."

"It is slow slogging, Karen. Sorry. Bill's file is the only one I have finished. I found nothing of note, thank God. After that, I have a priority on Romano, then the other two. I should have Joe done today. I have completed Terrance except for court records. Danny won't be finished until next week."

"Thank you, Susan. Let me know if anything pops up."

* * *

The week dragged by made worse by the minutiae Karen had to deal with. When Friday finally arrived, Karen put in a day's work until one o'clock, and then went to see Chief Tate.

"Chief, I am leaving now. This is it. The plan is set. I have called Tom Rose in Atlanta. They're set to go."

"What time will you meet with Joe?" asked Tate.

"I'm going to call him when I'm in the car to tell him to expect me around three. Tom said his guys will be there when I arrive."

"Karen, I hate to think he's the killer. You have to be careful. I'm sending Grace to the Atlanta PD separately, so that we will have one of ours present."

"I'll be careful, Chief. This is personal. I have to follow through."

"Please take care."

"Tom is going to call you when we arrest Romano. Ask Don to continue his work. That will be the decisive factor for a murder trial if he solves the ciphers. Please have

Susan keep working the background checks."

"Be careful."

I will be okay do not worry. I can manage myself, if he pulls anything."

"Well, you have our theory concerning this guy. Knockout drops in a drink."

"Chief, okay. I will not drink the wine. I will sip. See you later."

You won't be alone, Karen. Grace is leaving for Atlanta behind you. You just won't know it.

Karen began her drive to Atlanta. This was it. She hoped today would see the end of the nightmare. The torment of past few months was interminable.

Dear God, please let this be the last of the pain for me. Let us avenge the pitiful victims of Joe's hatred.

It was time to finish this business. Put this berserk killer behind bars. With any luck at all, he could be sent to the other side as quickly as a few years.

She dreaded the meeting with Romano. As she drove along, thoughts swirled in her head, which she couldn't control. How would the meeting end? She could not back out now. Was it right to endanger the baby? It was innocent in all of this mess. She could not turn back now.

Fear gripped Karen when she reached her destination.

I have to finish this. I have to stop him. I wish it were not this way. Why does it have to be you, Joe?

* * *

As Grace drove to Atlanta, she thought over the

disturbing events, which had happened in her personal life.

Her head was filled with thoughts.

My marriage did not end well. Phillip caught me messing around on him. He nearly killed me. He has gone away now. He left me in peace. I did love him once.

When she felt this way, thoughts just appeared. They formed with no logical thought pattern. Zip, zap, here and there. There was no connecting of the thoughts. A mixture of jelly beans just tumbling around in the bag.

Grace remembered the recent blowup with Karen that occurred in the office.

I did get involved with Bill. I slept with him. Why did I do that? Did Karen know then or did she just act surprised when Bill told her? How can she not hate me? I screwed up her life; that's not even considering our working relationship.

Nah, Karen screwed up her own life. I am not taking responsibility for that. Becoming involved with Romano was not professional or moral.

Nevertheless, she does not deserve what is going on now. Okay, she messed up. That does not give anybody the right to kill her.

As for the investigations to date, all the people we had interviewed around the six murdered women led to no suspects. Their profiles and alibis withstood scrutiny. Who could this evil killer be? How many more will happen? Well, maybe we have him this time, if I can find the car.

Romano is certainly high on my list. I tried to tell Karen that we should interrogate him. Bring him in. Make him sweat. She still carries the torch for him regardless of how much she protests. Dangerous ground, Karen. He is scum. Not taking responsibility for the fun he had is just scummy. He is leaving her to deal with the mess. Nice guy. Never be involved with a suspect. Then, she was involved with him years before. I have no idea if he took the breakup well or not. He may have been seething all these years just wanting revenge. Nah, that only happens in Hollywood. Maybe it does.

If Romano is the killer, it will not be the end. With Karen involved with him, the defense lawyers will have a field day. Assuming we could get a conviction, there will be appeals.

Grace's thoughts ground to a sudden stop when she reached Atlanta. Grace looked at her watch, 2:45!

Chapter Twenty

And they shall see his face; and his name *shall be* in their foreheads. Revelation 22:4

At last, Karen arrived at Joe's condominium. Locking her car, she headed up the walk.

Joe, gracious as ever, was already at the door.

"Come in, Karen. I was hoping you would come."

I'll bet you were.

"I'm actually happy we can meet to put our differences behind us," she told him.

"Please have a seat and make yourself comfortable."

Karen chose the comfortable platform rocker.

"Let me pour you a glass of wine. Do you have any preference?"

"Do you have Chardonnay?"

"I just bought a bottle this afternoon."

I bet you did. Is this how you lured your victims to their deaths?

"I'll be right back."

I hope the two detectives are here. They were supposed to be here by two.

Joe came back into the room carrying two glasses of wine.

"Here you go. You can use the coaster on the table beside you."

"Thank you, Joe. You are always the gentleman."

"I try; believe me, I try."

I bet you do, you seducer.

"Have you thought how we could develop some peace between us?" asked Karen.

"I have some thoughts around how we could handle this," Joe replied.

I will bet you have.

"What are your thoughts?"

"Well, what is happening with you and Bill with regard to your divorce?" Joe asked.

"Right now we are in negotiations. The two lawyers are butting heads. The major issue is the house. I want it and Bill wants to sell it. Of course, unless he continues to pay the mortgage, I can't swing it alone."

"How is that going to work out?" Joe mused.

"He's telling all his friends that the baby is yours and says he won't pay any child support."

"Isn't that up to the judge?"

"It is. If he can prove that you are the father, then he is off the hook. That is my lawyer's opinion.

"He's probably right. I checked with a lawyer friend."

I am sure you did.

"The lawyer said the issue is that some sort of alimony may be required. He earns so much more than you do, your standard of living would go down."

Boy, you really have been working the angles to get your ass out of this, haven't you?

"The judge may think my infidelity to Bill would negate that," said Karen.

"When do you go to court?" Joe asked.

"We are scheduled next month. By then I will be starting to show."

"Will you have to appear or can your lawyer handle it for you?"

"I'm not required to be present, but there is the baby issue."

"Well, good luck on that."

"Joe, could you open the slider a little. I am feeling a bit cramped for air."

"Sure, give me just a minute."

Joe slowly opened the sliding-glass door nearly five inches.

"Thank you, Joe "

"You're not drinking your wine."

"I'm sorry; I will now."

Karen slowly sipped at the drink. She felt nothing different from usual and took another sip.

"Joe, we've only discussed my divorce. What are your other thoughts?"

"I've been thinking, maybe it's time I settled down."

"What do you mean by that?"

What are you saying, Joe? Are you running out of whores to kill?

"Perhaps we could look again at each other in terms of commitment."

"What does that mean?"

"Do you think you care for me?" Joe asked.

"I thought I did. Your behavior and words the last time we talked made me think more about it."

"How do you feel today?" Joe probed.

"Do you care for me enough to work with me and rear our child?"

"I'm still not sure."

"Then your words earlier are nonsensical. You said you are thinking that you may want to settle down. Apparently, it is not with me. I know that I am not ready for another commitment."

"As I said before, can we go a little slower and see if love rekindles?"

"I'm not sure that will work."

"Why don't you finish your wine? We can agree to meet again."

Karen took the chance and drank.

"Well, Joe, if you can ever make up your mind, you can give me a call. I have more important things to do than waste my time with an indecisive man."

Karen rose out of the chair still holding her wine glass, when the room suddenly started whirling around. She immediately sank back into the chair, and dropped the glass. She heard the crash of the glass against the wooden floor as it shattered. Light slowly faded from her eyes as she began to lose consciousness.

Oh, God, he has gotten me.

Joe rushed over to her.

"Karen, are you all right?"

Suddenly, the two detectives came into the room and grabbed him.

"Why are you doing this?" Joe asked incredulously.

"Joseph Romano, I am detaining you on suspicion of murder," said Detective Hoffman.

Detective Kelly then gave the Miranda Warning to Joe.

"What? I do not believe this. What murder? I haven't done anything."

"We are taking you to the station headquarters where you will be interviewed. Are you willing to talk to us?"

"Not without my attorney."

"In that case, we will go to the Southside Jail. You can call your attorney from there," said Hoffman.

"I'll stay with her. Call for an ambulance," Kelly said.

Karen opened her eyes, and slowly the room came into focus.

"Who are you?" she asked groggily.

"I'm Detective Kelly. My partner and I have been watching this guy for the past month."

"Oh, that's right. You're one of Tom Rose's guys."

"Are you okay, Major Hunter?"

"Yeah, I'm okay. Where's Romano?"

"Detective Hoffman is taking him to jail. We are having a search warrant signed for this place. We will have that done later today."

Kelly called and cancelled the ambulance.

"Now I'm not sure he is the guy. I think my brief fainting spell may have been due to the wine itself. Maybe this gives us a chance to obtain a swab from him for analysis. He refused to give us a swab, recently. Perhaps he'll agree now," Karen said.

"What do you want to do now?" asked Kelly.

"I have a doctor's appointment scheduled for later this afternoon. I feel well enough to go to it."

"I'm going to secure this condo, and head back to headquarters for my report," said Kelly.

As Karen climbed to her feet, she still felt a little wobbly. Kelly gently took her arm to steady her.

"You sure you're okay? I can give you a lift downtown."

"I'm fine, just a little shaken."

Karen went to her car to call Tom at APD.

"Hi, Tom, thank you for your support. We have the problem we thought we might have. Romano did not spike my drink as far as I can tell. He did not make his move today. That was the risk of this whole plan. Tell the guys thank you."

"Detective Kelly called me to give me the story. He says you still want to hold him."

"Complete a search warrant. If you find nothing, let him go. I'll face the consequences of that."

"What do you want us to search for?"

"Check for syringes, Rohypnol or other date rape drugs, journals, diaries. Also, look for any paperwork for storage units. We have a witness who saw the killer dumping the latest body.

"A witness to the Reuben dump site recognized the car.

He said it was an Oldsmobile model, I cannot remember which one now. We were not able to track it down from DMV records, so it must be stored somewhere."

"We'll have the warrant typed and passed by the DA. Then off to the judge for signature."

"Thanks again, Tom. Your support is a blessing."

Chapter Twenty-one

He that overcometh, the same shall be clothed in white raiment; and I will not blot out his name out of the book of life, but I will confess his name before my Father, and before his angels. Revelation 3:5

Karen, still feeling a bit woozy, looked at her watch. It read 4:15.

Just have time to get to the appointment.

Karen pulled into the Adelphi Medical parking lot. The clinic building, an older wood-frame structure, was located at the end of Locust Street in an area transforming itself from residential to business. It was familiar to Karen. She had been there many times over the past years when she came to see Dr. Culver.

As she exited her car, Karen looked at the house next door, which was in tasteful colors. Its well-kept shrubbery and lawn showed that the owner took pride in his home.

Karen turned back towards the Clinic, and looked at the painted sign above the formal entrance door.

Sean has been investing some money into his business. A new sign, new windows, even a new walkway. The old door has been replaced and a 'Welcome' mat with pretty flowers added.

A strange feeling made her pause as she approached the Clinic door. Karen was nervous to see Sean again.

Why am I nervous? The April visit went well.

Karen shook it off. Reaching the door, she entered and

signed in for her appointment at the reception desk.

"I'll let Dr. Terrance's RN know you are here," the receptionist said.

"Thank you."

After waiting the usual half hour past the appointment time, Karen had her blood pressure and weight taken. She was then ushered into an examining room.

Dr. Terrance came into the room with his RN.

"Hello, Karen, it's nice to see you again," Terrance said.

"Good to see you again, Sean."

"I hope you have been well. Your blood pressure and weight look good. However, I think we should take another blood sample today. The April sample was fine, but I like to keep a check on it. Perhaps, we will take one more next month, and then one in August. Doris can take a sonogram, in August, if you wish. Otherwise everything looks great, Karen."

After Sean left the room, blood samples were taken. Karen went to the reception area.

While Karen was at the reception desk to make her next appointment, Sean came up to her.

"Thank you for everything, Sean. I had better get going. It's been a long day."

"Oh, Karen, can you wait for a couple of minutes? I have to give my RN some last instructions."

When Sean returned, he asked, "Karen, if you have some time, can you come over to my house? It is right next door. I told Jean you were coming today. She was not crazy with the idea, but she would like to meet you. The kids should be there also."

"Are you sure she is okay with this?

"She is fine. She was nervous with the thought of you being a patient, but she is over it."

"I do have a bit of time before I need to return, sure."

As they entered the house, Sean called out, "Jean, Karen is here."

There was no answer. Sean picked up a note lying on the dining room table: "Honey, I had to bring Karen to soccer practice. Jamie is at an after-school chess session. Love, Jean."

"I'm sorry Karen. Jean had to take my daughter; her name is Karen also to school activities. She should be back fairly soon."

"I'll be going along, then."

"Well, do you have time for a glass of wine?"

"I'd better not. Do you have seltzer water or Coca Cola?"

"I have Coke; I'll be right back."

While Sean was in the kitchen, Karen looked around at the furnishings.

Strange, this place has the feel of a bachelor. I don't see the woman's touch I expected. Interesting that he has a daughter named Karen, I wonder…

Sean brought the drinks, and both settled into well-worn, comfortable chairs. It was like old times as they began to reminisce over the good old days.

Chapter Twenty-two

Thou hast a few names even in Sar'dis which have not defiled their garments; and they shall walk with me in white; for they are worthy. Revelation 3:4

"Chief, has Karen left for Atlanta yet? I have some critical information."

"Yes, she's already left for the meeting with Romano."

"Oh no, I hope this whole thing works out," said Don

"Unfortunately, if nothing happens today, it still won't clear Romano. What news do you have?" Tate asked.

"I talked with her this morning over our latest ideas for deciphering the last line of the letter. I was going to deliver some encouraging news to her."

"What is the news?"

"I'm part way to the solution. This afternoon I spent more time on keyboards."

"What do you mean by part way?"

"I told Karen I had a feeling I know what the possible keyboards used for the last lines of the Mendosa ciphers may be.

"As I've explained to the group before, the first row of the keyboard sets the sequence of the second and third rows. It's this guy's method."

"Don, as I said, I'm very impressed with what you've done so far. How did you decide on the first row letter sequence?"

"I'm a little embarrassed to tell you. It wasn't scientific,

I can assure you."

"I can keep a secret. Tell me."

"I actually started to tell Karen the other day, but I was too embarrassed."

"Go ahead, Don"

"I hadn't been able to sleep well for several weeks. I'd been having strange dreams. One dream returned night after night. Finally, one night I woke up my wife to tell her."

"Well, tell me."

Don began his story hoping Chief Tate would not think he was slipping off the sanity bridge.

"You know that I've been trying to find a keyboard that would let me decipher the killer's name. In my dream, I had an answer, but I have strong negative feelings thinking that dreams having any credibility. Believing in dreams is just superstition."

"Well, think about it, Don. You have consciously been working this problem for the past several months. Why do you think your subconscious won't be aware, and help sort this out?"

"It's not scientific."

"That's nonsense. I remember an interesting story concerning a chemist researching some molecules. The molecular weights did not add up properly. The weights were lower than they should have been," Tate responded.

"And what happened?"

"He catnapped in his lab one day. In his dream, he saw

snakes slithering along the ground. Suddenly, one snake grabbed his own tail, forming a circle. He realized that organic molecules did not have to be straight chains; they could be cyclic. When he applied that idea to his molecules, the weights worked out. That's what dreams can do."

"So you don't think that I'm cracking up?"

"Of course not, let me tell you something. I have been having some nightmares of my own lately. They are haunting me. It's as though they are forecasting my future."

Feeling relieved, Don continued his story.

"Karen had broken the Vigenère cipher that we believed was the clue to the last keyboard for line seven of the Mendosa cipher. By using **hunter** as the keyword, Karen deciphered **RETNUHINOSAERTRESOL** as a result. I tried using various combinations of those letters for the first row of the straddling keyboard, but it never made sense.

"Then one night in my dream, a brightly lit straddling keyboard appeared. As I looked at it, the first row of eight letters and two spaces constantly rearranged themselves. Rows two and three of the keyboard remained the same. Suddenly, as I was looking at the keyboard, the letters froze and then flipped backwards.

ЯƎTИUHIИOƧAƎЯTЯƎƧO⅃

"It was then I saw a large mirror in front of me reflecting the keyboard. When I looked at the words in the mirror, the letters spelled **LOSERTREASONIHUNTER**.

"I now knew the first row read: **TREASON**. The next question was how the blank spaces were arranged with the leftover '**I**' in the row. It confirmed my thought that the killer's ego needs to show itself. I finally decided on the following keyboard sequence for the first row."

	0	1	2	3	4	5	6	7	8	9
		T	R	E	A	S	O	N	I	
0	B	C	D	F	G	H	J	K	L	M
9	#	P	Q	U	V	W	X	Y	Z	&

"So that's why you chose **TREASONI**. It was a dream!"

"That's the sad, unscientific reason."

"Perhaps unscientific, Don, but it appears it may be true progress on those lines," Tate said.

"It took me awhile to decide where the spaces might be. I set up a keyboard with blank spaces at the end of the first row. Next, I moved the blank spaces around to get nine keyboards."

"I'm impressed you were able to narrow down the problem to so few boards," Tate said.

"Deciding on the first row sequence of letters was the killer, no pun intended. The next issue I faced is how the killer used the keyword. I had to try the keyboards that I show you here. He may have used multiple keywords. I told Karen that I would test prime numbers: **2, 3, 5, 7, 11, 13, 17, 19, 23, 29, 31, 37, 41, 43, 47, 53, 59, and 61**. I told her I would also try the Fibonacci series as keywords.

"Here is what the keyboards look like:

	0	1	2	3	4	5	6	7	8	9		0	1	2	3	4	5	6	7	8	9
	T	R	E	A	S	O	N	I				T	R	E	A	S	O	N		I	
8	B	C	D	F	G	H	J	K	L	M	7	B	C	D	F	G	H	J	K	L	M
9	P	Q	#	U	V	W	&	X	Y	Z	9	P	Q	#	U	V	W	&	X	Y	Z

	0	1	2	3	4	5	6	7	8	9		0	1	2	3	4	5	6	7	8	9
	T	R	E	A	S	O	N			I			T	R	E	A	S	O	N	I	
7	B	C	D	F	G	H	J	K	L	M	0	B	C	D	F	G	H	J	K	L	M
8	P	Q	#	U	V	W	&	X	Y	Z	9	P	Q	#	U	V	W	&	X	Y	Z

	0	1	2	3	4	5	6	7	8	9		0	1	2	3	4	5	6	7	8	9
			T	R	E	A	S	O	N	I		I	T	R	E	A	S	O	N		
0	B	C	D	F	G	H	J	K	L	M	8	B	C	D	F	G	H	J	K	L	M
1	P	Q	#	U	V	W	&	X	Y	Z	9	P	Q	#	U	V	W	&	X	Y	Z

	0	1	2	3	4	5	6	7	8	9		0	1	2	3	4	5	6	7	8	9
	I		T	R	E	A	S	O	N			I			T	R	E	A	S	O	N
1	B	C	D	F	G	H	J	K	L	M	1	B	C	D	F	G	H	J	K	L	M
9	P	Q	#	U	V	W	&	X	Y	Z	2	P	Q	#	U	V	W	&	X	Y	Z

	0	1	2	3	4	5	6	7	8	9		0	1	2	3	4	5	6	7	8	9
		I		T	R	E	A	S	O	N				I	T	R	E	A	S	O	N
0	B	C	D	F	G	H	J	K	L	M	0	B	C	D	F	G	H	J	K	L	M
2	P	Q	#	U	V	W	&	X	Y	Z	1	P	Q	#	U	V	W	&	X	Y	Z

"I'll show you the thirty-two digits of the seventh cipher line in two parts."

"Don, the more you tell me, the more impressed I am."

"Thank you. For a keyword, I used prime numbers in their natural sequence up to 61 to cover the full cipher line.

You can see the results in the charts below. They give us a nonsense of letters. The question I now had was whether the problem was the keyboard, or the keyword.

“The plaintext is unreadable.

“First half:

Line 7	Prime numbers as key															
Letter Cipher	1	6	3	3	1	3	2	4	4	3	6	8	5	6	1	5
Key	2	3	5	7	1	1	1	3	1	7	1	9	2	3	2	9
Let. Cipher–Key	-1	3	-2	-4	0	2	1	1	3	-4	5	-1	3	3	-1	-4
Mod 10 (+)	10	10	10	10	10	10	10	10	10	10	10	10	10	10	10	10
Plain Text Cipher	9	3	8	6	0	2	1	1	3	6	5	9	3	3	9	6
Plain Text		U	I	O		D	T	T	E	O	S		U	E		X

“Second half:

Line 7	Prime numbers as key															
Letter Cipher	8	0	5	4	1	7	9	2	8	4	4	5	8	3	5	8
Key	3	1	3	7	4	1	4	3	4	7	5	3	5	9	6	1
Let. Cipher–Key	5	-1	2	-3	-3	6	5	-1	4	-3	-1	2	3	-6	-1	7
Mod 10 (+)	10	10	10	10	10	10	10	10	10	10	10	10	10	10	10	10
Plain Text Cipher	5	9	2	7	7	6	5	9	4	7	9	2	3	4	9	7
Plain Text	S		Q	N	N	O	S		V	N		Q	E	A		Y

“I then tried a Fibonacci series as a key. For the first half, to get:

Line 7	Fibonacci series as key															
Letter Cipher	1	6	3	3	1	3	2	4	4	3	6	8	5	6	1	5
Key	0	1	1	2	3	5	8	1	3	2	1	3	4	5	5	8
Let. Cipher–Key	1	5	2	1	-2	-2	-6	3	1	1	5	5	1	1	-4	-3
Mod 10 (+)	10	10	10	10	10	10	10	10	10	10	10	10	10	10	10	10
Plain Text Cipher	1	5	2	1	8	8	4	3	1	1	5	5	1	1	6	7
Plain Text	T	S	R	T	I	I	A	E	T	T	S	S	T	T	O	N

“And for the second half:

Line 7	Fibonacci series as key															
Letter Cipher	8	0	5	4	1	7	9	2	8	4	4	5	8	3	5	8
Key	9	1	4	4	2	3	3	3	7	7	6	1	0	9	8	7
Let. Cipher–Key	-1	-1	1	0	-1	4	6	-1	1	-3	-2	4	8	-6	-3	1
Mod 10 (+)	10	10	10	10	10	10	10	10	10	10	10	10	10	10	10	10
Plain Text Cipher	9	9	1	0	9	4	6	9	1	7	8	4	8	4	7	1
Plain Text		&	T		M	A	O		P	N	I	A	I	A	N	T

“You can see for yourself it also gives rubbish for plaintext. It’s still good news, though.”

“Well, how is that good news?”

“I guess news is relative. It is good news because I believe I can eliminate that straddling keyboard for now. I plan to try all the keyboards with the two math keywords I have shown you. If they don’t work, it’s on to other words.”

“Well, the killer did hint in the letters that prime and Fibonacci numbers were possible clues,” Tate added.

Just then, Tate’s phone rang.

“Hi, Chief, this is Grace. The sting worked. They just arrested Romano.”

“I am relieved. Go over to his place and assist them if you can. Keep your cell phone handy.”

“Will do.”

Later, Susan dialed Karen’s cell phone from her office. Susan’s call went directly to Karen’s voicemail.

“Hi, Karen, this is Susan. I am still trying to complete those background checks. Danny’s is the most difficult. I have Romano’s done. Terrance’s is nearly finished. Just some last minute checks, but otherwise it's done. Call me if you have a chance."

Meanwhile, Don continued his keyboard explanation to Chief Tate.

"When I tried the following two keyboards, they did not work either.

	0	1	2	3	4	5	6	7	8	9
	T	R	E	A	S	O	N	I		
8	B	C	D	F	G	H	J	K	L	M
9	P	Q	U	V	W	X	Y	Z	#	&

	0	1	2	3	4	5	6	7	8	9
	T	R	E	A	S	O	N			I
7	B	C	D	F	G	H	J	K	L	M
8	P	Q	U	V	W	X	Y	#	&	Z

"Then I tried the straddling keyboard below for line seven.

	0	1	2	3	4	5	6	7	8	9
	T	R	E	A	S	O	N		I	
7	B	C	D	F	G	H	J	K	L	M
9	P	Q	U	V	W	X	Y	#	Z	&

"I used prime numbers as the keyword again. What I obtained made no sense to me, but it was coherent.

"The first half above gave:

Line 7	Prime numbers as key															
Letter Cipher	1	6	3	3	1	3	2	4	4	3	6	8	5	6	1	5
Key	2	3	5	7	1	1	1	3	1	7	1	9	2	3	2	9
Let. Cipher–Key	-1	3	-2	-4	0	2	1	1	3	-4	5	-1	3	3	-1	-4
Mod 10 (+)	10	10	10	10	10	10	10	10	10	10	10	10	10	10	10	10
Plaintext Cipher	9	3	8	6	0	2	1	1	3	6	5	9	3	3	9	6
Plain Text		V	I	N	T	E	R	R	A	N	O		V	A		Y

VIN TERRANOVA Y

Line 7	Prime numbers as key															
Letter Cipher	8	0	5	4	1	7	9	2	8	4	4	5	8	3	5	8
Key	3	1	3	7	4	1	4	3	4	7	5	3	5	9	6	1
Let. Cipher–Key	5	-1	2	-3	-3	6	5	-1	4	-3	-1	2	3	-6	-1	7
Mod 10 (+)	10	10	10	10	10	10	10	10	10	10	10	10	10	10	10	10
Plaintext Cipher	5	9	2	7	7	6	5	9	4	7	9	2	3	4	9	7
Plain Text	O		U		K	N	O		W		M	E	A	S		#

"The second half gave this:

Line 7	Prime numbers as key															
Letter Cipher	5	9	2	7	7	6	5	9	4	7	9	2	3	4	9	7
Key	3	1	3	7	4	1	4	3	4	7	5	3	5	9	6	1
Let. Cipher–Key	8	10	5	14	11	7	9	12	8	14	14	5	8	13	15	8
Mod 10 (+)	10	10	10	10	10	10	10	10	10	10	10	10	10	10	10	10
Plaintext Cipher	8	0	5	4	1	7	9	2	8	4	4	5	8	3	5	8
Plain Text	O		U		K	N	O		W		M	E	A	S		#

"That gave me the following result:

OU KNOW ME AS

"Or put together, it reads:

VIN TERRANOVA YOU KNOW ME AS

“I have no idea who he is.”

“I have no idea who he is, either.”

“Chief, I’m going back to my office and try the Fibonacci series on the last cipher line. I will come to your office when I finish. It shouldn’t take too long.”

“See you in a bit, Don.”

Chapter Twenty-three

And when they have finished their testimony, the beast that ascendeth out of the bottomless pit shall make war against them, and shall overcome them and kill them. Revelation 11:7

As Karen slowly sipped her Coke, she began to feel slightly dizzy.

Sean was talking to her, but her hearing started to echo, and his words were sounding slurred to her. As he spoke, Karen was able to understand some of the words.

His words stretched out becoming softer and slower. Karen did her best to grasp their meaning. Everything in the room was starting to blur.

"Jean …is a myth…..I am not married……I have…….waited…….a…..long…..time….for…this ….chance……you….will…….not….get….away…today ….I…..am……going…..to……kill…….you."

As Karen's head swirled, she asked, "Sean why?"

Sean only answered with a maniacal laugh.

Karen panicked, afraid of losing control completely. Fumbling she reached for her firearm.

Sean arose from his chair and came toward her. As he did, she fired twice. Sean stumbled forward and dropped to the floor.

Karen's vision went black and she slumped back into her chair.

"I'm going to die."

As Dr. Terrance's RN was walking to her car, she heard

two gunshots from Terrance's house. Grabbing her cell phone, she dialed 911.

The call came into the Atlanta Police Dispatcher.

"What is the nature of your emergency?" asked the Dispatcher.

"Someone has been shot near the Adelphi Medical Clinic. It came from Dr. Terrance's house."

"Is the gunman still there?"

"I don't know, but please hurry."

"Don't go near the house. Stay where you are. The police and medics are on the way."

"Please hurry."

"Please stay on the line until they arrive."

"Who am I talking to?" asked the Dispatcher.

"Rita Wilkerson. I'm an RN here at Adelphi."

"Is he there with you at the Clinic?"

"No, he left a half an hour ago with a patient and went to his house."

"Can you see anything at the house?"

"I don't think so. I don't know if he is okay or not."

"Again, stay on the line with me until the police are there."

"They've just pulled up."

As two officers entered the house, the officers went into defensive mode with their firearms drawn. There was no response to the demands for someone to come out. Inching their way beyond the front door, the officers saw a man on the living room floor. It was obvious he had a gunshot wound. A woman was slumped in a chair. Beside her was a firearm on the floor.

"Send the EMTs in here and transfer the woman and man to Atlanta Medical," the lead officer ordered.

Retrieving the gun as evidence, the officer took Karen's handbag, and searched it finding her police badge and ID.

"This is an officer from Middlefield PD," he said.

* * *

Back at Middlefield, Don came back to Tate's office.

"Well, I have another name, Chief."

"We have two names. Do you suppose this has been a joke played on us?" Tate asked.

"For Line eight, I tried the prime numbers with the new keyboard, but again–no luck.

"When I tried the Fibonacci sequence, it worked. Again, I will show the first half:

Line 8		Fibonacci key														
Letter Cipher	4	3	4	8	3	7	9	2	6	8	8	4	6	4	1	3
Key	0	1	1	2	3	5	8	1	3	2	1	3	4	5	5	8
Let. Cipher–Key	4	2	3	6	0	2	1	1	3	6	7	1	2	-1	-4	-5
Mod 10 (+)	10	10	10	10	10	10	10	10	10	10	10	10	10	10	10	10
Plain Text Cipher	4	2	3	6	0	2	1	1	3	6	7	1	2	9	6	5
Plain Text	S	E	A	N	T	E	R	R	A	N		C	E		Y	O

"And the second half:

Line 8		Fibonacci key														
Letter Cipher	8	3	5	9	9	1	0	5	4	5	1	0	3	1	9	4
Key	9	1	4	4	2	3	3	3	7	7	6	1	0	9	8	7
Let. Cipher–Key	-1	2	1	5	7	-2	-3	2	-3	-2	-5	-1	3	-8	1	-3
Mod 10 (+)	10	10	10	10	10	10	10	10	10	10	10	10	10	10	10	10
Plain Text Cipher	9	2	1	5	7	8	7	2	7	8	5	9	3	2	1	7
Plain Text		U	R	O		L		D		L	O		V	E	R	

"That gives us the following result for the two halves:

SEAN TERRANCE YOUR OLD LOVER

"I think we should call Susan and let her know what we've found. She's been doing background checks on possible suspects," said Don.

Tate phoned Susan to come to the office. Moments later Susan arrived.

"Susan, do you know who these people are?" asked Tate.

"Oh no! Unfortunately, I do, now. When I tried to phone Karen today, I was going to tell her that I nearly finished the background checks. It took time to get some court records. I found that Sean Terrance's parents changed the family name from Terranova when he was a youngster," Susan said.

"Why did they do that?"

"I guess to blend in better. Of course, the records don't say why."

"I suppose people change names for a variety of

reasons."

"Chief, Karen has an appointment to see Sean Terrance at the Adelphi Clinic. Her appointment was at 4:30."

"My God, I have to call Grace! She called me when Romano was arrested, and said Karen was headed to her appointment."

Before Tate could dial Grace's number, his phone rang.

"Chief, this is Grace. There has been a shooting at Adelphi Clinic. Karen was going there."

"Get over there, Grace."

"I'm on my way to Atlanta. I will be there as soon as I can. Don cracked the code," Tate said.

* * *

Atlanta Medical admitted Karen to the emergency room. Nurses wheeled Terrance into surgery.

The ER physician examined Karen. She appeared to be unharmed, but she remained unresponsive. After five hours had passed, she slowly began to move and opened her eyes.

"Welcome back," said the duty nurse.

"Where am I?"

"You're at Atlanta Medical."

"Why am I here?"

"You fell asleep. The police brought you in here."

"I feel like I'm going to throw up."

"Here's a pan. Just relax. You should feel better in a bit. I'll ask Dr. Ritter to look in on you."

Chief Tate finally arrived at the hospital. Grace had been there with Karen shortly after her arrival.

In the ER room, Tate said, "Karen that was too close for comfort. Can you tell me what happened?"

"I don't know. I don't understand what happened."

"You were found at the Adelphi Clinic. Apparently the doctor was shot in the chest."

"How did that happen?" Karen asked.

Grace responded, "We don't have the answer to that yet. Chief is going to check with the ER physician. They are moving you to another room. I will stay with you."

"I will get back to you shortly. Grace, please have Karen sign an information release form. I know the doc will need that before he can tell me anything," Tate said.

* * *

"Nurse, can you tell me who the ER physician attending Ms. Hunter is?" asked Tate.

"Yes, it is Dr. Ritter. I will get him for you."

"Hello, Dr. Ritter. I'm Chief Tate from the Middlefield PD. Ms. Hunter is an officer in my department."

"It is very nice to meet you."

"Do you have any idea what Ms. Hunter ingested?"

"We took blood and urine samples for testing. I will not have final verification until the toxicology results are back.

"However, it is my suspicion that she ingested flunitrazepam, which is a benzodiazepine. You probably know it by its street name as rohypnol or narcozep. It is an intermediate acting hypnotic drug, sometimes called the date-rape drug. It can be measured in the blood to diagnose the level of poisoning. I suspect that she may have ingested enough to give a concentration of 30-60 μg/L in her blood, which would be enough to immobilize her. I have asked to test for a particular metabolite degradation product 7-aminoflunitrazepam to confirm flunitrazepam ingestion. Most likely, we will find small amounts of that metabolite; at least, that is my expectation.

"Of course, that is only my guess. It may not even be rohypnol. It could be chloral hydrate or a number of other drugs. We have to wait and see the results."

"Well, Doctor, that helps explain one piece of this situation. We have much more work ahead of us. We will need the toxicology reports. Will you test for other drugs if you are wrong?"

"Yes, they will also test for other drugs."

"Lastly, how long will she be here before she can be released?"

"I think only a few more hours. I'd like to wait until I get the results."

"Thank you, Dr. Ritter."

Based on Dr. Ritter's assessment of Karen, Tate called Chief Palmer of the APD.

"Tom, this is David Tate of the MPD. I think we need a search warrant for the Adelphi Clinic and Dr. Terrance's home next door. It appears Terrance drugged Karen Hunter, who was there for an appointment. Dr. Ritter from the hospital can confirm she was given knockout drops. We broke a cipher, and it has his name. At this point, I believe he is the serial killer we have been looking for. I'll have a detective call you with the details for the warrant."

"I just spoke with Karen this afternoon before she went to Romano's place. Is she OK? Do they expect Terrance to live?"

"Karen's okay, but I don't know if Terrance will make it. It doesn't look good."

"We'll get started on the warrants."

As Chief Tate returned to Karen's room, Grace left.

"Karen, how are you doing?"

"Alright, I guess. I feel somewhat nauseous."

Moments later Grace came into the room accompanied by Detective Holder from the APD.

"A police officer is here to speak with you."

"Are you alright?" asked the officer.

"I think so. My head is aching. I'm feeling a bit nauseous. I hope I won't be sick," replied Karen.

"Can you tell me what happened to you?"

"I can't clearly remember."

"How did you happen to be here today?"

"I only remember going to a doctor's appointment. My doctor asked me to go to his house. That is all I can remember. I am pregnant and he is my obstetrician."

"Did you shoot him?" asked the officer.

"Who?"

"The man who was shot is Dr. Terrance."

"What? Is he alive?"

"He is, barely. He is in surgery now."

"What happens now?" asked Karen.

“Karen, Captain Holder is from the APD and is here to take your statement,” Tate said.

“Ms. Hunter, this happened in Atlanta’s jurisdiction so there will have to be an investigation by the APD. In the meantime, I’ve informed DA Johnson and Superior Court Judge Romer of the incident. The APD is in the process of obtaining warrants to search Terrance’s home and offices,” Holder said.

“They have to look for any evidence of code writing ability as well as a search for a car he might have in storage someplace. A witness saw him dumping Lauren Reuben, and the witness can identify the vehicle. Susan is talking with detectives to include the car in the warrant. Chief Palmer of Atlanta PD has agreed to release you back to Middlefield. You will tie yourself to your desk until this has been resolved. Your firearm will be held for evidence,” said Tate.

“Oh, terrific, police can’t defend themselves these days without being dragged through the mud and indicted.”

“Come on, Karen. We sometimes see improper use of firearms by police. The politicians get so nervous they tend to go overboard. The citizens want police under control. It is only right,” Tate responded.

“I will say in defense, an officer in danger has little time for a split second decision, but it has to be right 100% of the time,” Grace said.

“We’ll talk about this at the station. In the meantime, detectives need your statement concerning the incident.

I've brought along Attorney Benton from the City council to be here for your interview. I will also be here."

"Thanks, Chief," said Karen. "We have to release Joseph Romano, Chief. We detained him because of my sting plan. The problem was, I fainted, and that set the plan into operation. Joe is innocent of this whole thing. I am embarrassed to have accused him."

"Detective Holder, you still holding Romano?" asked Tate.

"Yes. We have not arrested him, but put him on detention until we conclude Mrs. Hunter's statement today. Then we can decide to hold or release him," replied Holder.

"How is Terrance?" Tate asked.

"It's too early to tell. He is in critical shape. The surgeons are not hopeful. I have ordered a DNA sample profile. The hope is to solve the similar murder case we've had on our books for over eight years."

"Mrs. Hunter," said Holder, "I need to have your statement about the shooting today."

"Karen, before we start with this, I have to remind you of our policy. Since this happened in Atlanta, we will work with them. It will take some time," Tate said.

"Chief, can we obtain Karen's statement?"

"I'm not sure I'm up to it," replied Karen.

"Is the baby okay?" interrupted Grace.

"What baby?" Tate asked.

"Oh, I didn't tell you. I'm pregnant."

"Jesus, nobody tells me anything."

"We'll fill you in later, Chief," Karen said.

"Can we get back to business? I will video tape your statement. We will need to clear the room," said Holder.

"The Middlefield PD counsel is waiting outside. I asked him to accompany me to this session," Tate said.

"Is there a problem?" asked Holder.

"No, I just wanted him to be here in case anything in the future pops up. I think the more ears we have during this statement, the more it will benefit us. Karen has nothing to hide."

Chief Tate stepped out of the room, and soon re-entered with Counsel TJ Benton.

"Detective Holder, this is Attorney Benton from the Middlefield City Council. He is here to witness Karen's statement as her counsel."

"I am pleased to meet you," said Holder, unconvinced.

"Ditto, let's get started."

"Karen, this is Officer Dykstra and she will record your statement. Officer Brown will manage the video. When we are done, I will have you sign the document," said Holder.

Karen was ready to tell her story.

"Mrs. Hunter, please tell me what happened today at the clinic."

"I had made an appointment for today for my pre-natal checkup. This was my second visit to the Clinic. The appointment was for 4:30. I arrived at his office at 4:15; signed in. At 4:50, the RN finally called me in for blood pressure and weight. She led me to an examining room and

I undressed. Around 5:00 by my watch, Dr. Terrance came in along with his RN and examined me. He asked if I could stay a few minutes after we were done. I agreed. The RN and Dr. Terrance left the room. I dressed and went to the reception area. When he returned, he asked me to accompany him to his house to meet his wife, Jean, and we went next door."

"Then what happened?"

"This is where I can only vaguely remember now. He offered me a glass of wine, but I told him Coke or seltzer water would be better. He said his wife was due back after taking the kids to some school functions. I do not remember much after I started to drink the Coke. What happened after that is a blank. Who called the police?"

"His RN heard shots and called," Holder said.

"I must have blanked out. When I came to, I was here."

"How did you know to come to the hospital, Grace?" Karen asked.

"We had a call from the Atlanta PD. You didn't know, but I was already here for the Romano thing," added Grace.

"Anything else you want to add?" asked Holder.

"I'm almost done. I want to give you all information I can remember for this situation," answered Karen.

She continued her story.

"Some time ago, I was advised to review my life as much as possible to determine who in my previous life may have had a grudge against me. I went through the litany of previous boyfriends and yes, lovers. This review was done because of the personal tone of the two letters we received. They were addressed to me personally and were hateful."

"I know we set up the sting. Please continue the reasons for suspecting Romano," Holder pushed.

"His behavior and chemical background led me to suspect him. He and I were going to be married after college, but I dumped him for my husband, Bill.

"Romano moved on with his life, I thought. He never married, and I was not certain that he had truly gotten over it. I began to think that he had built up an uncontrollable rage, which he was able to mask well. For a long time, I could not believe he would kill someone else to get me. I never suspected Sean Terrance," Karen sighed.

"Why were you here to see Terrance?"

"When I was at State, women were referred to Adelphi Clinic for OB/GYN services. At the time, he was not associated with that clinic. An older doctor and his brother owned and ran the clinic. It was only this year, when I needed obstetrical services that I realized that Sean was now with the clinic."

"Was he one of your old boyfriends?"

"Yes, I had dated Terrance years ago. When I learned he was at the Adelphi, we talked regarding whether it was unethical for him to be my doctor. He assured me that the relationship would be strictly professional. With regard to the past, he said that as far as he was concerned, he knew I wanted to move on with my life after graduation. He said that he understood. I thought he was over it. I believed he later married and had children. I actually received an invitation to attend his wedding. I realize now that was a vicious scam."

"Is there anything else you want to add?" asked Holder.

"I think I'm done," said Karen.

"This interview is concluded. You are free to return home for now," said Holder.

Karen, Grace, and Chief Tate discussed her ordeal and the next steps for finishing the cases.

"Change of subject, Karen. Did Don ever tell you how he came up with the keyboards for the last lines of the Mendosa letter?"

"No, he started to tell me, but said he was embarrassed, so I didn't push it."

"It was a dream. He told me."

"Speaking of dreams, Chief, I had a dream about my dead brother Sebastian. In my crazy dream, my dead brother warned me that I would die if I didn't listen to him, but I didn't understand. He said 'Beware of the brothers'."

"What did it mean?"

"When I went for my appointment, something made me pause at the Adelphi Clinic door before I went in. It did not occur to me then, but I now remember Dr. Culver and his brother, John, started the clinic. Sebastian's 'Beware of the brothers' was telling me to be careful at Adelphi. I just didn't get it then."

Just then, the Emergency Room surgeon entered to say that Sean Terrance had died.

Chapter Twenty-four

Here is wisdom. Let him that hath understanding count the number of the beast: for it is the number of a man; and his number is Six hundred three score *and* six. Revelation 13:18

After returning home from the hospital, Karen dropped onto her bed. Sleep came quickly, and so did the dream.

Sebastian. I now understand what you meant. You said 'Beware of the brothers.' You warned me about the Adelphi clinic. I did not realize what you were saying until after. You were the one that made me pause at the clinic door, but I did not know why. You saved my life.

"NO, KAREN, YOU DID. I WAS THERE TO GUIDE YOUR HAND. I HAVE GIVEN YOU BACK WHAT I TOOK SO LONG AGO."

Karen awoke and smiled. ***Yes, Sebastian, you did give back me my life.***

On Monday, Karen met with the Unit.

"Karen, I'm so sorry to think that I might have been able to warn you, if I had worked this cipher a little harder," Don said.

"Let me tell you, Don. You have been outstanding through all of this mess. You have been the one person who offered us hope to solve these cases. That is not trivial."

"Thank you Karen. That means a lot to me. You had a lot to do with the solutions, yourself."

"Chief told me you had made great progress on the cipher. You realize that your cracking it makes our solution of these cases airtight. It also gives me my defense. I need to hear how you cracked the ciphers."

"Let me back up just a bit. I had a dream sometime ago that gave me the possible straddling keyboard. I was too embarrassed to tell you."

"I know, Tate told me," Karen said.

"Unfortunately I didn't complete this until after I heard what happened to you in Atlanta. I could have saved his life without putting you in danger."

"Well, maybe that wasn't meant to be, Don."

"Perhaps, I feel I let you down."

"Don, I never suspected Terrance. We were involved for only a year. I never thought he hated me for breaking off with him. It must have torn him apart."

"It is unbelievable to me that he loved you; then just went over the edge. I am just pleased you stopped him. He was sick. You weren't the cause, Karen."

"I guess you never really know a person. He always appeared to be such a nice guy who wouldn't ever injure anyone."

"It has been a long, painful ride. I, for one, am glad we have the killer. I guess the final nail will be a DNA check to our database. I don't have any doubts at this point."

"Thank you all for the incredibly difficult work you've done."

The APD obtained the appropriate warrants to search Terrance's home and offices. While searching through Terrance's home, the police found diaries tucked behind a row of books. In the diaries, the doctor had listed his murder victims' names and dates of deaths.

A note in the diary listed a storage space numbered 345 at the Sure Locker Company on Willard Avenue. In the large storage space, was a gray Oldsmobile Ciera. Inside the car were syringes and vials of succinylcholine. Found in the trunk of the vehicle were books on cryptanalysis along with scads of trial ciphers.

Chief Tate assembled the MCU for a post-investigation wrap-up.

"From all we have learned, this is the how he operated."

- **His diaries confirm that our assumption that Terrance knew his victims was wrong.**
- **He met his victims at bars in Savannah and Atlanta during the St. Patrick's festivities.**
- **He lured them into his car with promises of alcohol or drugs.**
- **He would then drug them with Rohypnol.**
- **While drugged, he drove them to Atlanta to his house.**
- **He kept them drugged while he raped them.**
- **When he was tired of them, he injected succinylcholine.**
- **He then dumped them in the eastbound lane along I–16 within a few hours of their deaths.**
- **Reuben was the exception. She was killed in a hotel room in Savannah.**
- **He had intended to dump her in the westbound lane of I–16 to confuse the police, but he was spotted by Spelling.**
- **He panicked and dumped her in the eastbound lane as the others.**

* * *

Five days later, the Middlefield Police Department held a celebration to show its appreciation for all the work that was done to solve the murders. In attendance were the City Council, Mayor, and other delegates from the GBI.

The Mayor, never to miss a publicity opportunity, awarded medals of outstanding performance of duty to Chief Tate and the Major Crimes Unit.

In addition, the Mayor presented special letters of merit to Don and Marcus for their work in solving the ciphers.

"Chief, I have some not good news."

"What's that?"

"Grace has handed me her resignation. She says she wants to go to Big Sky country."

"I knew after your dust-up with her, she would leave. She told me she would stay on long enough to finish the murder cases. I think it's better for you both."

* * *

Later that month, Karen screwed up her courage and called Joe.

"Hi, Joe, this is Karen; please don't hang up on me."

"Hello, Karen. I see from the papers you folks finally did your due diligence and caught the right person. Was there no choice? Did you have to kill him?"

"It has haunted me terribly, and probably will for the rest of my life. It was me or him."

"I understand. No one wants to kill another, cop or not."

"Thank you for that, Joe."

"So why are you calling?"

"I was wondering if we could have dinner again sometime. Earlier I called you to apologize for the trouble that day, but I understand why you did not call back. I probably would not have either. I am sorry for thinking it was you. I would like to be friends at least, Joe."

"Tell you what, Karen. I will come to Middlefield and you can take me to dinner. I have to see how I fit into your world. When is the baby due?"

"The baby is due in late October, in three months. The ultrasound says a girl with all the fingers and toes."

"How is the divorce coming?"

You are Always the scientist. We were talking about the baby, you jerk.

"Bill has actually been nice through this. He is deeding his portion of the house to me. I will buy out his half. We still have a mortgage, but I believe I can handle it. I am elated. I love that house, but I hope I can hold onto it."

"I will be down Friday night around seven."

Epilogue

And they sung a new song, saying, Thou art worthy to take the book, and to open the seals thereof: for thou wast slain, and has redeemed us to God by thy blood out of every kindred, and tongue, and people, and nation. Revelation 5:9

On July 6, Karen was admitted to the Middlefield Hospital. She had miscarried her baby. The strain of the past several months had taken its toll. With sadness unique to a mother, Karen named the child Maria and buried her. She was unable to share the depths of her anguish. When Karen told Joe of her miscarriage, he was sympathetic and caring, but it transformed all that was meaningful with Joe. As time went on, they realized they had nothing in common.

Joe Romano continued his teaching and research career at Tech. His role as a father never materialized, and each day he wondered how he could have ever suggested an abortion to Karen. It was only after Karen's miscarriage that he understood the bond formed by mother and child. He had come full circle in his thinking. Life was too precious to throw away and too tenuous to take for granted.

The citizens of Middlefield were relieved that the killer was gone. It was worse to realize that he had not used firearms, axes, or other violent methods of death, but had used his training and skills as a doctor. His training allowed him to be a healer. Instead, he had used a poison, one that not only killed, but also provided terror to his victims as they fought to take their last breaths.

Most citizens felt that Terrance's violent death to be justice delivered. There would be no long years of appeals robbing the citizens of a justice needed and deserved; the heroic efforts of a Middlefield Police Unit and a vulnerable officer had taken care of that.

For Karen, the death of Sean Terrance by her hand continued to haunt her dreams. She rued the day she took the life of another human being—evil or not.

The City of Middlefield settled down after the MCU solved the serial murders. Life went on, but it would not be the last murder the city would see. Soon, the City would need the efforts of Middlefield's Finest to resolve another mystery. For Karen, the work would continue to tax her skills and her dedication to her career.

Afterword

And no man in heaven, nor in earth, neither under the earth, was able to open the book, neither to look thereon. Revelation 5:3

In the second letter concerning Lauren Reuben, Terrance wrote fourteen cipher lines with the last two lines identical to those in the Mendosa Letter. During the course of the investigation, Don did not have enough time to solve the first twelve lines of the Reuben letter. Don and Karen's approach concentrated on the last two lines of the Mendosa letter knowing that solving those lines would be the best use of their time and effort.

They believed the killer used different straddling keyboards in the Reuben letter. The solution of the first twelve cipher lines from the Reuben letter were left to other cryptanalysts to work. Again, line thirteen was identical to line seven of the Mendosa letter and was solved. Line fourteen cipher of the Reuben letter was also identical to line eight of the Mendosa letter meaning the plaintext was the same.

Karen and Don believe the keyword Terrance used to encipher the twelve line numeric ciphers may be the date 2011.

He probably did not use the same keyboard for each of the cipher lines. Solution of the Vigenére ciphers should give the straddling keyboards.

The Reuben Letter Victor ciphers and the Vigenére ciphers are:

JEJNBDIB TACJBYSN UACOVHOW IICKAHAN HARJGEEB YRXJFQTN YNNNBIAC HEJEFDOC KTNKAIIA HOWEFJEJ IACABDRR KKGUQQBTBZWNKZELOXE

38636321479039593841491578222820
93691574039572410246039292743153
63963016536905413201386413902969
58914382584988574369840409444300
56526573618591185987121805036158
69186585768502693460455183536219
88675661382932148593103269626307
44159997087323974745747663940790
50235149399438802849596258444743
85930294727588476307020976425434
93699811305388274097086555076874
67050494623579939886740484626528
16331324436856158054179284458358
43483792688464138359910545103194

The Vigenère ciphers do not have the same encrypting keyword in the Reuben letter as used in the Mendosa letter. Since he used **HUNTER** in Mendosa's letter, a possible thought is that he may have used **KAREN** as the key for the Vigenère ciphers in Reuben's letter.

Don is seeking support to decipher lines one through twelve. Lines thirteen and fourteen, of course, have been solved. Please see if you can solve the others. For those new to ciphering, Don suggests that you may want to set up a spreadsheet as he did to simplify your deciphering work for the Victor ciphers. It is in two parts due to page space limitations.

Decipher Example: Line 1, First half																
Letter Cipher	3	8	6	3	6	3	2	1	4	7	9	0	3	9	5	9
Key	2	0	1	1	2	0	1	1	2	0	1	1	2	0	1	1
Let. Cipher–Key	1	8	5	2	4	3	1	0	2	7	8	-1	1	9	4	8
Mod 10 (+)	10	10	10	10	10	10	10	10	10	10	10	10	10	10	10	10
Plain Text Cipher	1	8	5	2	4	3	1	0	2	7	8	9	1	9	4	8
Plain Text		L	R	E		U		B	E	N	I	S		M		Y

Decipher Example: Line 1, Second half																
Letter Cipher	3	8	4	1	4	9	1	5	7	8	2	2	2	8	2	0
Key	2	0	1	1	2	0	1	1	2	0	1	1	2	0	1	1
Let. Cipher–Key	1	8	3	0	2	9	0	4	5	8	1	1	0	8	1	-1
Mod 10 (+)	10	10	10	10	10	10	10	10	10	10	10	10	10	10	10	10
Plain Text Cipher	1	8	3	0	2	9	0	4	5	8	1	1	0	8	1	9
Plain Text		L	A	T	E	S	T		V	I		C	T	I		M

About the Author

Jon A Sanborn, writing as J A Sanborn, has written six mystery novels: *The Lost Cipher, The Orion Factor, Death Comes to Ely, The Stillwater Incident, Of Friends and Others, and Recollections – An Olio of Short Stories.*

The author holds a BS degree in chemistry and a Ph.D. in computational chemistry from the University of Massachusetts Amherst.

He is a U.S. Navy veteran who served in an antisubmarine squadron, VS-34, aboard the antisubmarine aircraft carrier, USS Essex, CVS-9, at the peak of the Cold War during the Cuban Missile Crisis in 1962.

He has had a career spanning thirty years in various management positions in high technology corporations as well as fifteen years in academic settings teaching chemistry.

After retirement, he formed Swift River Publishing to provide publishing services for his own novels, and for people who have written manuscripts and wish to have them published at modest cost.

He has had a lifetime interest in physics, chemistry, ciphers, codes, and mystery stories: fact and fiction.

He and his wife live in Savannah, Georgia with a spoiled tuxedo cat.

www.ingramcontent.com/pod-product-compliance
Lightning Source LLC
Chambersburg PA
CBHW062027170626
46813CB00001B/316
9780996808200